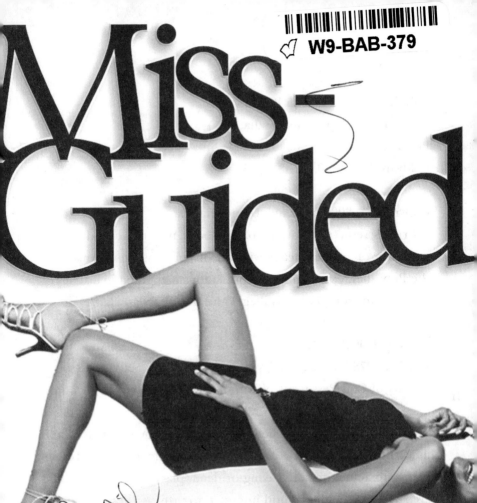

Miss-Guided

A Novel by

Renee Daniel Flagler

Aspicomm
BOOKS

A Division of Aspicomm Media

Renee Daniel Flagler

Published by Aspicomm Books
A Division of Aspicomm Media, Inc.
PO Box 1212
Baldwin, NY 11510

ISBN 0-9760466-1-X
ISBN-13 978-0-9760466-1-5
Library of Congress Control Number 2006900246

II

Printed in the United States of America

DEDICATION

For Daddy & Laila

ACKNOWLEDGEMENTS

By the grace of God, I made it around the block a second time with my sophomore novel. Thank you, Father. I've enjoyed every step of this process, no matter how grueling. It's truly a blessing to live your dream. Don't ever wake me up!

Special thanks to my editor Susan Herriott. May you have many years of happy living! Life is so fulfilling when you enjoy what you do. Brian Walker, my designer for life, as always you visualize my thoughts so eloquently. You are the best. Thanks a mil, man!

To those special people who read the manuscript and helped this story blossom, Les Flagler, Valorie Daniel, Cora Daniel-Hall, Lorie Balbosa, and Marion Grant, thank you dearly.

To my husband, my partner in love, life and friendship, Les Flagler, you are the best thing that has ever happened to me. To my mother, Eva Daniel; my father Benny Daniel; my sisters Cora Daniel-Hall, Valorie Daniel, Patricia Daniel and Eileen Daniel; and my brother, Rodney Daniel, there are no stronger advocates for my achievements. Thank you for your unrelenting encourage-ment and support. Milan and Laila, I live every day for you! To my soldiers, LaShawn Daniels, Jereema Daniels, Javon Daniels, Richae Leon, Nicole Ranger, Richelle Leon and Lil Les, I love you. Little Ron and Tyrese, I love you and hope to see you soon. To the rest of my family, Pamela Doran and Karen Cumberbatch, you can't even begin to imagine how much I appreciate you. Thank God for girlfriends, Dana Hogan Brown, Lorie Balbosa, Janice Boyd, Dani Bethune and Janeen Goodson. No matter what, you ladies have always had my back at every turn. Special thanks to those I never thought I'd be this close to at this point in my life. How blessed I am!

I have so many people that I wish to acknowledge this time around that I could fill a book with my gratitude alone. To Carol and Brenda of C&B Books Distribution, words cannot express how thankful I am for the two of you and the things you do for people like me. Knowing you is a blessing. To Vickie Stringer, thank God for you, for being successful yet still being dedicated to others in their journey of success. To Crystal Lacey Winslow, thank you for always availing yourself and thanks for the great quote! A special thanks to Phil Andrews, my PR Director, VIP Stylz and Heather Covington. To C. Rene West, Caroline McGill and Meisha Holmes my sisters in the struggle, let's keep moving on up. Special mention to Anthony White, Takesha Powell, Nancey Flowers, Patrick Paine of Bestseller Book Store in Hempstead, Tonia Weiters of Excelsior Consortium Companies, Massamba and Nelson Ninn. May we all enjoy immeasurable success!

Chapter 1

Kennedy Divine paced her spacious living room after trying to reach Andre on his cell phone for the past three hours. It wasn't like him not to call back immediately, and she wanted to know just what kept him. Kennedy had already left several messages, and her instincts told her that he was up to something. She continued to pace the room and press the redial button, then threw the phone down on the caramel-colored leather couch, retrieved it and dialed Andre's number one last time. Finally someone answered, a woman.

"Hello," the strained feminine voiced greeted. Kennedy was speechless. She assumed immediately that the woman on the other end was none other than Indira Lewis, Andre's ex-wife.

Again the woman spoke in a quiet tone as if she were in pain. "Hello? Who's calling?"

"Uh… hello. I'm sorry. May I speak to Andre, please?" Kennedy began her pacing ritual once more.

"He just stepped out. May I ask who is calling?" Indira's voice gained strength.

Kennedy couldn't resist. "Excuse me, but is this Indira?" She stopped pacing and placed her available hand on her hip.

"Yes, it is. Who's asking?"

"This is Kennedy. I just find it odd that you would be answering his cell phone, especially since he assured me that the two of you haven't been together in months. From what I understand the two of you were divorced months ago," Kennedy cracked a window to stabilize her rising body temperature.

"Divorced? That's interesting, considering the fact that I gave birth to our baby girl just hours ago. We are certainly still married," Indira said, her response bordering on irritation.

Kennedy couldn't believe her ears. Did she sense sarcasm or apathy in Indira's tone? Anger and disbelief fought to win over her emotions. She removed the telephone from her ear and stared directly into the receiver. Kennedy paced some more, holding the phone in a choke hold. She huffed and brought the phone back to her ear.

"Well, Indira, the last thing I want to be accused of is being a home wrecker. I don't mess around with married men. Oh, and don't bother telling Andre that I called. It won't be necessary." Kennedy held the phone for a moment longer, not sure if she wanted to say more.

"Kennedy?" Indira questioned quietly.

"Yes, Indira?"

"Um...Thank you."

Kennedy smirked. "You are most certainly welcome, and all the best with the new baby." She slammed the telephone down on the receiver and covered her face.

Andre and his wife had a baby! A few hours ago? Her eyes stung from the threat of tears that she refused to allow the chance to descend. Kennedy sat and looked around the townhouse. Reminders of their affair stood at attention. She had sensed Andre's lies yet hadn't had the proof to make a just accusation. She thought of Indira's expression of gratitude on the phone. How stupid could that woman be? How did he explain his disappearances, weekend getaways, and week-long stays on sun-drenched islands in the Caribbean?

Kennedy poured a glass of her favorite Merlot to ease the sting. This certainly marked an end to their fairy tale romance. Andre lied to her when he said he was divorced and yet it was now very clear that he wasn't. Kennedy had a rule, no married men! More than being considered a home wrecker, Kennedy refused to play second fiddle to any woman.

The morning sun poured through the windows, bathing the room in light. Kennedy lay sprawled across her scarlet chenille chaise, French-pedicured toes hanging off the back and the phone to her ear as she listened to Lacey Alexander. Lacey was Troy Alexander's first cousin and the family gossip. The only part of the conversation that Kennedy found interesting was the fact that Troy's estranged but wealthy father was dying. As Lacey talked, Kennedy's mind began to stray as she closely examined her fingernails, appraising the perfect lines of her French manicure. A welcome knock shifted Kennedy's attention and gave her an out from Lacey's continuous chatter.

"Lacey, there is someone at my door. I'll call you back later." Kennedy hit the 'talk' button to disconnect the call and threw the cordless phone on the couch before Lacey could respond.

Swinging her feet to the floor, Kennedy slipped into a pair of raw silk house shoes—a souvenir from a recent trip to Bali with Andre. Kennedy sauntered towards her front door, stopping to study her image in the mirror on the wall of the entryway. Admiring her reflection from each side, she ran her fingers through her closely cropped hair and smiled in approval at the sight of her flawless skin. She often joked by describing herself as looking the way she took her coffee, light and sweet. She stood on her toes and looked downward in the mirror to get a glimpse at the rest of her, to ensure that she was indeed presentable.

The visitor jolted Kennedy's attention by delivering frantic blows against the door. Kennedy whipped her neck towards the door and sucked her teeth.

"Just a minute!"

Despite the urgent banging, Kennedy took her time opening the door. Andre Lewis pushed passed her and walked into the townhouse. Kennedy stood sideways, staring at him with her hands folded across her ample breasts, and her lips pursed.

"I told you when you decided to finally call me back last night that I was finished with you, Andre! What part of that did you have trouble comprehending?"

Kennedy had not moved from her position near the door. She placed one hand on her hip and the other on the door knob.

"Kennedy, please. Just listen."

"There is nothing more for me to listen to. Don't you get it? I heard all I needed to hear from your wife. And by the way, don't you think you should be getting back to the hospital? It must be close to feeding time."

Andre sighed and searched the ceiling for the right words. Kennedy wondered how he intended to explain his way out of this situation. After pacing a few steps, he started.

"Kennedy, I knew you wouldn't see things the way they were. I told you I am not with her. I only intend to be there for our baby. You have to understand that."

Kennedy stared at Andre through slit eyes. As mad as she was, she was still taken by his undeniable masculinity and good looks. The epitome of tall, dark, and handsome, Andre stood an overwhelming six feet four inches with the body of an athlete. Kennedy could see the tension in his strong jaw line. His dark eyes framed with thick, short lashes narrowed and his full nose flared rhythmically.

"First of all, there is nothing for me to understand. *You* need to understand that I don't tolerate lying. And your ass has been lying to me from day one. First, you lied about leaving your wife, you told me you were divorced and now you have a brand new baby. When were you going to tell me about the damn baby, Andre?"

Kennedy felt herself becoming excited, which she didn't want to happen in front of Andre. She tightened her grasp on the door knob and stepped back to allow Andre space.

Andre ignored the hint. He rested his weight on one leg, sighed, and placed his hands on his hips.

"I know you Kennedy, and this is not what you want." Andre tried to inch closer to Kennedy. He extended his hand to hers.

Kennedy slapped his hand away and walked from the door back into the townhouse, leaving the door ajar. Sunlight poured through the door and illuminated her back before she took a seat on the soft leather sofa and crossed her legs. After pondering her next words, Kennedy glared at Andre.

"Andre, what makes you think you know what I want? Now you have a brand new bundle of joy and your business is not even yours. I no longer have a need for you." Kennedy smiled as

Andre's mouth fell open. "Oh yes, sweetheart, I know all about the business. I check out my prospects thoroughly. Never once did you mention anything about having a partner."

"Excuse me?" Andre asked incredulously. His eyebrows met as he cocked his head to the right. After a moment of thought he continued. "So that's all I was to you, a prospect?"

Andre stood frozen in his position and gnawed on his bottom lip. He shook his head from side to side before he headed towards the door. He stopped suddenly and turned back to Kennedy.

"You know, Kennedy, money isn't everything. But you will have to learn that the hard way, won't you?"

Kennedy challenged his stare, unmoved by his statement. Andre shook his head once again and left. Kennedy ran to the door and swung it shut. She peered though the tiny peephole to watch Andre march away. As he pulled off, his tires screeched against the concrete. Kennedy fought a strong urge to call him back but she knew she had to stick by what she had done. She'd let him go and would try her best to forget about him. Besides, after what Lacey disclosed in their chat earlier, she had another mission to accomplish.

Miss-Guided

Chapter 2

Dina Jacobs curled her petite frame on the weathered black leather couch and stared absently at the big-screen television, flipping the channels as Carl moved through the apartment. She pushed her straight, shoulder length hair away from her almond eyes and focused on Carl as he prepared himself for the evening. Hanging out with the boys was this week's excuse, but as far as Dina was concerned, that was another one of his lies. The husky scent of Carl's expensive cologne hung in the air. Decked out for a night on the town, he hummed as he prepared himself for the night. This only infuriated Dina more. She wished that Kennedy would hurry up and get there.

When Carl told her that he wouldn't be spending the evening with her yet again, Dina called Kennedy so she could get out as well. The intent was to see what Carl would do or say because she really didn't feel like going anywhere. Yet it seemed as though he didn't care one bit.

Dina's eyes continued to follow Carl around while he added his finishing touches. "Carl, you are not right."

"Oh, come on with this, Dina."

"Every time I turn around, it's you and your boys."

Carl huffed in the mirror, dropped his hands to his sides and turned towards Dina.

"Listen, baby, how about I take you shopping tomorrow to make up for tonight? I know you wanna hang out, but baby, I already made plans."

Carl turned back to the mirror to check himself out one last time.

"That's what you always say," Dina said into the pillow she hugged. She extended her full brown lips into a childlike pout.

"Whatever, Dina."

Her brown eyes filled with water but refused to give way to her tears. Carl pulled his wallet from his pants pocket and quickly counted his money. He patted his side pockets for his keys and noticed they were on the coffee table. Grabbing his keys along the way, he leaned toward Dina and planted a quick peck on her pouting lips, then dropped a couple of hundred-dollar bills for her on the maple coffee table. Dina didn't move. Just then the bell rang and she thanked God for small favors since she knew that Carl would have commented on her lack of affection. She jumped up and headed for the door, hoping it was Kennedy, but wanting to know who it was in case it wasn't.

Dina opened the door to let Kennedy in.

"Hey, Ken. It's about time. I thought you forgot about me."

Kennedy was effortlessly eye-catching in her fitted cashmere, v-neck sweater, deep blue bootleg jeans, and stilettos. Suddenly Carl was right on Dina's back, staring Kennedy down. His wide grin nearly split the upper half of his face from the bottom.

"What's up, Ken? Looking good, as always."

"Hi Carl," Kennedy said. She turned to Dina, "You ready?"

Dina stepped aside to offer Carl room to exit. Carl remained in place and watched Kennedy as she stepped further into the house. Dina could see him appraising Kennedy from head to toe. She wanted to scream. Instead of getting mad at Carl with his blatant disregard for her presence, she became furious with Kennedy for always getting the attention. What was so special about her?

Dina grabbed her bag from the couch and dragged Kennedy by the arm toward the door.

"Let's go."

Just as she and Kennedy reached the door, Carl called behind them.

"Oh Dina, I'll check with you tomorrow. I'll pick you up around three."

Dina's face twisted with anger.

"What the hell is that supposed to mean? I was planning to come back here, like I usually do."

"Nah, just go to your mom's house. I won't be in 'till late anyway. This way, I can get my sleep and be fresh when I see you, all right, babe?"

"Whatever, Carl! Let's go, Kennedy." Dina couldn't believe his audacity. She knew he was up to something.

Once in the car, Kennedy asked, "What's up with you and Carl? You didn't look too happy in there."

"He's pissing me off, Ken."

Dina turned to stare out of the passenger window. She mulled over commenting on how Carl was staring at Kennedy and decided against it. She knew she was wrong for getting mad at Kennedy. It was just her jealousy. Kennedy was truly her best friend in the world.

"I know he's up to something. Since when does he want

9

me to go to my mother's house after hanging out?"

"Well, I have never been one to tell anyone to leave their man, but you have to look out for yourself, Dina. He is definitely exhibiting some signs."

"I know. I'm not as stupid as you may think. I really do care for him, and I'm not ready to lose him."

"Who are you fooling, Dina? You care about his money, and *that's* what you have a problem walking away from, not him."

Dina's mouth fell open. She quickly closed it and thought of what to say. She came up short and began to stare out the window again.

After a few moments she finally responded. "It's not just the money, Kennedy. I do care about him. If I didn't, then why else would I put up with all of his garbage?"   "Money will make people do a lot of things," Kennedy said.

"I guess you would know," Dina said snidely.

"You know what they say, 'birds of a feather, flock together.' Your problem is that you get too wrapped up."

"What?"

"Dee, if it's about the money, you have to keep your emotions in check. You don't do that, and that's why you end up getting hurt a lot."

"Oh, yeah, you're the expert. Teach me how to get the cash and leave my heart out of it."

"That's pretty much what you have to do," Kennedy said. "When feelings get involved, it takes the focus off the money, and then you are forced to choose between love and money. When does it ever happen that you really have both?"

"Well, thanks, Madame Money Bags. I will be sure to keep that in mind."

The girls picked up their girlfriend Angel Simmons and headed to Manhattan for dinner and cocktails at their favorite trendy grill in the Village.

On the way back, Dina instructed Kennedy to take her back to Carl's place.

"Are you sure you want me to drop you there?" Kennedy asked.

"Yes. My car's there, remember?"

"Oh, I forgot."

Dina wanted to see what mischief Carl was sure to have gotten into. Why else would he suggest she go home? She had been staying at his place for the past two weeks.

11

Using her key, Dina went in and sat on the couch to await his return. She wanted to be the first thing Carl saw when he walked in. The time on the microwave was visible from where she sat in the living room. It read 3:54 a.m. Carl would be in soon. Dina waited on the couch in the dark until she fell asleep.

She woke with a start. The sun beamed strips of light through the blinds, hindering her line of sight. Dina squinted her eyes to shut out the bright rays. She rubbed her eyes and focused her line of sight on the microwave for the time. It was after eight in the morning. Dina looked around for signs of Carl. She couldn't believe he wasn't home yet.

After quickly brushing her teeth she resumed her position on the sofa so that she would definitely be the first thing Carl saw when he walked in. Another two hours passed before he arrived, looking like he'd just rolled out of bed. Dina was so upset she didn't know where to start. Poised and standing with her hands on her hips, she waited for Carl to notice her. He closed and locked the door, then turned around and flinched, obviously startled by Dina's presence.

"I thought I told you to go to your mother's house last night?"

"Why, Carl? So you could hang out with some nasty woman all night?"

"Baby, I told you I was with the boys."

"Well, why the hell does it look like you just got out of bed? What, are you sleeping with your boys now? What, you're on the DL?"

"You're not funny, Dina."

"Then what's going on, Carl?" Dina's chest was heaving.

"Just calm down, baby. I had a little too much to drink, so I crashed at Mark's house. I didn't want to drive home like that."

"Bullshit, Carl. You were with another woman. Who do you think you're fooling?"

Dina closed the distance between her and Carl. He stepped back a few paces.

"I can't believe you. I'm going back to bed," Carl snapped and walked off

When he attempted to walk by Dina, she grabbed his arm. Dina pulled him close and sniffed, getting a light whiff of the musty scent of sex that still clung to his body. She stood back and folded her arms across her chest.

"Drop 'em, Carl."

"What?" Carl asked, clearly baffled.

"You heard me. I'm nobody's fool. Drop 'em."

"You can't be serious! You want me to drop my pants? For what?"

"You smell just like sex. If you have nothing to hide, just drop 'em. What's the problem?"

"You're crazy!"

Carl's eyes grew wide as he stared at Dina as if she had spoken a foreign language. He shook his head and moved his hands to his hips. It looked as though he was giving deep thought to what Dina just said.

"You *are* crazy, and I don't have time for your crazy-ass games. I'm going to bed, you do what you want."

Carl rushed to his room and closed the door. Dina quickly followed on his heels but didn't reach the door in time and watched it slam in her face. The door nearly bent under the pressure of Dina's wild banging.

"Open this damn door, Carl! You think I'm stupid? Open up!"

"I'm not feeding into your games, Dina. Find something to do with yourself," he yelled from the other side.

"You can't hide in there all day. My ass will be right here when you open this damn door."

Dina took a seat right in front of the door.

Chapter 3

Kennedy sat thinking about Andre, Indira and the new baby. She had gotten a little too close to Andre and actually felt betrayed. He wasn't like her other boyfriends. She was truly attracted to him, not just his status.

A knock at Kennedy's door startled her and she somewhat hoped it would be Andre. She spotted her girlfriends Dina and Angel through the peep hole and opened the door. She turned immediately so that her face wouldn't clue them in on anything.

"Hey, you!" Kennedy greeted as she made her way back to her sleek living room.

"Hi, sweetie," Angel said in her usually cheerful tone.

"Hey, yourself. Are your ready?" Dina asked as she quickly scanned the house. Something she did each time she came over.

"Ready for wh…" Kennedy's hands covered her mouth. "Oh, my goodness! I forgot all about today." Dina and Angel exchanged looks and looked back at Kennedy. "I am so sorry, girls. I just have a lot on my mind."

"I can't believe you forgot, Kennedy. Don't tell me you can't go now. I was depending on you to drive." Dina huffed and flopped down on the sofa.

Kennedy turned her lip up at the mention of her driving. Dina was good for always having a reason for Kennedy to drive. Kennedy knew that it was because she drove a late model Mercedes ML 350, and they received more attention when they went out in her car than when they rode in Dina's Honda Accord.

"I didn't say I wasn't going," Kennedy put her hands up in surrender. "You know I don't miss an opportunity to shop. But I will have to call Troy and ask if he can drop Evan off a little later or just let me pick him up when we get back. I'll go call him now and get myself ready. Just give me a few minutes."

"Well, I didn't realize we were taking Kennedy's car. Let me go and get my stuff out of your car, Dina. I'll be right back." Angel turned to Kennedy and said, "And you, Ms. Thing, make it snappy."

Kennedy swiftly ran upstairs to get herself ready. First she called Troy to let him know she needed to pick up their son at a later time. She grabbed what she needed to take with her. Kennedy quietly climbed back down the stairs and jumped to the base. The movement startled Dina, who dropped the piece of mail she had been examining on the coffee table. It was an envelope addressed to Kennedy from Troy, which contained his monthly check for Evan.

"Dina, why are you so damn meddlesome?"

Dina just sat there with a blank face, looking like a deer caught in the headlights. "What?" she asked, trying to sound innocent.

"Don't act like I didn't see you snooping through my damn mail. You are about the nosiest person on earth."

"Okay, you've got me. Troy takes good care of little Evan, huh?"

Kennedy glared at Dina, placing her hands on her hips.

"And that would be none of your damn business, wouldn't it?"

Just then Angel stepped back into the house with her copy of *Lucky* magazine.

15

"Okay! I'm sorry!" Dina said.

"Yeah, I know." Kennedy said, rolling her eyes.

"Girl, I know you weren't snooping through Ken's mail?" Angel questioned.

"Yes. She was! Can you believe her?" Kennedy said and glared at Dina once again.

Angel's mouth dropped and she shot Dina a disappointed look. Dina snarled.

Kennedy knew Dina had to know the amount of the check because Troy never put anything else in the envelope. She made a mental note to again remind Troy to use some method of concealing the contents of his mailings.

"I'm ready!" Kennedy snatched her keys from the mantle and headed towards the door before glaring at Dina once more. If the fire that shot from Kennedy's eyes were tangible, Dina would have been burned to a crisp right there on the couch.

Dina stood and fidgeted as she tried to straighten out her short skirt, and then headed for the door as well.

"Well, let's get going. There is a pair of sandals in Michael Kors that has been calling my name all week. They even left a message on my answering machine, saying that they were waiting on me," Dina announced as she nervously swayed passed Kennedy.

Kennedy rolled her eyes.

The trio was on their way to SoHo for an afternoon of shopping. As tradition would have it, after perusing many shops and street vendors for 'must haves,' they would select one of the area's hip bistros for light fare and a few cocktails. As much as Kennedy tried to focus on her present company and the conversation, her thoughts bounced back and forth between Andre and the news about Troy's sickly father.

After dropping off the girls, Kennedy called Troy to let him know she was on her way. Kennedy pulled up in front of his mother's well manicured split-level home, where Troy and Evan had spent the evening having Sunday dinner with his family. She noticed Troy's four-year-old Ford Expedition in the driveway—typical of him.

"Still driving that truck," she said out loud.

It was his practicality that had bored her to stitches when they were together.

Troy's family lived in a secluded section of Rosedale, where the houses were more impressive than the rest of those in the neighborhood. Kennedy sat for a few moments to ready herself for interaction with Troy's family. From where she sat in the car, she visualized the familiar scene play out through the living room's large picture window. She could see the family milling about in the large living room and dining area. Some were seated at the table chatting. A few men were seated comfortably on the sofa and love seat watching television, most likely a game of some sort. Three children darted from one end of the window to the other, then out of sight completely.

Laughter and conversation greeted her as she stepped along the walkway that led to the front door. She hesitated, huffed, then rang the bell. The sound permeated the bustle of the family gathering. Sturdy thuds emanated from the inside, then drew closer to the entry. After a few short clicks, the door opened to reveal Troy's stout but pretty mother. Mrs. Alexander offered an icy, "Hello, Kennedy." Then she stood for a moment to take Kennedy in before turning to announce her arrival. Troy appeared, towering behind his mother, and then replaced her in the doorway.

"Evan, sweetie, your mother's here. Make sure you get all your things," Mrs. Alexander announced as she walked away.

"Come in," Troy offered, and stepped aside.

"No, thanks." Inside seemed frigid in contrast to the cool spring air that swathed Kennedy as she stood on the porch.

Troy stepped his lanky frame outside to accompany her on the steps. Kennedy felt him observe her. He smiled. Kennedy, no stranger to attention, watched Troy as he watched her. She tried to gauge his thoughts while she focused on his dark, slightly slanted eyes. The slightly slanted eyes and the rich reddish-brown complexion were courtesy of the Native American share of his ancestry. The full lips were undoubtedly compliments of his African lineage.

"Have fun today with the girls?" Troy asked as he leaned against the porch railing. He fingered his carefully trimmed goatee.

"Yes. You know me when it comes to shopping. It's always fun."

She noticed the way he wet his lips and hunched his shoulders against the cool evening air.

"Evan asked me today why he had to have two houses instead of one."

Kennedy smiled at the thought of her son's 'life' questions.

"How did you handle that one?"

"I think I did well." He smiled and the moonlight danced across his perfect teeth.

"I am sure you did." Kennedy smiled back.

Just then Evan came barging through the front door toting bags. He hugged Kennedy's knees. The spitting image of his dad, little Evan began to chatter.

"Mommy, Mommy! I had so much fun. Dylan and Auntie Courtney slept over Daddy's house, and yesterday we went to breakfast, and I had pancakes with chocolate chips! Auntie Courtney took us to Jillian's, and Dylan stayed over again last night. Today we went bike riding and then came to Grandma's house. Grandma bought me some clothes and..."

"Whoa, pudding, sounds like you've had a great weekend."

Kennedy smiled at her son, then looked at Troy and laughed.

"I did, Mommy."

"Hey, pudding, do Mommy a favor and put your bags in the car? Mommy wants to talk to Daddy for a minute, okay?

"Grown people stuff, huh?" Evan confirmed.

Kennedy chuckled. "Yes, sweetie, private stuff. Between adults."

Evan turned to his dad and reached up for him. Troy picked up his boy, hugged him, and gave him a kiss on the cheek. Evan ran off with Kennedy's keys and lugged his bags to the car. Kennedy watched her son open the car with the remote alarm and toss his belongings into the back seat. Evan ran back into the house to say his good-byes and fetch the rest of his bags.

Kennedy turned to Troy, who was already staring at her. She turned away from him slightly and placed her hands in the back pockets of her close-fitting jeans.

"Listen, Troy, to be honest, Evan has been hitting me with some of those 'hard' questions as well lately. I think maybe we should get together and talk about how we should deal with these questions. You know, sort of make sure that we present a united front."

"What about tomorrow night after work? Do you want me to come to your house?"

Kennedy was taken back by his quick response.

"Tomorrow? Well, okay. I guess I can drop Evan by my mother's and we can meet at..."

"Are you scared for me to come to your house?" Troy interrupted then smiled, his bright teeth again glistening in the moonlight.

"Are you kidding me? My house will be fine. Come over around seven." Kennedy waved her hand at him and looked towards the stars.

"That's dinner time. Should I bring Chinese food?"

They both laughed. Kennedy was certainly not a cook. Thanks to many restaurants and her mother's great cooking skills, she and Evan ate well.

"No. I like Thai, and make it six thirty because I have to get Evan and have him in bed by at least nine."

"Fine, I'll see you tomorrow." Troy's look turned serious and he starred at Kennedy.

Not one to feel uncomfortable since she was used to getting attention, Kennedy returned Troy's gaze. He was still just as good looking with his smooth nut brown skin, chestnut brown eyes, keen nose and deep dimples. Troy's wealthy background is what first attracted Kennedy to him. The fact that he wasn't hard on the eyes helped tremendously. Yet despite his family's financial status and his ownership of a car stereo and alarm shop, he possessed a laid back nonchalant demeanor. For Kennedy that was the deal breaker. Predictable and subtle was how she described him. It all summed up to boring for her and the lack of adventure served as the catalyst for their inevitable break up.

Kennedy leaned in to spot Evan approaching the door. She knew he had intentionally waited inside to avoid interrupting their 'grown people talk." Troy gave Evan one last hug and walked them to the car. Once Kennedy and Evan were all settled in the car, she glanced back before pulling off. Troy was standing in the yard watching them.

Chapter 4

On his way to the hospice for veterans to visit his father, Troy decided that it was time to let Kennedy know how he felt. Thoughts of Kennedy preoccupied his mind and he had contemplated getting back with her for a long time. The right approach was imperative. The fact that he and Kennedy were cut from very different cloths remained a challenge. Yet that's what intrigued him about Kennedy the most. She was an adventure.

As the elevator doors opened, Troy stepped aside to offer a small, round lady room to board. Surprised but pleased she turned to Troy and offered a nod and a toothy smile. The harder she smiled, the more her eyes closed. He smiled back and assumed that she must have had at least six more teeth than that of the average adult.

When the elevator doors opened at the fourth floor, Troy turned to the woman, smiled, and told her to have a nice day. He looked down at the visitors pass he obtained from the patient information desk, then looked at the directional signs on the wall to determine which way to go. Blinding light bounced back and forth between the stark white walls of the corridor. The sterile environment summoned Troy to straighten his posture and step cautiously. The quiet made him uneasy. He rounded a corner and encountered a nurse's station. A petite Indian nurse with a soothing, sing-song West Indian accent asked if she could help him.

"Yes, thank you. I'm looking for room 404." Her pleasant demeanor made him smile.

"You're here to see Mr. Alexander. I am so glad. He hasn't had many visitors, ya know." She smiled at Troy. "You must be his boy?"

"Yes. His son."

"Striking resemblance. You can follow me. I was just going that way to check on him, ya know." She reached for her portable blood pressure monitor and rolled it down the hall towards his father's room. She waltzed inside the room and said hello.

"Mr. Alexander, you have a visitor today. Your boy come to see you. How you feelin' this morning?"

Troy was frozen at the door. His father's groan was barely audible. The sight of the machines, tubes, and monitors entering and exiting his father's body was more than he could stand. The nurse took special care in taking his blood pressure and temperature. When she was all done, she turned to see that Troy still hadn't entered the room. She gathered the cord of the monitor and approached him. Her expression showed compassion.

"It's okay, honey. Go on in. At this stage we just try our best to make him as comfortable as possible. Don't let all that stuff discourage you. It's all right." She gently touched his back.

Troy cleared his throat. "Thank you."

The nurse left and Troy took tiny steps until he reached his father's bedside. An earthy smell rose to his nose. It appeared that Mr. Alexander was asleep until he stretched out his hand. Troy looked at his father's withered hand and touched it. He was afraid to apply pressure. He thought the slightest amount would crush him. A single tear descended his right cheek, and he was overcome with grief. Troy stared at his father through soggy eyes. Once a tall and burly man, he was now a feeble shell. His red-brown complexion was ashen with a gray overlay. Dried tear lines left a trail of crust from the corner of his eyes to his ears. His once firm skin hung loosely from his frame. His deeply set chestnut brown eyes sank further into his face.

His father struggled to speak. "Hey, son," He cleared his throat.

"H...hey, dad. How you feelin?" Troy fought back more tears.

"Just as good as I look. Ha," his father teased, then coughed. His voice was raspy, yet his slight southern accent rang through. Troy smiled.

"Still got your sense of humor I see."

"Yep, gotta have something to keep you going round here."

His father suddenly began a coughing fit. Troy just stood over him and watched. He was awed by his father's quaking body and hypnotized by the rise and fall of his dad's flimsy chest. He couldn't think of anything that he could do to help. Troy turned his attention back to his father's eyes—eyes that mirrored his own. Mr. Alexander closed his eyes and attempted to settle his labored breathing. Troy blinked in an effort to deter the fresh batch of tears that threatened to fall.

His father's eyes opened slowly and a single tear escaped and crept down the side of Troy's face. Troy lifted his head and directed his attention to the pasty ceiling.

"Whew!" his father sighed.

Troy turned his attention back to his father. When he had finally gotten his emotions under control, he asked, "Is there anything you need?" then blinked several times to keep the water at bay.

"Just get a little ice water. I'll be fine."

Troy poured his father a cup of cold water from the pitcher on the cluttered bedside table. After a few sips, his father's voice gained a little strength.

"Son," he said and cleared his throat. "I'm so happy to see you. I have a couple of things I really wanted to talk to you about."

"We don't have to do this now…"

"Yes, we do. I don't have much time and I need to do what I can, when I can."

"Okay Dad," Troy said, taking the seat next to his father's bed. The words, 'I don't have much time,' replayed in his head.

Once again Troy focused on the pasty ceiling, blinking back potential tears. The seat suddenly felt restricting and Troy rose to his feet, shifting his weight to and fro while holding his right fist in his left hand. Standing didn't seem to help him to manage the weight of the words his father spoke. The sense of finality they represented felt like a bolder had been laid on his chest. Troy released the air building in his lungs and took to the seat once more. "Don't have much time," rang in his ears like church bells.

"Listen son, I know I haven't been the best father. And I damn sure wasn't the best husband, but that's another story." Mr. Alexander paused for a long while. He batted his eyes and pressed his lips together. It looked as though he was holding back tears. "Anyway…I have made my share of mistakes in life and some of my living just wasn't right. But I have made amends with God."

Troy was shocked at his father's revelation. His father had never been a religious man. As a matter of fact, even when his father and his mother were still together Troy couldn't recall see-ing his father attending a single church service. Troy wondered what was coming next.

"I want you to know that I have always loved you and your sister very much." Troy wondered if this was the first time he actually heard those words from his father. "You made me proud, whether I deserved to be or not. And, as far as your Mama is con-cerned, I didn't know it then, but I've never met a woman like her in my entire life. I never stopped loving her." Mr. Alexander looked upwards, blinking rapidly, and took a deep breath. His voice cracked. "She may not have understood, but that's why I never granted her a divorce. I wanted to be sure that if something ever happened to me, you all would be well taken care of. After all I put her through, it was the least I could do."

His tears began to flow freely. Troy sat still, listening.

"Go over to that door there and get that black bag."

Troy got up and obediently followed his father's instruc-tions. There was a wall of cabinets for the patient's belongings. The small, black duffle bag was visible as soon as he opened the door.

"That's it. Now bring it on over here."

"What's this for?"

"Put it here." His father patted the bed along the side of his leg. Troy placed the bag down. "Open up the side zipper inside the bag and you'll find some keys."

Troy searched, retrieved the keys, and held them up for his father to see. "These?"

"Yep. Those are for you."

"What for?"

"Hand them here and let me show you."

There were five keys on the ring: one for each of his father's three real estate offices, one for his home in Jamaica Estates, and one to a safe deposit box at his bank.

"This one here is for my safe deposit box at the bank. It has your name on it." Mr. Alexander paused and took another deep breath. "Inside the box you'll find my will, insurance papers, and financial records, the deeds to my properties and my house, and a few other important papers. I don't want anyone else viewing these documents but you, you hear? If anyone has questions, you can tell them to see my lawyer."

Troy stared at the keys. His father's life and fortune was in his hands. Troy contemplated whether or not he wanted the responsibility.

"No problem, Pop."

"Wait...there's more. There's a woman. Name is Lela. I had taken up with her a while ago. She's stood by me through most of my sickness. I left her a little something as a token of appreciation, something that would help her out a little. Everything else goes to you, your mom, and your sister." He suddenly stopped speaking.

Troy jumped to his feet. "Pop? You okay? Should I call somebody?"

After a few moments Mr. Alexander replied, "Boy, I'm all right. Just need to catch my breath, that's all. Anyway...I have everything spelled out. Most of the money goes to your mama, and some goes to you and your sister. I want you to sell the house in Jamaica Estates and take over my properties. As far as the real estate offices are concerned, I know you aren't into real estate, so if you wish, you can sell the businesses, give your mom and sister some money and invest the rest. Set Evan up for college, you know." He hesitated again. "Lela's an agent at the office over on Union Turnpike—a special lady. Been there for me in these times, you know. I left a little something for her. I want you to make sure she gets it," he huffed. "That should cover everything."

"I'll take care of it," Troy said, and they sat in silence for the next few moments.

He needed to speak to his sister, Courtney, but knew that he had to be careful about how much he revealed to her. Troy also knew just why his father had chosen him. If his mother and sister knew about Lela getting anything, they would be furious. Troy sat with his father for a while longer, chatting about various topics. It had been a long time since he and his father sat and just talked. Every now and then his dad would pause, go into a coughing fit, or wince from pain. In a single visit they had reconnected. It was sad that it had taken so long, especially since Mr. Alexander wasn't guaranteed to see the year out. From that day forward, Troy visited his father as often as possible.

Chapter 5

Kennedy and Evan arrived at her mother's house at exactly six o'clock Monday evening. Grace Divine's Lexus SC 430 was parked in the narrow driveway, but she wasn't answering the door. Kennedy huffed and knocked again—hard. Just as she was about to turn and go back to the car the door opened. The inside of the house was dim. Her mother peered through the door. Kennedy peered back.

"Do you have any idea how long we have been standing out here ringing and knocking? You knew we were coming." Kennedy was disgusted.

Grace sighed. She closed the door to release the chain and opened the door again to let her daughter and grandson inside. Kennedy and Evan stepped in the well kept home.

"Hi, Grandma," Evan chimed.

Grace tightened her pastel-colored silk robe, flicked a few loose strands of her long hair away from her face and reached out for her grandson.

"How's my baby doing?"

Evan and Grace shared a quick embrace.

Grace held Evan at arms length and stared at him. Kennedy rolled her eyes.

"You are becoming more and more handsome every time I see you. Are the girls chasing you around the school yard yet?" Evan blushed.

"Yuck, Grandma. No and I hope they don't start!" Grace

threw her head back and laughed.

Kennedy felt Grace checking her out. Then she heard the shower come on upstairs and listened to the rhythm of the water change beats. Kennedy wondered if he was one she'd met before. She turned her attention to her mother. Grace focused on Evan and placed her hand upon his shoulder.

"Come on dear, I have something special for you in the kitchen. Say good-bye to your mother now."

Grace led Evan to the kitchen in the back of the house. She glanced back at Kennedy standing in the living room. Kennedy glared at her, then directed her glare towards the steps that led to the bedrooms.

"What time should I expect you back?" Grace asked.

"Around eight." Kennedy swung around and bolted through the front door, slamming it shut.

She reached the car and had to take a moment to put her rage in check. Kennedy didn't want her attitude to carry over into her meeting with Troy. She had important business to tend to.

Just as she pulled into her designated parking spot, she noticed Troy's Expedition roll to a stop and park. She jumped out and invited him with a motion of her hand. Troy came in behind her with bags from the nearby Thai restaurant on Merrick Road. The aroma stole through the air.

"Oh, that smells great. I can't wait to dig in."

Kennedy kicked off her stiletto pumps and removed her waist-length suit jacket. Troy carried the food to the kitchen and placed it on the countertop. Kennedy joined Troy in the kitchen and pulled out a set of paper plates, plastic forks, and real glasses. They prepared their plates, and went into the posh den. Kennedy flicked on the evening news. Minutes passed filled only with the sounds of them consuming their tasty repast. Kennedy set her plate aside and reached for the remote, silencing the anchor that announced breaking news.

"Evan asked me last week if you will ever come back to live with us permanently."

Troy stretched his eyes and smiled. "What did you tell him?"

"I just told him that for now this is the way things will be, and I just assured him that no matter what, his parents love him very much."

"What a cop out. How did he take that?"

Kennedy chuckled. "He said, 'Mommy, I know that, that's not what I asked.' I said wow!"

"Well, when he asked me, I said you never know what the future holds."

Kennedy held her head to the side and stared at Troy. "What's that supposed to mean?"

"It means that we don't know what the future holds. To be honest, I know that one day we'll get back together."

Kennedy was taken back by his confidence. "And how are you so sure of that?"

"It's not just because of Evan. We had a good thing going." Kennedy looked away. "We still have it good. I have friends who can't be in the same room as their kid's mother—let alone hold a decent conversation. Things never got that bad between us. When you left, we just worked everything out on our own. We never had to go through the court system to determine how our son would be taken care of. We didn't have to practice being cordial to one another. It came naturally."

"True, but what does that have to do with us getting back together?"

"Plenty…"

"Wait, Troy," Kennedy interrupted. "Are you trying to say something here?"

"Ken, I never stopped caring for you. And once Evan was born that solidified what I felt for you even more. Contrary to what you believe, being the mother to my son did grant you a permanent residence in my life. What happened to us was over three years ago. I've gotten passed it. I think we have both matured in a lot of ways, and I think it's about time for us to give it another try. If it doesn't work, then so be it. We will still be Evan's parents. But instead of meeting to determine how to deal with Evan's growing pains, we could deal with them together—as they come."

Kennedy stared at Troy. Since she and Troy broke up, she had not entered into another serious relationship. She always kept a safe emotional distance from the men she dated. Kennedy had motives and her goals would not be met if she fell too hard for her prospects. At least that's how she played it until Andre came along.

"Troy, I'm not sure if I get what you're saying right now."

Troy moved towards Kennedy until his lips were a breath away from hers. Kennedy straightened her back. Troy moved even closer and met Kennedy's gaze, eye to eye.

"I want you back, Ken."

They continued the gaze until Troy broke it with a tender peck. Kennedy didn't respond. Troy planted several more soft kisses, then caressed her cheek. Kennedy's eyes closed and Troy pulled her in for a more insistent kiss. Kennedy allowed Troy to continue.

Troy guided her onto her back and moved his lips across hers. Kennedy gave him a slight response. She needed to remain in control. Once she was ready she surrendered to the passion that stirred inside of her. She pulled Troy onto the Persian area rug that decorated her polished wood floors. Kennedy covered Troy's body with hers. She aligned herself with his body and spoke softly. "So you want this again?"

Troy managed a breathless whisper. "Yes."

"Show me. Make me believe you want me."

Troy wrapped his strong arms around Kennedy's body, rolled her on her back, and proceeded to demonstrate just how much he wanted her. Kennedy took pleasure in Troy's unselfish manner of lovemaking. He hit all the right spots until they reached their sensual peaks together. Then they lay side by side, basking in the afterglow. Kennedy sensed Troy watching her and smiled.

"So, do you believe me now?"

"I guess."

"So where do we go from here?"

"Right now, I'm going to pick up Evan from Mommy's house. As far as you and I are concerned, I need some time to think things over. I'll call you."

Kennedy hopped up from the floor, grabbed her clothes and headed to the bathroom. Troy looked disappointed. That made Kennedy smile, pleased to have this power over Troy. When she returned, Troy was still lying on the floor naked. She threw him a towel.

"Lock up on your way out."

Chapter 6

Dina threw down the cloth she was using to wipe down the kitchen table and raced for the telephone. She wanted to catch it before Carl did. She was too late. They answered at the same time.

"Hello," they said in concert.

"Hello?" the female caller said. She sounded unsure.

"Dina, I got it," Carl yelled from the bedroom. Dina ignored him.

"Who's calling?" Dina asked and the caller hung up. She huffed and slammed the phone down on the receiver. She folded her arms and leaned her back against the wall. It had been just over a month since Dina officially moved in with Carl. He had made the suggestion after they fought about his night out with the boys. Dina was tired of all the women callers. She knew she had only been there a short time but felt that as long as she and Carl had been going out, there shouldn't be so many loose ends. She heard Carl's cell phone ring and the bedroom door shut. She marched right to the door and tried to open it. The door was locked.

"Carl, open this door now!" She could hear him carrying on a conversation inside, but she couldn't make out the words.

Carl took his time and finally unlocked the door. Dina pushed passed him glaring. Carl simply nodded and smiled.

"I don't see anything funny, Carl. Who the hell was that? And what was so important that you had to lock the damn door?"

Dina's chest was heaving, and her perfect nose flared.

"Dina, relax. That was a friend. And for your information, I closed the door because I knew your crazy ass would do just what you did, come barging into the room."

"What's with all the women calling, Carl? I'm not stupid."

Carl walked up to Dina to embrace her. She pushed him away.

"Answer my question, Carl."

"Dee, that was just a friend." Carl approached Dina again and pulled her to him. Dina didn't push him away this time, but she kept her arms crossed and she pouted.

"Don't baby me."

"Dee, just listen. It was an old friend and, I explained to her that I live with my girl now, that's all. Why would I ask you to come and live with me if I was playing games?"

"Huh, I'm still trying to figure that out." Dina said, then turned on her heels and left the room in a huff.

She no longer felt like cleaning and decided that she needed to get out of the house for a little while. She had no clue where she would go. Kennedy was out with Evan and Troy, and Angel was out of town on a business trip, so she had no one to call.

She thought about going to her mother's house but changed her mind. Their relationship was already challenged. Not to mention that Dina's mother Judy, didn't like the idea of Dina moving in with Carl. At this point, their relationship was more than strained. Dina also didn't get along with her sister, Dionne, so calling her was out of the question. She felt stuck. Dina

35

flopped down on the living room sofa and sulked. She turned on the television and started flipping the channels. Carl came into the room and stood directly in front of her. Dina sighed and cut her eyes at him.

"Could you move, please? You are blocking the television," Dina said.

"This is not going to work unless you at least try to trust me," Carl said.

"You have to give me a reason to trust you."

"If it's that bad then why stay?"

"You want me to go?" Dina was on the verge of tears.

"I never said that. You're always so busy jumping to conclusions. You get yourself all worked up before you ever know what's really going down."

Dina huffed again and the tears began to fall. Carl sighed and shook his head. "Come on, get dressed. We're going out."

Dina wiped her tears with the back of her hand. "Who said I wanted to go anywhere with you?"

"Just get yourself together so we can go."

"Where are we going?"

"Don't worry about that, just get dressed. Throw on something cute, and look good for your man. We're going to hang out today."

Dina's anger melted. She was happy to be the one Carl chose to hang out with for a change. Lately, he had made more of an effort to be attentive to her. She allowed herself to get so caught up in the thought of him cheating on her that she'd let it get the best of her. Maybe this was just what they needed. She got up, showered, and put on a white strapless top adorned with a yellow rose, a knee-length denim skirt that accentuated her feminine lines, and a sexy pair of yellow sandals. She'd bring along her matching denim jacket just in case it became cooler as the night progressed.

Carl stepped out looking rather dapper in gray slacks and a bold-stripped, gray and white, button down shirt. Looking good and smelling better they jumped into Carl's oversized Yukon Denali and headed out. Dina was happy at last.

Once inside the car, Carl put in the Chocolate Factory CD by R. Kelly and sang the title track to her as he drove and held her hand. They drove to City Island and dined on lobster and crab legs. Dina nearly drank a bottle of Chardonnay by herself. After dinner, they headed over to a popular club and lounge in the heart of the Flatiron District in Manhattan.

As they parked and exited the car, Carl asked Dina to place his keys and cell phone in her bag. When they entered the club, Dina said, "Babe, I need to go to the little girl's room. Find us a spot and I will be right back." Carl nodded and planted a sweet peck on Dina's lips.

Dina entered the rest room and raced for the large handicap stall at the opposite end. Once inside, she pulled out Carl's phone and began to go through the numbers, first checking the names stored, then checking incoming and outgoing calls. She made note of the call that came in earlier that evening and wrote down a few of the other numbers. One name in particular caught her attention, Tamara. She couldn't recall why that name sounded familiar to her. Hoping she hadn't spent too much time examining the contents of Carl's cell phone, she went to the mirror, checked herself, and applied a light coat of gloss to her lips before heading out.

Dina exited the ladies room in search of Carl. She found him at a table near the bar sipping his drink and bobbing his head to the music. Just then a scantily dressed, well endowed woman approached Carl and began rubbing the back of his head. Dina stopped and watched a moment. She wanted to see how Carl planned on handling his guest. The woman's flirtatious smile widened as Carl spoke. Dina had enough and began a brisk walk in their direction, stopping close enough to make the visitor and Carl uncomfortable. The woman stared at Dina as if she was intruding. Dina raised her brows. Carl chimed in immediately.

"Chanel, this is my girlfriend, Dina."

Carl took Dina by the hand and drew her closer to him. Dina bumped the woman purposely and sat on Carl's lap. The woman turned her lip up. "Dina, this is Chanel, Rob's sister. You remember Rob, right?"

"I don't recall." Her response was dry.

Dina reached for the drink across the table that Carl ordered while she was in the bathroom. Dina sized the woman up and determined she was no threat. Dina was much prettier even though the woman was overdeveloped in a few key areas. She looked sloppy and unkempt. Dina knew that was a major turnoff to most men, especially Carl.

"Whatever, Carl, I'll see you later. I'll tell Rob that I saw you. Take care of yourself."

Chanel waved her too-long, acrylic nails haphazardly and departed, but not before cutting her eyes at Dina.

Carl and Dina watched her abundant assets sway away. Carl turned his attention back to Dina.

"You need to relax," he said.

"What's that supposed to mean?" Dina asked.

"You know what I am talking about. Why do you think that I'm after every woman out there or that they're all after me?"

"I don't think that," Dina whined.

"Yeah, you just don't trust me."

Dina stayed quiet for a moment. "Babe, how about we dance?"

Dina stood and took Carl by the hand. Carl sighed, took one last sip of his drink, and accompanied Dina to the dance floor. They danced for the next hour. The wine Dina consumed began to take toll on her bladder. She excused herself once more and headed to the ladies' room. Just as she entered the crowded room, Chanel approached the door to leave. The two women spotted one another and the staring match began. Dina cut her eyes at Chanel, lifted her chin, and made her way to the nearest stall. She relieved herself, freshened up, and exited the rest room. When she came out, she saw Carl seated back at their table. Chanel approached him once again with a wide-grinned smile.

Dina hastened her steps in their direction. She could see Chanel smile and run her hand along Carl's inner thigh. Carl didn't flinch. Dina pushed passed the patrons in her way, leaped towards the table, and grabbed Chanel by her long ponytail. Chanel screamed and tried fanatically to remove her hair from Dina's grasp. Dina refused to let go and wrung her hand around the girl's ponytail. Dina dragged her to and fro. Chanel finally got hold of Dina by the leg. Dina fell flat on her behind. Chanel's hairpiece accompanied Dina to the floor. Chanel was left with a short wad of hair jutting from the center of her head.

Chanel's eyes widened with horror at the sight of her ponytail in Dina's hands. Dina saw the horror in Chanel's twisted expression; but before she could move, Chanel pounced on her, and successfully landed several hard blows. Chanel's punches were flowing so rapidly, Dina was hardly able to block them. The two continued the tussle. They rolled down the two steps separating the tables from the dance floor, and knocked two unsuspecting dancers to the floor. Carl ran to the feuding women to break them up. By the time security managed to break through the crowd of onlookers, Carl managed to pull them apart. Chanel reached for Dina one last time, catching her by the front of her shirt, and exposing her bare breast to the entire club. Dina recovered and reached toward Chanel once again. Because of Carl's hold on her she couldn't reach her with her hands; so she lifted her foot and delivered a swift, hard kick right between Chanel's thighs. Chanel howled in pain and dropped to the floor, cupping the center of her womanhood. Carl carried Dina out of the club. She looked a mess.

Outside, Dina tried to collect herself. She pressed her hair down and adjusted her clothing. Carl grabbed her by the hand and dragged her to the car. The clatter of her heels against the concrete echoed through the darkness of the night. Carl opened the passenger-side door and threw Dina into the car. He marched to the driver's side, swung the door open, jumped in, and slammed the door shut. He turned to Dina and pointed his finger in her face. He came so close that Dina fought the urge to bite his finger off.

Carl bit his bottom lip, took a deep breath, and stared at her. His jaw tightened. Finally he swung his body back around and jammed the keys into the ignition. Dina sat silent with her arms bent across her chest, her hair awry, her face bruised, and her shirt soiled. Carl threw the car into gear and pulled off fast, jerking the SUV forward. Thick, tense silence rode with them all the way home.

Chapter 7

Kennedy leaped out of bed and ran to the door in her close-fitting tank and panties. Who could be banging at her door at this time of the night? she wondered. The knocks permeated throughout the entire house.

"This better be an emergency."

Kennedy peered through the peephole. The porch light wasn't on, so all she could see was Dina's frame. What was Dina doing at her door at this time of the night? Kennedy flipped the locks and swung the door open, stepping behind it so no one would see her in her scant lounge wear. Dina raced inside, still flustered from the events of the evening, and began pacing the living room.

Kennedy was in awe at the sight of Dina. Her shirt was ripped, her cheek bruised, and her hair stood awry.

"What the hell happened to you? I know Carl didn't do this."

Dina seemed to snap out of her pacing trance and simply stared at Kennedy with no response. Kennedy moved towards Dina to examine her bruised face more closely. Tears began to fall from Dina's eyes under the scrutiny of the examination. Kennedy shook her head and sighed.

"Sit down. I'm going to make us some tea. When I come back, you need to tell me what the hell is going on."

Dina flopped on the couch and grimaced. Kennedy headed to the kitchen, preparing herself mentally for what she was about to hear. She got the kettle going and realized that all she had on was her tank and panties. Kennedy started to go and put on more clothes but figured it wasn't necessary. It was only Dina there and she was her best friend.

Kennedy came out of the kitchen with two steaming cups of chamomile tea only to find Dina fast asleep across the couch. She placed the hot cups on the coffee table and shook her friend gently. If she needed to sleep, then she could go to the guest room and be comfortable. Dina woke with a start and began swinging punches, knocking Kennedy back a few paces before she grabbed a hold of Dina's flailing arms and shook some sense into her.

"Dina, girl, it's me. Relax!"

Dina collected herself and looked around as if she didn't know where she was or how she'd gotten there.

"Oh my goodness, Ken, I am so sorry."

"What's up with you, Dee?"

Kennedy handed Dina the cup of tea, hoping it would calm her down.

Dina took a sip. After a few more quick sips, Dina appeared to calm herself. She took a deep breath and placed her cup back on the coaster.

"Would you believe I was in two fights tonight?"

"Two fights? With who?" Kennedy was puzzled.

"Let me explain." Dina pulled her legs to her chest and got comfortable on Kennedy's leather love seat. She hugged her legs and took another deep breath, then lightly touched her bruised cheek. Dina explained the events leading up to the fight with Chanel in the club, revealing every detail.

Kennedy shook her head from side to side as she listened

43

to Dina convey the fine points of the evening.

"Carl was pissed. He practically threw me in the car and drove home so fast I didn't breathe until we got to the house. Neither of us uttered a word all the way home." Dina took another sip of tea and continued. "When we got to the house, we got into it. He was screaming at the top of his lungs. 'I can't believe your ass. You're supposed to be a lady, my lady, and you're out there brawling like a low-life half wit from the streets.'"

"He's right, Dee. You said the chick wasn't competition. Why fight? You definitely let jealousy get the best of you. Look at us. We are not the type of women that need to fight for any man. Girl, I can't believe you."

"Kennedy, that girl knew what she was doing. She did it on purpose. I wasn't going to let her get away with that. And Carl was too damn stupid to notice."

"Well, I agree with him. What else did he say?"

"I can't even remember. But when the screaming match got really heated he grabbed me and shook me so hard I thought my head was going to fall off. I don't even think he realized what he did because after he shook me, he just stood there staring me in the face. Then he let go, stomped into the bedroom, and slammed the door shut. That's when I grabbed my car keys and left. I came straight here."

Dina's voice trailed off at the end of her sentence, and she held her head down. Silent tears began to roll once again. Kennedy came over to the love seat, sat by Dina, and held her in her arms.

"Ken, I don't know what the hell this relationship is turning into. I've never acted like this over a man before."

"There's always someone that brings out a side of you that you never thought existed."

"I love him, Ken. I don't want to lose him but he makes me crazy sometimes. When I saw that damn girl touch him, I could feel fire rise in my insides. My mind went blank, and I just lost it. And he thinks I am the one who's wrong." Dina laid her head on Kennedy's shoulder and released her tears.

Kennedy didn't say a word. She just held her friend. Any words that she had for her friend were much too harsh for her current fragile state. She'd let her get some rest tonight and talk to her about the situation later.

"Kennedy, why is it that you never seem to have these kinds of problems with the men you date?"

"I told you before. I never get too wrapped up into men. Love is for soft folks."

"Yeah, you're far from soft," Dina chuckled. Kennedy smirked.

Dina rested back into Kennedy's arms. The two sat quietly listening to the ticks of the clock in the kitchen. When Dina's heavy breathing gave way to a soft snore, Kennedy knew that she was again fast asleep. Kennedy tried to carefully steal herself away from Dina without waking her. With Kennedy's movement, Dina snuggled deeper into her friend's embrace. Kennedy tried again. This time Dina woke with a pensive look. Staring directly into Kennedy's face, Dina smiled a wry smile, pulled Kennedy to her, and kissed her square on the lips. Kennedy pulled away immediately and jumped off the couch. Dina looked baffled by Kennedy's response then, her jaw dropped, her eyes stretched open, and she cupped her mouth with her hands.

"Oh my goodness, Ken, I am sorry. I..."

Kennedy just stared at Dina, wondering what the hell just happened. Her friend had just kissed her like she was a man—her man. Kennedy threw her hand in the air and walked off, leaving Dina seated on the couch with her mouth hanging open.

Chapter 8

Troy had taken a day off from work to handle some of his father's business. Lela, his dad's girlfriend, would take over the Union Turnpike office and purchase the building from him for a reasonable amount. Troy let Lela place the other two locations on the market to be sold. He had no interest in real estate so there was no need for him to hold on to those businesses. Realtors from those offices would move to the Union Turnpike location or find other places to work. The money would be dispersed between his mother, sister, and himself. The sale of the two offices was expected to generate over seven hundred and fifty thousand dollars.

William Alexander also owned several multi-family homes throughout Queens and Brooklyn. Troy would be responsible for working with his father's property management firm to keep up with the homes. The firm collected rent and maintained the buildings. Troy's dad also had a sizeable portfolio of investments, cash, and several hefty insurance policies as well as a secret one just for Lela. She would be well taken care of as a result of William's passing. Yet what Lela was due to receive didn't compare to what he was leaving to his wife and children. Troy was sure that his father's intentions were motivated by guilt.

During one of his visits, his father divulged a few details about his relationship with Lela. To Troy's surprise, Lela was the reason his mother kicked his father out nearly fifteen years ago.

Lela was about ten years younger than Troy's dad. She had come to work at his real estate office fresh out of the real estate training course. Outside of her beauty, her apparent sweetness and innocence struck a cord with Mr. Alexander. Using this front, she reeled him in. Late hours at the office turned into overnight stays. After hours, the office became their forbidden playground. Eventually Mrs. Alexander came to realize that there was a lot more going on at the office than selling homes.

One day, Mrs. Jean Alexander came to the office. The moment she stepped in the door the receptionist made feeble attempts to stall her. Mrs. Alexander marched straight to the back of the office. As she approached her husband's door, she heard light laughter then silence, a womanly chuckle and more silence. Finally she could hear pleasure-filled sighs and deep groans seep through the cracks in the door.

The receptionist frantically attempted to contact Mr. Alexander on his phone and warn him about his wife's visit, but he didn't answer. Mrs. Alexander came back to the front, gingerly placed her purse on one of the realtor's desk, and then eyed the metal chair from the waiting area. Grabbing the chair by the back, she dragged it through the office, picked it up over her head, and slammed it against the door. Mr. Alexander came rushing through the door screaming, "What the hell is going on here?" He halted in his tracks at the sight of his seething wife.

"Baby, wh…What are you doing here?" Mr. Alexander sputtered as he tried to block Lela from Jean's view.

Lela was fully dressed but hadn't had enough time to close the buttons on her shirt, leaving bare cleavage exposed. Jean pushed passed William, barged into the office, and quickly looked around taking in all of the evidence. Disheveled papers were scattered across William's desk. One high-heeled, black shoe looked as if it was carelessly flung across the floor. Jean's ample chest rose and fell heavily as she assessed her surroundings. Everyone appeared to be glued to their spot. Jean tossed sharp glares back and forth between the cheating couple. She had seen all she needed for one afternoon. Anger tightened her throat and all Jean could do was simply point a finger at her husband as she slowly approached him. He took a few steps back and she drew nearer. With narrowed eyes, Jean stared him down and he pleaded with her to understand and at least let him explain. Without saying another word, she straightened her back, lifted her chin and walked out of the office. Labored steps carried her back up front to the reception area where she brushed off her clothes and slapped her hands together signaling her declaration of the end. Gracefully she grabbed her purse, and stepped outside without ever looking back.

49

After the initial shock wore off, William ran after his wife and followed her home to plead for a second chance. When he reached the house she met him at the door with a steak knife, left her mark upon his head, and packed his clothes. In the midst of her pain-filled ranting, he learned that Jean's visit was planned by Lela, who called and advised her that William wanted to take her out to lunch.

That evening, William brought his overnight bag back to work with him. When he returned to his office to tell Lela she had to go, she was sitting on his desk with her legs crossed, shirt open and a cynical smile on her lips. William turned and walked out leaving her right where she sat.

Over time Lela continued to work on him until she finally won him over. William decided that if they were going to be together, it would be on his terms, then promised Lela that he would never divorce his wife and that his children would always come first. Occasionally she would attempt to convince him to divorce his wife and marry her but he held his ground.

"Because of that girl, I made the biggest mistake of my life. Then I fell in love with her," William admitted to Troy.

Troy believed he would never be weak enough to jeopardize his family in the manner in which his father had. That was, of course, once he got the family he always wanted—with Kennedy.

Chapter 9

More than a week had passed since the kissing episode at Kennedy's place. Dina was embarrassed and couldn't bring herself to call her friend. What must Kennedy think about that night? Dina had high-tailed it out of Kennedy's house as soon as she heard the door to her bedroom slam shut. That left her with no choice but to go back home to Carl. She surely couldn't show up at her mother's house at that late hour looking like she had lost a fight with a gang of garden tools. Life with Carl hadn't been easy, but they finally made up over the weekend. Dina apologized for acting out, and Carl apologized for shaking her. They spent Saturday evening at home making up with one another.

Now that things were back to normal with Carl, Dina knew she needed to work things out with Kennedy. She decided to invite Kennedy out to dinner—her treat. She'd be sure to invite Angel as well to absorb some of the tension. Both girls agreed. Kennedy made no mention about the prior week, and they all decided to meet at one of their favorite after-work spots in Chelsea.

Dina was the first to arrive. Still nervous about confronting Kennedy, she tried to take the edge off with a chocolate martini. Eventually Angel came scurrying in, apologizing for her lateness.

Out of breath, Angel announced, "My train just stopped in the tunnel and sat for about twenty minutes. No announcements, no explanations, nothing. Don't you just love New York?" Then she chuckled and ordered a Merlot. "What's the matter, sweetie, you don't look too happy?"

"Just overwhelmed. You know, work, life, man, etc," Dina said.

"Well I can relate to the work and life part, but I don't exactly have a man right now, remember?" Angel said, chuckled, then got comfortable in her chair.

"Girl, are you sure you want one?" Dina asked and both girls laughed.

"Ah, sweetie, is everything okay with you and Carl?"

Dina hesitated. Even though Angel didn't have a man, her life always seemed so calm and perfect compared to Dina's. Dina never felt very comfortable disclosing the mishaps of her life to her bubbly friend who never seemed to have any drama of her own. Kennedy, on the other hand, created drama so Dina didn't feel so exposed sharing things with her.

"Same ole, same ole," Dina said.

Just then Kennedy came prancing in, commanding the attention of both male and female patrons. Dina rolled her eyes. Kennedy donned a flowing, colorful halter top with a spilt up the center, revealing her pierced belly button. Her fitted jeans accentuated her curvy hips and round bottom.

"Hey, sweetie, how are you?" Angel gave Kennedy a friendly hug and a real kiss on the cheek. Not one of those fake air kisses that most women give. "You look so cute, as always. I love that shirt."

Dina wished Angel wouldn't throw compliments at Kennedy the way she did. She was the last person that needed to hear about how good she looked. Kennedy air-kissed Angel and sat down.

"Hey, Dee. What's up?"

"Hi, Ken."

Kennedy swung around and ordered a drink. Dina told the hostess that their complete party had arrived and they would like to be seated as soon as possible. The hostess showed them to a table immediately. On their way to the table, Kennedy said she had to go to the ladies' room. Dina told Angel she had to go too and they would meet her at the table.

Dina stepped into the ladies room behind Kennedy, who hadn't said more than 'hey' since she arrived. Dina sighed and tried to put the words together in her head.

"Ken, listen. I…I'm not sure what to say about last we…"

"Don't bother. You flipped out for a minute. Just don't let that shit happen again."

Kennedy painted on a fresh coat of gloss and headed for the door. Dina really had to use the facilities, so she headed for an empty stall. Kennedy could be so abrasive at times. At least that was out of the way. Now she could go on with life as usual.

When Dina got back to the table, there was a fresh round of drinks for all the ladies. Still troubled by the incident and somewhat annoyed at Kennedy's flippant remark in the bathroom, Dina decided that she was going to let it all hang out that night. She needed this night out more than anything.

"It's been a few weeks, so what's been up ladies?" Angel asked.

"Troy wants to get back with me," Kennedy said.

Both Dina's and Angel's eyes opened wide. Angel smiled.

"You're kidding me?" Angel's expression showed she was truly surprised.

"I'm not surprised at all, he's always wanted her. You can tell by the way he acts when she is around. Poor guy, don't know what he's asking for," Dina teased.

Each girl chuckled.

"What's that supposed to mean?" Kennedy asked.

"Ken, you know you're a mess. That man can't handle you. I don't know how you made it so far before, " Dina continued and chuckled.

Angel said, "She's right, Ken. You know you are a little hot to trot."

"I'm considering it," Kennedy admitted.

"Really," Angel asked.

"Whatever," Dina said.

"Well, girls, I think I may have found someone myself," Angel said.

"Go, Angel," Kennedy sang.

"Well, tell us about him," Dina said and immediately regretted making the statement.

Angel went on for the next ten minutes or so, raving about her new friend. He was so cute, had a nice body and best of all, he's a Dentist. After multiple attempts to get Angel to go out with him, she had finally agreed. They would have their first date the following weekend. The more the girls talked, the more Dina drank. After a while they started to get on her nerves with their stories of how great their lives were. Either they were telling lies or simply trying to torture her.

The girls ordered a few appetizers for the table to serve as their meals, and they drank some more until they were served. No one seemed to notice Dina's altering state.

"So wait," Angel said. "Let's get back to you, Kennedy. Are you really thinking about getting back with Troy? That's so sweet. I know little Evan will love that."

Dina rolled her eyes again and belched up some of her appetizer. She swallowed it, sending it back where it belonged. Their lives were flourishing while hers was slowly spinning out of control. Why wasn't she ever the bearer of the good news?

"Yeah. Partly for Evan's sake," Kennedy said.

"Are you doing it for you or for Evan?" Angel asked.

"For both of us," Kennedy admitted.

Dina had had enough. "Ooh. Watch out, Ken, you might end up falling in love," Dina said stretching out the word love like a six year old. "Love is for suckers or soft people, remember? That's what you told me."

"I think somebody exceeded their drinking limit," Angel teased.

Kennedy stared at Dina across the table. "I have a soft side."

Dina laughed loud. "Oh yeah? Where?" She slurred.

"Dee, please. I just try to help you avoid getting tangled in the webs you so eloquently weave. What, do you think I'm incapable of being in love?" Kennedy asked.

"Yeah, pretty much. You're a frigid bitch," Dina replied and rolled her eyes.

Angel's eyes stretched yet again. "Whoa! Dee. Relax, sweetie. I think the martinis are getting the best of you."

"Let her vent. She needs to get it out. She's dealt with a lot lately. Angel, you know Dina, and you know me well enough to know that this stuff does not bother me."

"Not to mention, Ken, what qualifies Troy to be considered for a second chance? He's doesn't look like he's rolling in the dough like your usual prospects. How long will it be before you kick him to the curb like last season's boots?"

"Whatever, Dina." Kennedy was clearly becoming annoyed with Dina's snide comments.

"Dina, sweetie, are you all right?" Angel asked. She appeared to be genuinely concerned.

"Angel, please. Cut it with that sweet, mushy shit." Angel's eyes stretched wide but she didn't say a word and Dina continued, "You know Kennedy as well as me. How long do you think it will be before she gets bored with him? Troy's not her type. He's one of the few good ones," Dina said directing the last statement to Kennedy by way of her agitated expression, then she took another large gulp of her drink.

"Okay, Dee, that's enough. Chill out, all right," Kennedy said.

Kennedy's indifference angered Dina more as the liquor swam in her stomach and altered her sense of reason. The gates holding back her emotions ruptured under the weight of her misery and flowed freely with the aid of the liquid courage.

"Kennedy, please. Don't tell me when enough is enough." Dina slammed her hand on the table, then repositioned herself to face Kennedy directly. "One day you will realize that people are made of more than just money. You always have something to say to me for loving Carl. You criticize me for going through my ups and downs with him, but apparently you don't care that it takes more than a damn trip to an island somewhere and a fur coat to maintain a true relationship. The messed up part is that you always end up with the good ones. If only they knew that you didn't give a shit about anything other than what's in their bank accounts, they wouldn't be bothered with your ass. You always treat me like I don't know enough to handle myself, like I'm stupid because I want more from a man than his money. I am not stupid. I want to be loved. I want to be more than a high-priced, high-maintenance, cold-hearted money chaser!"

"Dina, you don't mean that." Angel placed her hand across her forehead and shook her head back and forth. "Ken, she's tipsy. Don't pay her any mind. Dee, relax please."

"The truth is, Dina, you don't know what you want. You think you want love but I know how important money really is to you. You wouldn't be so 'in love' with Carl if he didn't have money. All of a sudden you're so much better than me because you claim to have a heart. Don't give me the bullshit. I know what motivates you, and I know where your intentions lie. You're just not genuine enough to own up to them." Kennedy said then she opened her Christian Dior purse, pulled out a fifty-dollar bill tossed it on the table, and left.

Chapter 10

More than a month had passed since Dina's blowout at the restaurant with Kennedy and Angel. She had yet to speak to either of her friends. Angel called her nonstop to check in on her. Angel must have thought that Dina lost her mind. She was trying to be Dina's psychoanalyst with her bubbly self, but the last thing Dina needed was Angel's counsel. She loved Angel dearly, but right now she didn't give a rat's ass about what Angel had to say. It was time to talk directly to Kennedy.

Dina didn't remember all that she had said that night, especially after the martinis took over her ability to think and speak coherently. Angel had been the one to tell her exactly what had transpired. Dina knew Kennedy was furious with her and didn't want to go near the raging flames. She wanted to give Kennedy time to simmer down. After all the terrible things she'd said, Dina felt that she deserved the lashing Kennedy had given her that evening. And she admitted there was quite a bit of truth to Kennedy's accusation.

Things with Carl were still like a roller coaster—up one day, down the next. Her jealousy was getting the best of her. Everywhere they went, Carl knew some woman in the vicinity. A woman who had to make sure Carl saw her too. A woman determined to make her presence known. She hadn't had anymore fights, but she and Carl sure had some knockout arguments. They fought constantly.

For a week, Dina had gone as far as to forward Carl's calls

from his cell phone to hers. Every time he received a call, it went straight to Dina's voicemail. Carl mentioned to Dina that people said they called his number but didn't get him, but couldn't understand why. It's possible that he assumed there was a problem with the service. When he voiced the fact that he thought his phone was on the blink, Dina secretly stopped forwarding the calls. She had received a few female callers but nothing that sounded suspicious enough to act on. Dina promised herself that next time she would not forward the calls for such a long period of time.

Kennedy was the only person Dina could talk to about her and Carl's fanatical relationship, and she decided it was time to stop the madness and get her friend back. She figured Kennedy wouldn't answer if she called, so she decided to drop by and talk to her face to face. Since it was Saturday morning she assumed Kennedy would probably be home cleaning her house.

When Dina pulled up, Kennedy was just entering her townhouse with a few bags in her hands. Dina quickly parked and ran towards the door calling Kennedy's name. She turned and made eye contact with Dina, but continued to walk through the door. She left the door open. Dina let herself in and met her in the kitchen.

Kennedy put down her bags, put her hands on her hips, and waited for Dina to speak.

"Ken, I'm sorry," Dina blurted.

"You sure are a sorry ass," Kennedy laughed. "Don't think I am going to keep taking your snide ass comments. I'm the one who's there for you when you go through your bullshit. I am tired of catching your daggers when you get pissed off or drunk."

"I know, Ken. I didn't even realize all the stuff I said that night. Angel called me and told me what I said. She filled in the blanks for me."

Kennedy started putting the food she bought away. Dina joined in and helped.

"People say a drunken tongue speaks the truth. So I guess that's how you really feel. You should have said something before," Kennedy said without looking directly at Dina.

"I didn't mean all of that. I was just being mean. Sometimes I feel like my life is always spinning out of control while everyone else is living la vida wonderful," Dina said then lowered her eyes.

"I will not join your pity party. No matter what you think I think about you, you are not stupid. You know what you need to do, but you simply choose not to," Kennedy said.

Dina kept her eyes lowered as Kennedy played on that piece of her heated monologue from that drunken night.

Dina started to pout and swing from side to side like a little girl. "Ken, are you my friend again?"

Kennedy looked at Dina acting girlish and hugged her.

"It's been a while. What's up with you?" Dina asked, but before Kennedy could answer, Dina looked around and asked, "Where's Evan?"

"Evan is with Troy this weekend. But I do have some news that I'm sure you'll love." Dina's eyes widened. Kennedy got a kick out of baiting Dina with the lure of gossip. "Troy and I are officially back together."

"Really?"

"Yes, really."

"You mean it this time, Ken? I know you."

"Don't worry about me, Dina."

Dina hung out at Kennedy's place for a few hours. She helped her clean while they talked about what they missed in the past month and brought each other up to date on the status of their love lives. Dina was surprised to see that Kennedy appeared to be sincere with rekindling the flames with Troy. Not only was Troy genuinely a nice guy, but he was damn good-looking too. Maybe Kennedy could change. Maybe she did have some warmth somewhere inside of that pulsating boulder she called a heart.

"So, Ken, now that you are all down with the soft folks in love..." Kennedy shot Dina a playful glare. Dina laughed and continued, "Have you officially kicked all other prospects to the curb?"

"Actually, yes."

"Wow, this is for real," Dina said, genuinely surprised as she helped herself to one of Kennedy's Granny Smith apples.

"I told you."

"Well I wish you the best."

Dina looked at her watch and determined it was time to head back home. Carl had no idea where she was, even though he hadn't bothered calling to find out.

"I gotta run, Ken. I'll call you later."

As Dina left she noticed a familiar face approaching Kennedy's door. Then it hit her. Andre. Kennedy's former prospect –the one with the wife and new kid. She turned around and ran back inside.

"Uh, Ken, you have company. Andre is on his way to your door right now."

Kennedy looked surprised, "You sure it's him?"

"Yes, Ken, I remember those biceps. You better go see what he wants."

"I thought you were leaving?"

"I was, but I just got some incentive to hang out a little longer."

"Go home, nosy. I need to get him away from here anyway. Troy and Evan should be on their way back from the movies soon."

"All right, all right. I'll leave. But you better call me and let me know what's up."

"Get out!" Kennedy pushed Dina to the door.

Andre had just reached the porch.

Chapter 11

Kennedy wondered what made Andre show up on her doorstep after all this time. She constantly fought to push him from her thoughts and surely didn't need him coming around to complicate things. One thing was for sure, he wouldn't see her sweat.

"Bye, Dina. I'll call you later," she said as she pushed her nosy friend out of her front door.

Andre greeted Dina and stepped aside to let her by.

Kennedy had a number of things she could have said to Andre. Cordially she chose, "What brings you by, Mr. Lewis?" Kennedy could never deny him his hard body and good looks. He reminded her of Godiva's dark chocolate.

"Hello, Ms. Divine." His voice was deep and smooth like rich-colored velvet.

"What can I do for you?"

"Can I come in?"

"Not really."

Andre sighed. "I really need to talk to you."

"How are the wife and kid?"

"Kennedy, please. Can I come in and talk to you?"

Kennedy figured it couldn't hurt. The sooner she let him in to talk, the sooner he could leave. She sighed before saying, "Come on in, but please make it brief, I have a lot on my plate today, and I'm expecting company."

He started with small talk. "You look great as usual."

"Cut to the chase, Andre."

"Okay, okay." Andre rubbed his hands along the sides of his pants. "Can I have a seat at least?"

Kennedy shut the door and led Andre to the living room. She motioned for him to have a seat on the love seat and took her seat on the couch.

"I'll get straight to the point."

"Please do."

On the outside, Kennedy was hard. Inside she was fighting to keep her emotions in tact. Emotions that began to stir the moment she saw him. The richness of his voice almost softened her. Thoughts of Indira and the infant wrestled to keep her focused.

"I miss you, Ken. You wouldn't believe how much. Indira and I are no longer together. We weren't really together when she had the baby. Things hadn't been good even before the baby. We got caught up, that's all. One thing led to another, and she ended up pregnant."

"Wow, that easy huh?"

"Please, hear me out. I told her from the beginning I would be there for the baby, but there was nothing more for us."

Kennedy was half listening and it showed. Andre stood and that got her full attention. He made his way over to the couch she was sitting on, sat next to her, and took her by the hand. Kennedy rolled her eyes.

"Baby, all I'm asking is a chance to show you I am for real. I told Indira how I feel. She's already accepted it. I need you, baby. Let's work it out."

"Andre, I have moved on and so should you."

"You have somebody already?" Andre asked incredulously.

"What do you mean *already?* You've had somebody else all along." Kennedy reminded him. *The nerve of this man,* Kennedy thought. "Baby, we can do this. My life is on track. Indira knows where she stands. My interest is caring for my baby girl. The business is doing well and I'm in the process of buying out my partner. How about we go away for a long weekend—give us a chance to reconnect."

Kennedy was touched, but she couldn't show Andre. Besides, she had to stay strong and stick to her guns. What she had coming with Troy wasn't worth passing up for Andre. No matter how much he still affected her, she wasn't going back to him. That chapter was closed.

"I'm sorry, Andre. Wife or no wife, business or no business, we don't have a future. Understand that."

"I know you don't mean that, baby. I know how you feel about us. Can you just throw it all away?"

"Maybe you should have thought about all of that when you hid the fact that your wife was pregnant. I had to find out from her directly. No, I can't do this again!"

"Baby, the trip. Let me take you away and give you a chance to think it over."

"Andre, don't you get it? There's nothing for me to think over. We don't have a future. I don't care about your business. I don't want you anymore. And, you know what? You were falling apart before all of this came out anyway. The end was already near. You knew what it took to keep me, but you weren't handling your business properly. Instead of screwing your wife behind my back, you should have been taking care of me the way I need to be taken care of."

Andre's face twisted with rage. Kennedy realized she had stuck a nerve and kept digging.

"Yeah, I need my man to be focused. You let the prospect of a night of pleasure cause you to lose your focus. Who needs a man like you? Why don't you go back to Indira? She's obviously weak, I'm sure she's more your speed."

"You don't have to be so nasty, Kennedy."

"What's wrong? Can't handle it like a man?"

"Watch yourself, Ken."

"Watch myself?

"Yes, watch your mouth. All of that is not necessary." Andre said slowly. His anger had clearly risen to the surface and his lips pursed to a thin line.

"Don't tell me what's necessary," Kennedy shouted.

"Why do you have to be such a bitch?"

Kennedy, stunned by his reference, lifted her hand and delivered her open hand to the side of his face with as much force as she could muster. She attempted to slap him again, but this time he caught her hand mid-air. Andre's gnawed on his bottom lip. Kennedy's hand was tied by his tight grip, so she continued with her assault verbally.

"Get off of me."

Andre stared at Kennedy as if he wanted to slug her one good time. She continued to taunt him, "Oh what are you going to do, hit me? Go ahead. Prove to me once again how much of a man you really are."

Andre's face made strange contortions. Apparently he'd had his fill of insults for the day, but his rapid change of expressions jarred Kennedy. She had gone too far.

"Now I'm not a man? You weren't saying that when I was buying you furs and paying your mortgage. I guess that's all you really cared about. Without that I'm nothing to you huh? I guess you are just like your mother."

Kennedy's jaw dropped. Andre's face continued a series of transformations. She tried to get away from his grip, but he held on strong. "I'll show you how much of a man I can be. You think you can just say whatever the hell you want to people. You are nothing but a high maintenance gold digger. I've got a man for you right here, baby."

Andre grabbed Kennedy's free arm in the same hand that held the hand she'd slapped him with. With his other hand he ripped open Kennedy's tank top. Kennedy began kicking and screaming in an attempt to release herself from his hold. Andre held tighter.

"Get off of me." She caught a glimpse of his eyes and was gripped with fear.

Andre wore the look of a deranged man as he slung insults in a pitch slightly higher than the normal tone of his voice.

"I got your man for you. Let's see how much respect you have now."

Andre ripped Kennedy's bra from the center and pulled at her sweat pants. Kennedy yelped and managed to free one hand to hold onto her pants. Andre was too strong for her and pulled her pants down. She was down to her panties and getting more scared by the second. Kennedy tried to knee Andre in the balls. Andre covered himself and continued in his pursuit.

He spat as he spoke, "Yeah, bitch, I'll show you how much of a man I am."

Andre fumbled to free his erect manhood from his pants. With her back held firmly to the couch, Kennedy squirmed to keep him from entering her. She fought until there was no more fight in her. Then she fought some more.

Andre pressed his large frame on top of her and rammed himself inside. He showered her face with saliva as he sputtered curses at her. Kennedy felt and heard her skin rip when Andre finally succeeded in forcing his way inside of her, robbing her of her sense of dignity. Kennedy cried out and tears sprang from her eyes.

She screamed, "No, Andre. Please no."

It appeared as though another entity had taken a hold of Andre as he continued to thrust himself in and out of Kennedy. She freed her hands from his powerful grasp and scratched at Andre's face. Kennedy carved rich red lines from his forehead to his eye and down his cheek. She closed her hands and turned the scratches into punches, rapidly landing one blow after the other. Andre lifted his arms to block the onslaught of Kennedy's reign. He convulsed, grabbed a hold of Kennedy's flailing arms, and released his life-giving fluids inside of her.

Andre jumped up and looked down at Kennedy. She had balled up in a fetal position and cried as she rocked back and forth.

"Oh God, Kennedy. I'm sorry." Andre's hands flew to his mouth.

"GET OUT!" She cried and winced from the immense

pain. "Get out of my house. I'll kill you for this," she howled releasing a piercing wail akin to that of a wounded animal.

Andre stood over her shocked. Kennedy spotted pain in his eyes and took in the scratches and bruises she managed to bestow. He reached for her. She found strength and leaped on him, hurling blows at an astounding pace. Andre tried to shield his body from the rage. He backed away until he was out of her reach, then bolted for the front door. Kennedy's body quaked. Her knees had forsaken her and sent her crashing to the ground. Kennedy stayed there and cried some more. When there were no more tears, she dragged herself to the kitchen, retrieved a freezer bag from the drawer, and crept to the bathroom to clean up.

Kennedy took a cloth and swiped at the blood between her legs. She dug deep enough to extract some of the semen he left behind. With the same cloth she cleaned his skin from beneath her nails and placed the cloth in the baggie. She carefully climbed into the shower and tried to scrub away the disdain. The water from the shower mixed with her tears. When the rest of her skin was raw from rubbing too hard, she exited the shower, cleaned up the rest of the evidence around the house, and stored the baggie in the back of the freezer.

Chapter 12

"Ma, I want to invite Kennedy to our BBQ for the Fourth of July. Is that okay with you?"

Troy's mother threw him a blank stare.

After a while she asked, "So you two are really back together?"

"Yes." Troy looked square in his mother's face.

Mrs. Alexander stood from her seat at the table in her spacious eat-in kitchen and walked toward the bay window overlooking the lush greenery garnishing the backyard. Still quiet, she placed her hands on her hips and sighed. Troy simply waited.

Troy believed his mother's dislike for Kennedy was a result of her being what most would consider a diva. She once told Troy he would be better off with a woman that was a little more humble. Troy found out his mother's real thoughts of Kennedy when his cousin, Lacey recapped a conversation that her mother had with Troy's mother. Mrs. Alexander had plainly expressed her dislike for Kennedy and referred to her as a money-grubbing, high-priced whore.

"Ma, there's more."

"I'm going to ask Kennedy to marry me."

Mrs. Alexander's neck snapped in Troy's direction, snatching her attention away from the greenery. She stared at Troy for moments before asking, "Are you sure about this? Is that what you really want?"

"Again, yes. I love her, and she's my son's mother."

Mrs. Alexander dropped her hands to her side, walked back to the table and took her seat. "What about that sweet girl you were dating a few months back?"

"Ma, I haven't been serious with anyone since Kennedy and I broke up. Now I know you don't really like her, but she's who I want to be my wife, and I just want you to be with me on my decision."

"Troy, honey, I'm not going to sit here and pretend that I like that woman. I have my feelings and reservations, and that won't change, so don't expect it to."

"I understand where you are coming from, Ma." Troy got up and kissed his mother on her forehead. She smiled.

Troy's only sister, Courtney, walked in the kitchen, looking and smelling as fresh as a spring blossom. "Hey, Ma. What's up, Troy?" she greeted as she walked over to give their mother a kiss.

"Your brother wants to marry that woman," Mrs. Alexander said and shook her head with her hands on her wide hips.

Courtney smirked and asked, "Who Kennedy?"

Troy reared his head back and asked, "Yes Kennedy. Who else would she be talking about?"

Courtney swung around and threw her hands up in surrender. "I have no comment. If that's what you want so be it. Far be it for me to tell you who to marry," She added as she checked the pots on the stove to see what their mother cooked.

Knowing how his mother and sister felt about Kennedy, Troy decided that he had done enough talking. His obligation was to let them know what he wanted and that's what he did. At a later time he would talk more about this to his sister. Even though she wasn't completely fond of Kennedy, she was more cordial to her than their mother had ever been or was ever likely to be.

"Okay, ladies, let me go before the bashing begins."

Both women displayed mock expressions of innocence. Courtney couldn't hold hers too long and burst out laughing.

"Don't worry, Troy, we won't bash your haughty girlfriend. And I promise I'll be cordial. You gave me that same respect when I was dating Mike, and you couldn't stand the ground he walked on. Remember that, Ma?"

"I didn't like his ass either. Where do you all find these people?" their mother retorted.

"It's not that I didn't like him, but I knew what he was about. He was a player or at least he thought he was. And, he was a pathological liar. Remember he told you all about the Benz that he claimed he had but didn't drive because he always got pulled over? What about the lies he told about his career? That punk worked at the mall and had you thinking he was an investment banker. Even after he found out that I was your brother, he was still trying to get over with his stupid lies, and he knew that I knew better. I went to school with that cat."

"I'll admit he was pathetic. The last straw was when I found out that the nice townhouse that I thought was his really belonged to his cousin who was always out of town on business. You know he called me a few weeks ago and told me he got a new apartment and asked me to come by. Of course I turned him down, but later I found out his new apartment was really his mother's basement. He moved to the basement from his room upstairs. Can you believe him?"

The roar of laughter filled the kitchen. Even Mrs.

Alexander found that one funny.

"I am glad I let that loser go."

"Yeah, but I had to make you see the light."

"You're supposed to, big brother."

"Whatever," Troy said, then kissed his mother and sister good-bye.

His mother asked, "Did you have plans for me to attend this wedding of yours?"

Troy sighed and left.

Chapter 13

Kennedy pulled her mother's late model-Lexus into a parking spot that was just three doors shy of Andre's storefront office on Jamaica Avenue in Queens Village. It was 5:15 in the evening. Andre's office closed at five, but he often stayed late depending on his client's schedules. Fortunately for Kennedy, this wasn't a late night. Andre walked out the front door with a briefcase and a few files in hand. He carefully placed his package on the ground and pulled down the gates to his brokerage company. Andre fumbled for his keys a few minutes and locked the gates. He double checked the locks that secured his business, grabbed his belongings, and jumped in his shiny black Mercedes Benz.

Kennedy slowly pulled into traffic, careful to stay a few cars behind Andre. She followed him on a short drive into a handsome neighborhood of grand homes and well-manicured landscape. Andre turned onto a block guarded by a "Dead End" warning sign. Kennedy slowed her pace in an effort to remain inconspicuous. She pulled over and parked as she watched Andre's car disappear into a spacious two-car garage near the end of the block. Kennedy decided to sit for a while and see if there was any activity.

After two hours of spying, the garage door gently rose, giving way to Andre's luxury vehicle. Kennedy saw a woman, who she assumed was Indira, carry a baby's car seat to the back seat of the car. Indira wore a stunning gown with her hair swept up. Andre emerged upon the scene wearing a black tux. Indira turned her attention to Andre and adjusted his tie. She stretched upwards on her toes and planted a sweet peck on Andre's lips. Andre double checked the doors then got into the car himself. Kennedy had seen all she needed to see. When Andre and Indira drove pass, Kennedy leaned over in the car as if she were looking for something. When the coast was clear, Kennedy approached the house and noted the house number.

Kennedy's mission was accomplished. She confirmed that he was indeed back in business with regards to his company and his wife.

Chapter 14

When Dina reached Kennedy's home, she expected her to be ready to go. Instead she found Kennedy still in her silky loungewear.

"What's the deal here, Ken? Carl, Angel, and Dr. Dentures are in the car waiting, and we're already an hour late."

Kennedy scrunched up her face and questioned, "Dr. Dentures?"

"Yeah, Angel's new beau. You know, the dentist guy that Angel told us about."

"Oh. Funny," Kennedy said laughing. "Who gave him that very special nickname," she asked knowingly.

Dina just gave her a look and both girls started laughing. Anyone could tell that was Dina's doing.

"Kennedy, why aren't you dressed? I spoke to you an hour ago, and we're already late for the BBQ."

"I don't want to go."

"Why."

"Don't feel like being around Troy's stuffy-ass mom. Everyone knows we're not very fond of one another."

"Troy would be so disappointed."

"And he'll get over it."

"Aw come on, Ken. You made all of us get ready for this thing, and you pull this at the last minute. That's not right." Dina marched over to Kennedy. "Get up and get dressed. You're going, whether you like it or not. I canceled other plans for this."

"I'm not going! Let's go somewhere else."

Dina was exasperated. "Fine, we will go somewhere else after you have made an appearance. But you have to show your face. Troy doesn't deserve this."

"Troy will get over it like he usually does. Besides, Evan is there already. That's all they want. They aren't interested in me, and I don't feel like being bothered with their snobby, phony asses anyway."

"Did you just call somebody else snobby?" Dina chuckled. "Well if that isn't the pot calling the kettle black."

"Call it what you want. I don't feel like being bothered."

"You are such a spoiled brat. Get up and let's go." Dina looked towards the steps leading to the bedroom. "Do I have to go and find you something to wear?"

"No, don't go in my room. You have a bad habit of snooping around and looking for things that have nothing to do with you. I'll get dressed, but I am not staying. The only reason I am bothering is because he invited all of you there. I don't want to waste your time."

Dina sighed and walked to the car to let the others in waiting know that they would have to wait a little longer. When she got back inside, Kennedy was stylishly dressed and ready to go. Her face was fresh. A glow of tinted gloss garnished her full lips. Luminous, sizeable diamond studs adorned her ears. Her mango-colored wrap dress stopped a few inches above her knees and showed a hint of her strong thighs. Kennedy snatched her keys from the table and picked up a small natural-colored Christian Dior purse that matched her shoes. She topped off her attire with amber-tinted sunglasses.

"Cute shades," Dina complimented.

"Troy's mother won't see me rolling my eyes at her. Let's go."

When they arrived at Troy's mother's house for the huge, annual Fourth of July BBQ, Dina spotted Kennedy's mother right away. She was just as stunning as Kennedy. Dina felt that usual twinge of jealously fill her insides. Mrs. Divine was impeccably dressed in a polka-dot belted tank dress that teased her ankles. The wide belt cinched her waist and accentuated her fit shape. Mrs. Divine's wide-brim summer hat fashioned an exceptional match to her designer purse and shoes.

Seated next to her was the perfect complement to a woman of her style. A very distinguished gentleman was tastefully dressed in a gray linen two-piece suit. The short-sleeved button-down shirt hung gracefully over his matching gray pants. He drank in Mrs. Divine's presence like she was an aged fine wine. Being the social butterfly that she was, Mrs. Divine held the attention of everyone in her vicinity. Her graceful moves mesmerized her audience—men and women alike. From the other side of the yard, Mrs. Alexander watched her in disgust.

Dina scanned the yard for Troy. She watched Troy practically jump out of his skin when Kennedy entered the yard. His smile spoke volumes of his admiration for her. He drank of her essence in the same way the distinguished gentleman did with her mother. Like mother like daughter. Dina wondered what was so special about the two.

"What's up, Dina? Angel?" Troy grabbed Kennedy by the hand she barely held him back.

"Hey, Troy," Dina greeted. "You remember my boyfriend, Carl?"

"What's up, man?" Troy and Carl shared a half hand-slap and half hand-shake.

The very bubbly Angel chirped, "Hey, Troy. Long time no see." She leaned in and gave him a peck on the cheek then introduced her beau, Dr. Dentures. His real name was Patrick Saunders.

Troy held onto Kennedy's hand but Dina noticed that her attention was elsewhere, as usual. This time it was on her mother holding court across the yard. Dina assumed she was wondering the same thing that crossed her mind. What was her mother doing here? Troy hadn't missed a beat. It looked like he had invited everyone. The revelation suddenly hit Dina. Troy was going to propose. Why else would he invite all of them to his mother's annual July 4th shindig? Dina rolled her eyes and sucked her teeth.

Troy wasted no time. He led Kennedy over to the DJ's booth, and whispered something to the DJ. The DJ handed Troy a microphone. Kennedy was still focused on her mother. Troy asked the guests for their attention and turned to Kennedy. When the realization hit Kennedy, her eyes grew as wide as saucers, and her bottom lip nearly hit her perfectly-pedicured toes. Troy's mother's back straightened like a board, and she stood on her feet. Mrs. Divine was still engrossed in her tale. Angel and her sensitive self burst into tears before Troy said his first word.

"Hello everyone! You all know Kennedy. For those who don't, this is my girlfriend, Evan's mother." A few heads nodded in recognition.

Mrs. Divine had finally turned her attention to the matter at hand. A smug smile danced across her lips.

"Everyone that knows me knows how I feel about Kennedy."

Troy pulled a crimson velvet box from his pocket and took a deep breath. He turned to face Kennedy. Her surprised expression had faded. They stood face to face. She showed no emotion. For a moment Troy looked pitiful and unsure of himself. He turned to look at the guests once again and wiped his hands along the side of his pants. Dina noticed an array of emotions plastered across the faces of the guests, ranging from tears of joy and pure delight to shock and discontentment. Dina thought the entire ordeal was rather funny. She chuckled and Carl asked what she was laughing at.

"Nothing. Just listen," she said to Carl.

"Kennedy, you of all people know how I feel. Now that we are back together, I want to make sure we stay together. Will you marry me?"

"Yes!" Evan yelled and leaped up and down. Dina laughed along with the rest of the guests and was moved by his excitement. "Mommy! Say yes!"

Kennedy smiled at Evan then turned her attention back to Troy. It was apparent that she hadn't been prepared. The question hung in the air during Kennedy's silence. The guests awaited her response. Finally Kennedy answered.

"Yes, Troy. I will marry you."

Troy looked relieved and embraced Kennedy. She seemed preoccupied and looked towards her mother. Mrs. Divine flashed an approving smile, winked, and lifted her drink to salute her daughter. Troy's mother stood frozen in her spot. Mrs. Divine looked in Mrs. Alexander's direction and rolled her eyes. Dina watched Lacey eye Mrs. Alexander's response and whisper a comment to the girl standing next to her.

Mrs. Alexander unglued her feet from her position and moved her stout legs in a swift motion towards Troy and Kennedy.

"I need to speak to you inside," Mrs. Alexander demanded through clenched teeth. She motioned for Troy to follow her into the house.

Dina caught Kennedy roll her eyes at Mrs. Alexander behind the shadow of her shades. She zeroed in on each gesture and enjoyed watching the mounting tension fill the yard.

Dina looked around for Carl. When she spotted him, he was at the bar being served by a pretty girl that she hadn't noticed until then. Before she could head in his direction, Carl had started back towards her. Briefly she wondered why Carl couldn't be more like Troy. She deserved to have a great guy that seemed to love her more than life itself. Dina quickly dismissed those thoughts. She feared they would serve as the catalyst to another bout of depression.

Dina shifted her focus back to the buzz that Troy's proposal created. She was entertained by the guests' reactions. At first Dina didn't want to stay long, but with all the drama filling the space, she had no intention of leaving until she got an encore of the fat lady's performance.

Chapter 15

"What was that all about?"

"Ma, what do you mean?"

"You said you wanted to invite her here, not propose to her." Mrs. Alexander's chest was heaving.

"What difference does it make? I told you I wanted to marry her."

"Well you didn't have to make a spectacle of my annual BBQ. I wondered why you had that woman come here today."

"Who? Mrs. Divine?"

"Yeah. Like mother like daughter. You see the way she's prancing around over there with that man. I wonder how long he's been around and what she's going to end up getting from him."

"That's not right, Ma. You barely know Mrs. Divine."

"I know all I need to know. The apple never falls too far from the tree."

Troy raised his hands to his head and tried to calm himself. His mother was getting on his nerves. He'd never anticipate that she would respond this way. She went on and on about how much of a mistake it would be if Troy followed through with this marriage to 'that woman.'

"I can't stand either one of them. Those women mean you no good."

Troy felt like his head could bust. He looked outside to see if anyone heard their conversation. His sister was doing her best to keep the party going. He was sure that everyone noticed the intense way his mother walked in the house, summoning him behind her. He didn't want to be disrespectful, but he had to make an attempt to put this situation at bay.

"Ma, listen. This is not the time, nor the place."

"Boy, this here is my house. I'll tell you what's appropriate and what's not. That damn proposal wasn't appropriate. That's for sure."

"I don't know what you want me to do. I love Kennedy, and I want to marry her. I know you don't like her, but I didn't expect you to act this way, especially since I already told you that I wanted to marry her."

"You said nothing about proposing to her here, at my party, in front of my family and friends, without warning me."

Troy thought his mother was being completely unreasonable. He hadn't realized the depth of his mother's detest for Kennedy until now. But he knew what he wanted. Neither his mother, nor, anyone else, would be able to stop that. He decided that the best thing for him to do was to take a nice vacation and marry Kennedy while they were away. Mrs. Alexander probably wouldn't have come to the wedding anyway. Troy never imagined he would get married without his family present, especially his mother. Right now he saw no other way.

Troy's mother went on and on about how he was making a mistake. She knew what 'their' types of women were capable of.

"Does she even want to marry you?"

Troy looked puzzled. Weren't you outside when she said

yes? he thought. "If she didn't want to marry me, I don't think she would have said yes."

"That's what you think. She's up to something. I know these women. It's the same kind of woman that your father ran off with."

"Ma, is that what this is about?" Troy smiled for the first time, and the pain banging in his head eased a bit. "You and Dad's relationship? I'm not Dad, and Kennedy is certainly not you."

"Huh, that's for sure. But you're right about not being your dad. You were cut from a different cloth. Kennedy's more like your dad. They need adventure. She'll get bored with you and do exactly what your father did to me. She'll be gone like before just as soon as you stop buying her nice things. You deserve better. She's nothing but a high-class whore, just like her mama."

Troy had enough. His mother had just called the woman he loved, his fiancée, and her mother, a whore. This conversation was going nowhere fast. Troy decided he needed to go. As he walked out the door leading to the backyard his mother called out to him. He ignored her, the ranting and the onslaught of insults about Kennedy and her sassy-assed mother. The banging in his head returned with fury.

When Troy stepped outside, Kennedy was on the other side of the yard talking to her mother. Troy watched Mrs. Divine admire the three-karat oval-cut diamond flanked by baguettes. She turned Kennedy's hand from side to side to capture all of its elegance. Kennedy looked his way and Troy's heart skipped a beat. On the other side of the yard, Courtney was serving one of their older aunts but stared in his direction. He knew she was waiting for some indication of what went on inside. Troy rolled his eyes upwards and shook his head. Courtney flashed him a look filled with empathy. Troy smiled at her, and Courtney winked back. He knew she understood. Their mother was a wonderful mother but at times she was capable of being exceptionally perverse.

Mrs. Alexander's voice boomed as she approached the back door. Troy wanted to get away, fast! He jogged towards Kennedy, grabbed her by the arm, and started towards the gate. Unfortunately he hadn't moved fast enough. His mom met them at the gate.

"Kennedy, I don't know what you're looking for, but I've got my eye on you. I only have one son, and I'll be damned if you think I am going to stand around and allow you to ruin his life."

The scene gained the attention of every guest in the yard. Kennedy stood unscathed. Mrs. Divine was now at her feet. She stepped quickly until she reached Kennedy's side. Kennedy held her lips tight. But that did nothing to keep her mother quiet.

"How dare you speak to my daughter like that? Who do you think you are?"

Kennedy smirked as her mother proceeded to offer Mrs. Alexander a rapid-fire tongue lashing.

"Ma, please," Troy pleaded. He looked for his sister among the audience. She was right on his heels.

"Mommy, this is not the time, nor the place," Courtney said.

"I'm tired of everybody thinking they know when and where I should speak my mind. I'm gonna tell it like it is, whether you like it or not." Mrs. Alexander turned her attention back to Kennedy and Mrs. Divine. "That's right, the apple don't fall too far from the tree. Your daughter's nothing but a money grubbing, high-maintenance..."

Before Mrs. Alexander could finish slinging insults, Mrs. Divine hauled off and delivered a fresh smack to the side of her fleshy face. Mrs. Alexander's hand flew to the side of her cheek. All chatter and movement ceased immediately. A few guests gathered their things and hurried out of the yard. Others stayed to see how the scene would play out. Mrs. Divine was surprised with her own outburst and stood with her mouth gaped open. Mrs. Alexander slowly slid her hand from her cheek to her side. Her entire face had reddened. She closed her hand into a fist. Without warning, she administered a ferocious uppercut to the left side of Mrs. Divine's jaw, knocking her off her feet. Mrs. Divine hit the ground with a thud. Kennedy ran to her side. Her gentlemen friend lifted her off the ground and carried the unconscious grand diva to his late-model Cadillac.

Troy watched fire dance in Kennedy's eyes as she followed the gentleman out of the yard to the car. Dina and their crew trailed behind. Troy turned his attention back to his mother who was still standing with her fist closed. Mrs. Alexander's full chest continued to heave up and down. She appeared to take slow, controlled breaths. The guests left in droves, and the family went inside the house one by one until only Courtney, Troy, Lacey, and Mrs. Alexander remained outside in the yard. Even the smoke from the grill chose to blow in a more composed direction.

The pounding in Troy's head was so pronounced he was convinced that the others could hear it. He sighed and walked out of the yard. When he reached the front, he walked right passed his SUV and just kept walking.

Chapter 16

Kennedy waited for Andre to leave his business before going inside to drop off her special package. Kennedy stepped into the mortgage brokerage firm holding a beautifully wrapped box in both hands. She greeted the receptionist with a warm smile.

"Is Mr. Lewis in?"

Kennedy was happy to see a new receptionist. The old receptionist was incredibly loud and overzealous in everything she did and Kennedy wasn't in the mood for her theatrics today. She was a horrible employee who spent more time on personal calls and doing her nails, than she did answering the phones and working. Andre had finally made a smart decision of his own

"I'm sorry, ma'am. You just missed him."

This one was more mature and very polite.

"No problem. Can I leave this package for him?"

"Sure," the woman took the package from Kennedy and admired the elegant wrapping. "This is beautiful wrapping paper. Who should I tell him…"

"Oh don't bother. I want it to be a surprise." Kennedy flashed a sinister smile.

The receptionist's face lit up. She got excited as if something in the box was for her. If she only knew!

"He'll be surprised. I'm sure. I'll just leave it in his office."

"Thanks so much," Kennedy said in a cheerful tone. She flashed her award-winning smile one last time and left.

Surprised was an understatement. When Andre opened that package his life would flash before his eyes. This special delivery consisted of pictures of Andre, his wife, Indira, and their baby on various occasions. Others showed Indira leaving her place of employment, and a few of them showed Kennedy and Andre on one of their many vacations. Each photo was marked with the date. There was also a large envelope with 'DNA/Evidence' written across the front in bold black letters. Inside were printed images of Kennedy's torn, blood-stained panties, her ripped shirt, and the piece of bloody cloth she used to clean herself with after the vicious assault. She had also included a list of instructions. Andre was to make payments totaling $250,000 to Kennedy over a specified period of time. If he failed to comply, the authorities, his wife, father-in-law, and the accompanying list of clients would also receive a special delivery, and a criminal as well as a civil suit would also be filed against him immediately.

At the risk of loosing everything he had, Kennedy was sure he'd have no problem with meeting her terms. The best part about her additional probing was when she found more information about his business partner, who also happened to be his father-in-law. No wonder he didn't leave his wife and he probably never planned to.

Kennedy sat in the car and awaited Andre's return. She wanted to be sure he received his package today. Andre returned less than twenty minutes later. Once he stepped inside, Kennedy pulled her mother's car up so that she could see into the establishment through the door. She watched as the new receptionist led him towards the surprise waiting for him in his office.

Kennedy pulled off and headed back to her mother's house to switch cars. Along the way, her cell phone rang. Kennedy smiled and let the call go to voicemail. She checked her voicemail and of course it was Andre. He'd left a breathless message pleading for her to call him right away. Kennedy laughed out loud as she listened to the frenzied message, then she tossed the phone onto the passenger's seat. The phone rang all the way to her mother's house.

Kennedy pulled her mother's car into the driveway and jumped out. She opened the door with her key and yelled for her mother.

"Mom, I'm putting your key on the table. I'll see you later."

Kennedy wanted to hurry and get out of the house. She was tired of hearing her mother rant about the incident at Troy's mother's BBQ. She'd gotten over that ordeal the next day and wished her mother would move on as well. As far as she was concerned, her mom should not have slapped Troy's little fat mother in the face. Then she wouldn't have gotten knocked out. That was a bad scene for a woman of Mrs. Divine's stature. Kennedy was upset with both of the women but didn't want to keep living the scene over and over again. None of that would change anything anyway.

She thought about Troy's proposal. It certainly caught her off guard; but the more she thought about it, the better it sounded for assorted reasons. Troy would soon come into a lot more money. As his wife, she could quit her job as a medical records examiner and spend her days doing as she wished—mainly shopping.

Kennedy chose her occupation because she wouldn't have to be tied down to a desk for forty hours a week, but most importantly she relished in the high level of interaction with private doctors. Kennedy figured she'd find a rich, desirable doctor that would turn her into a well-kept woman. However despite the many physicians that flirted with her constantly, she had casually dated only two of them; and only one of them was what she would consider really attractive. Money mattered, but looks was an uncompromising prerequisite. For some reason, most of them were married. She didn't realize how much skipping grad school had cost her until she met all those doctors who met their wives while studying. Those women had airtight plans for snagging a soon-to-be, well-to-do husband. It was too late for that now. Troy would have to be her meal ticket. Kennedy thought about setting herself up with hefty a wife fund just in case she decided to move on to more exciting things in life.

Between Andre and Troy, Kennedy's life was taking a financial turn for the best. Not to mention, what could tick off Troy's mother more than for Kennedy to share her last name? That motivation was just as stimulating as the potential monetary benefits.

When Kennedy finally reached home, she answered Andre's call by simply saying, "What?" then she began her usual pacing ritual.

"Kennedy, why are you doing this?"

"Why did you rape me, Andre?" Kennedy snapped.

"Can we meet?"

"No!"

Andre took a deep breath. Kennedy imagined the hot air filling the space around the receiver. She sighed, checked her watch, and started towards her front door.

"Is there anything else we can work out?"

"Did you give me any options when you ripped my clothes off and rammed yourself inside of me? Why should I work anything out with you? You violated me! I didn't deserve that, Andre. I cared about you."

Kennedy surprised herself with her admission. She felt her temperature rise and her voice become unsteady. She was beginning to break down yet refused to allow her true emotions to filter through the line. Andre couldn't know how affected she was.

"Ken."

"Andre. There is nothing to discuss, work out or negotiate. My terms are final." She swiped at the tears stealing their way down her cheeks and made her best attempt to keep the pain out of her voice.

"Kennedy, I'm sorry. Please…"

"Andre," Kennedy paused to collect herself. "It's a little too late for that. Just get me my money, or else," she said through clenched teeth and punched the 'talk' button on the cordless phone to end the call.

Just as she hung up, Evan came barreling through the door. Kennedy waved at the bus driver who brought Evan home from day camp.

"Mommy, are you sad?" Evan asked with a concerned look on his face.

"No, pumpkin. I'm not sad. In fact I'm pretty happy!"

Chapter 17

Dina was driving home from work when her cell phone rang. Usually she had her earpiece on ready for calls. This time she wasn't prepared. She frantically dug in her purse with her right hand as she drove with her left. As soon as she retrieved the phone, which had somehow floated to the very bottom of her bag, it stopped ringing. "Missed Call" flashed across the display. She cursed the phone. After a few minutes, the cell phone's mechanical voice announced, "You have a message."

Dina journeyed through the contents of her bag to retrieve her earpiece. Once she was all set, she checked the message. An unfamiliar female voice had left a quick message for Carl: "Hey Carl, this is Tamara. Call me as soon as you get this message."

There was that name again. Tamara. Her name and number were stored in Carl's cell phone. The call highly piqued Dina's interest. Who was this woman, and what did she want with her man? Now Dina had her number in her call history. She would be sure to find out who the caller was.

Dina decided to reverse the call forwarding back to Carl's phone. Instead of forwarding Carl's calls to her cell phone for days at a time, Dina had begun to do an hour or so here and there. She had almost gotten caught before and didn't want to risk that again, so she decided to simmer down on the call screening.

As Dina drove, her curiosity grew. She couldn't hang

around waiting to find out who the woman was, so she decided to return the call herself and do some investigating. She gave it more thought and determined she would wait and call back from Carl's phone. Dina was interested in knowing how well Carl knew this Tamara person. A great indication would be to see how she answered to his calls.

When Dina arrived at home, Carl was already in from his job as a stock broker and was taking a shower. She could hear him singing in the shower while the water tapped against his skin. She tipped into the bedroom to find Carl's shirt, tie and slacks scattered across the bed. Dina glanced towards the bedroom door to make sure he was still singing in the shower. She quietly opened his nightstand drawer where he kept his wallet and cell phone. She picked up his cell, walked through the living room, and stepped outside. She closed the door gently behind her, leaving it slightly cracked so she could still hear him.

Dina's sweaty fingers tapped the keys until she found the one that displayed his contact list. She pressed the number eight to retrieve the list of names beginning with the letter 'T,' and Tamara's name was the first to come up. She pressed talk. After two short rings Tamara answered.

"Yeah." That was all she said.

Dina didn't want to speak first. She wanted Tamara do to the talking so she could figure out what their connection was. Dina tried to think of what to say next. Then she thought about just hanging up.

"Carl, can you hear me?" Tamara asked.

Dina read the familiarity in Tamara's voice when she called Carl's name. It came out easily, as if she called the name all of the time. Dina pressed the 'end' button. Her insides became warm. She was about to start crying when the cell phone rang. It startled her and she looked at the display. It was her again. Dina wasn't sure what she would do. She didn't count on having to actually speak. She answered in a deep man-like voice.

"Hello."

"Carl, can you hear me now?" Tamara joked then released a hearty, weightless laugh. Dina sensed the buoyancy in her laughter and wished she could feel so free. Attempting to maintain her front she chuckled. "Anyway," Tamara continued, "I'm coming in Friday night at eight. Are you going to pick us up at the airport?"

Dina flipped the phone closed and walked back inside. Carl was out of the shower but still in the bathroom singing. Dina hastened her steps into the bedroom and put the cell phone back in the drawer. Her head was spinning now. Was this person a relative? Carl hadn't said anything about picking up anyone up at the airport on Friday. More than that, he'd never mentioned a relative named Tamara.

Dina heard the bathroom door open and ran to the living room. By the time Carl came out of the bathroom, Dina looked as if she was just walking in.

"What's up, baby?" Carl greeted as he stepped towards her and continued singing. He was obviously in a very good mood. He leaned in and gave her a peck on the lips.

Dina focused on the glistening water droplets decorating his chest. He wore nothing more that a towel. A tantalizing, manly fragrance emanated from his moist body.

Unable to make eye contact, Dina returned a quick, 'Hi.'

"What's the matter, baby? You had a bad day?"

Dina's words were caught in her throat. The thought of Carl entertaining another woman both scared and enraged her. She needed to get to the bottom of this situation fast. She needed more time to think without Carl in her face or anywhere within her immediate vicinity.

"Traffic...you know. The drive home was the worst. The usual."

"I see."

Carl spun around on his heels and continued his melody as he headed for the bedroom to get dressed. Dina fussed around in the kitchen, trying to keep from breaking down. She didn't want to be in the same room as him. Carl entered the kitchen wearing boxers and a wife beater, holding the remote in his hand. Dina walked out. She ran into the bathroom and sat on the toilet fully dressed, trying to compile her thoughts. Her mind ran rampant. She couldn't seem to pull any logical string of thoughts together. It was going to happen again. She knew it!

Dina couldn't help but think the worst. Dramatic scenes of Carl with this other woman played in her head. She sat on the toilet sinking further into a state of depression.. Familiar questions came back to haunt her. Why couldn't someone just love her the way she wanted to be loved? How come she could never hold anyone's attention for too long? As a child she was unable to hold even her mother's attention long enough to obtain affirmation that she was truly loved or wanted. Dina's mother usually made her feel like she was in the way.

When she begged for her mother's attention, her mother would yell, "Cut the shit and get out my face." She treated Dina and her sister Dionne that way regularly, but when one of her dates came over, she'd act like she deserved the award for mother of the year for at least a few minutes. She'd find someone new and the cycle would begin all over again. If she had put half the time and effort into dealing with her daughters as she did pleasuring her men, their family would be a lot more stable. Dionne eventually tired of vying for her mother's love and stopped caring for anyone and everyone, including Dina. But Dina couldn't shake the need. She still yearned for love and attention.

Dina's mind was going way too far. She snapped back to the present. Nothing had happened yet. It was just a simple call. She could be anyone. Before she sunk into this well of misery, she needed more information. She could be getting all upset over nothing.

Dina hadn't noticed Carl standing in the bathroom watching her. It startled her when she realized his presence.

"Who were you talking to on my phone?"

"What?" Dina was shaking.

She tried to get up from the toilet, but her legs had fallen asleep. She punched them to jerk the feeling back into them. The glare Carl delivered inspired the pins and needles in her legs. Dina felt trapped. She wanted to run but couldn't move.

"You know what I'm talking about, Dina."

Dina tried to move again. Slowly she managed to stand, holding on to the towel rack for support. Carl stood firm in his position blocking the door. Dina was still at a loss for words. With all the thoughts spinning out of control in her head, she couldn't produce a single coherent sentence. She wanted out. She wanted answers but didn't want to answer Carl's question. She wanted to quiet the sound of her mother's voice telling her how much of a nuisance she could be. All she could manage was a tear. A lone tear calmly descended her right cheek before the left eye caught on. Carl sighed when the rest of the tears came.

Dina decided that she was not going to answer Carl's question. Not now anyway. There was too much going on. She usually wallowed in her state of depression alone. She couldn't break down in front of Carl. That would drive him away for sure. She had to get out of this conversation. She wanted to avoid him now and see how things would play out by Friday. Would he pick up this mystery woman at the airport?

"Dina. Look at me. I'm talking to you, and you're staring off into space." Dina snapped her neck in his direction. "Why are you even answering my phone?"

Why not, Dina thought and decided to say it out loud. She finally found her voice.

"Why not? What's supposed to be the big deal if I am your woman? You got something to hide?"

"It isn't about that. It's about you always snooping." Carl pointed the phone at Dina as he spoke. "You keep that up and one day you will find something, and you won't like it." Carl turned around and stormed off into the bedroom.

Dina was enraged. Forget about letting the situation sit. Her rage gave her the strength to step up and keep his pace.

"What's that supposed to mean? You have something to hide?" Dina spoke to his back as he stepped lively.

"No, I don't. But I get pretty damn tired trying to prove that to you. I can't do this anymore."

"Can't do what anymore?" Dina was right up on Carl.

"This," Carl said and waved his hand around the room. "You do have something to hide, Carl!" He sighed. "Who is Tamara?" Dina said.

"See what I mean. You know what? I am not going into this with you right now because you won't hear me. All you care about is who you think I'm sleeping with. No matter what I do, you can't believe that I'm doing the right thing. I might as well be sleeping around. You don't believe me one way or the other anyway. What am I wasting my time for if you're never going to trust me anyway?"

"Oh, so being with me is a waste of time?"

"Did you even hear me?" Carl asked incredulously. Carl threw his hands up and said, "I'm going out."

Carl searched the room for something to wear while Dina ranted on. She was pissed because he was totally evading the issue about Tamara. He must have something to hide and if he wouldn't tell her, she'd find out her own way.

"Go ahead Carl, go. I'll call her myself."

Carl stopped in his tracks. "Dina, don't do anything stupid."

Dina ignored him and ran to get her own cell phone. She quickly searched the call history to find Tamara's number and called her. Before Tamara could finish saying hello, Dina began to dig into her.

"Hello, Tamara? Yeah. This is Dina, Carl's woman. I was wondering why you needed to have Carl come and pick you up at the airport on Friday. You two have something going on..."

Carl's bottom lip hit the floor. Dina couldn't care less. She kept going.

"...because if you do, let me know now...what?...Oh really...Okay...I see...Whatever...Well I'm letting you know where I stand...If you want to speak to Carl, then you need to call him back on his phone. Bye."

Carl was standing before Dina with his eyes closed and his hands on his temples.

"Why haven't you told me you have an ex-wife and a daughter?"

Carl took a deep breath, held it for a long time and finally let it go. "How did you get Tamara's number..." Carl was cut off by the sound of his cell phone ringing. He left Dina where she stood, walked into the bedroom, and closed the door behind him.

When Dina tried to open the door, it was locked. She could hear Carl talking on the other side. She banged on the door. Carl ignored her knocks. She screamed at the top of her lungs. Carl still didn't answer. A few minutes went by and Carl finally emerged from the bedroom. There was fire in his eyes. The look on his face disturbed Dina. Carl stared blatantly into Dina's eyes and through her soul. She felt bare. Her palms started to sweat again, and her anger turned into uncertainty mixed with a speck of fear.

"Thanks, Dina. Once again your antics have caused nothing but trouble. Yeah, I have an ex-wife and a daughter." Carl moved toward Dina as he spoke. For each step forward, Dina took a step back until she was up against the wall. "Yes, a daughter that I haven't seen for the past five years because of women like you who can't live without drama. I was going to explain everything to you before she got here. I didn't know until you said it that she was coming on Friday. I've been trying to get her to let me see my daughter for years and you just messed that up. Now she's not coming, and who knows when I'll be able to talk her into coming again. She took my daughter away because she didn't want her involved in this type of drama. Now after years of making changes you have managed to put me back at square one."

"Carl, I didn't..."

"Of course you didn't, but do you ever ask? Or do you always jump to your own conclusions and react like a maniac?" Carl finally turned away.

Dina could see that he was hurt. She wished she had never forwarded any of his messages. He held his head down. When he looked back at Dina she saw hatred in his watery eyes. Carl walked back to the bedroom and turned his attention to Dina just as he made it to the door.

"Dina, I've tried to make this work. Now I know it won't. You've got some issues that you need to work on. I can't do this."

Dina ran to Carl and held him from the back. Carl shrugged her off.

"Carl, please don't to this." Dina cried hard as she pleaded. "I can change."

Carl didn't respond. Dina continued to implore him while he dressed. Carl stuffed his wallet into his back pocket, clipped his cell phone to his belt, and grabbed his car keys.

"Have your things packed by the time I get back so I can take you back to your mother's house." Carl walked out the door.

Dina ran behind Carl. The door shut in her face. She punched the door in defiance until the sides of her fist split and bled. Eventually, she mustered up enough strength to lug herself around the apartment and find the cordless phone. Dina's chest heaved and collapsed as she cried. The emotional pain had manifested itself into intense physical pain. Her head and chest ached and her knees buckled under the weight of her circumstance. She found the phone and dialed her mother's number. Five rings later, Mrs. Jacobs' husky voice rang through.

"Hello?" Dina sniffled and collected herself. Her mother quizzed, "Who is this?"

"Ma, it's me, Dina." Her mother didn't reply. The silence was uninviting. Dina knew she was waiting to see what she wanted. She also knew her mother waited to hear what would make her daughter call out of the blue, whimpering.

No show of emotion from her mother's side. No 'what's the matter, baby,' like most mothers. Just annoyed silence waiting to see what the nuisance wanted this time.

"Ma, I need to come back home."

"Okay, but not tonight. Call me in the morning." Mrs. Jacobs hung up.

Chapter 18

Kennedy lay across her cozy love seat with Evan at her feet. Together they watched one of his favorite shows from the Disney Channel. Evan giggled as he enjoyed the show but Kennedy's mind was elsewhere. The ringing phone snapped her out of her thoughts and brought her back to the den. Evan jumped up.

"I'll get it, Mommy." He answered the phone before she could object. "Hello...Hi Auntie Dina...yes...hold on, she's right here." Evan handed the phone to his mother.

Kennedy didn't feel like being bothered and hoped the conversation wouldn't take long. She grabbed the phone and greeted her friend with a short, "Hey." Kennedy heard Dina sniffling and knew this would take much more time than she was willing to spend.

"What's wrong, Dina?" Kennedy asked with indifference. She routinely assumed that her dramatic friend was up to her usual antics. Dina started bawling. Kennedy's eyes popped open. She knew something was really wrong.

"Dina, where are you? Talk to me."

"I...I...can I...come? I need you, Ken," Dina cried. She spoke as if she was completely winded.

"Come on. How far away are you?"

"I...I'll be there in less than ten minutes."

"Do you need me to stay on the line with you," Kennedy asked. She didn't like the way Dina sounded. She had been through this with Dina many times before.

"N...no." Dina hung up.

Kennedy apologized to Evan for having to cut their quality movie time short. She told him to prepare himself for bed because he had to get up for camp the next morning. His sparking brown eyes offered her the sad puppy dog look, and he pushed his lips out to an exaggerated pout.

"Don't try that with me, mister." Kennedy grabbed him and tickled him until he was on his knees begging for her to stop.

Evan was a very well trained and independent child. He headed to the upstairs bathroom to shower and brush his teeth. Kennedy heard a car pull up and opened the door for Dina to come right in. When Dina walked in, Kennedy was stunned by Dina's wide bloodshot eyes, untamed hair, and overall despondent look. She was even more surprised when she noticed the overnight bag Dina dragged behind her. Kennedy led Dina to the den, checked on Evan, and prepared the routine pot of herbal tea for her and Dina.

When she returned to the den, Dina was lying with her face buried in the crevice of the couch. Kennedy could tell by the way her body shook rhythmically that she was crying again. She left her alone for a while and tended to Evan. Kennedy left Evan in his room, sporting Spider-Man pajamas and watching television. When she went back downstairs, Dina was in the same position.

Kennedy rubbed Dina's back, and the shaking became more prevalent. Dina sat up and Kennedy put her arms around Dina's shoulder. The girls both cocked their heads to rest upon one another.

"He kicked me out, Ken. It's over," Dina said before her lip began to tremble.

"What happened?"

Dina replayed the particulars of the evening for Kennedy. Without interruption, Kennedy listened to the entire story. She decided she would save her hard-nosed input for another time and just let Dina vent. She felt bad for her friend but summed the entire situation up to being the result of Dina's unreasonably jealous behavior. She pitied Dina this night but knew that no matter the outcome, this wouldn't be the last time.

Mrs. Jacob's dismissal was typical. Kennedy had experienced her behavior first-hand in the past. Her own mother never would have done anything like that. Dina's dilemma coupled with Kennedy's own issues had her mind spinning but she had to keep her issues to herself. She couldn't share her problem with anyone until she decided what she was going to do.

Dina asked Kennedy if she could stay with her for a while until she could find a place of her own. Kennedy understood. She wouldn't want to go back to Dina's mother's house either. Kennedy really didn't want Dina to stay, but she couldn't turn her away. She had a lot to deal with and having nosy Dina around was not part of the plan. The girls drank their tea, and Dina fell asleep on the sofa.

Kennedy left Dina in the den and went to her master bathroom to clear away any evidence of her own issue. She emptied her bathroom wastebasket directly into the large outside garbage bin. She doubted Dina would go that far to find anything. Until she determined her course of action, Kennedy's pregnancy would be a secret.

Chapter 19

Troy was mentally, emotionally and physically spent. Between dealing with his mother's badgering about marrying Kennedy, handling his father's business and trying to win Kennedy over, Troy's level of tolerance had severely diminished.

Troy had always been the beloved son, the child that could do no wrong. But now, Mrs. Alexander insisted Troy was making the biggest mistake of his life, and she didn't miss an opportunity to remind him. She was adamant about letting him make his own decisions in life but was sure to let him know exactly how she felt about them. His sister, Courtney, hadn't said much. Troy and Courtney respected each other's decisions and that was that.

Troy avoided the last Sunday dinner because he was tired of hearing his mother attack Kennedy's character. He loved Kennedy and that's all that mattered. She was the mother of his son and would soon be his wife whether people liked it or not, including his mother. He told her she'd get over it. She told him that she would be waiting in the distance for the day Kennedy revealed her true colors because he would need his family to help him stand.

Mrs. Alexander's warnings swam around in his head as he drove towards the hospice to see his father. She didn't know Kennedy like he did, and Troy felt that if she got to know her better, maybe she would like her more. The only problem with that was getting Kennedy to spend more time around her. It would take a whole lot to convince her, especially after his mother knocked

Mrs. Divine out cold in front of a yard full of people. Troy thought he'd never hear the end of that incident. Fortunately the novelty of the event had finally worn off. Mrs. Alexander bragged about that one for weeks, telling their family and friends, "That woman had the nerve to smack me in my face, in my yard. I knocked that bitch out right where she stood." For someone who rarely cursed the word 'bitch' fell out her mouth with ease every time she spoke of Kennedy and her 'sassy-ass' mother.

Troy looked up and realized that he was only a block away from the hospice. He made it there in record time, probably because of the heavy thoughts that accompanied him along the way. Just as he approached the middle of the block, another SUV was pulling out. Troy quickly swung into the spot, thankful for the stroke of luck. He had allowed extra time to find parking. Normally he could spend at least twenty minutes searching for a spot and could still end up parking blocks away from the hospice since there was no parking on the hospital premises. He hated parking in Manhattan parking lots for several reasons: first, because of the extra charge for oversized vehicles: and second, because he always left with new dings and scratches on his truck. He summed it all up to highway robbery and lack of consideration. So he decided to avoid it all together.

When Troy reached his father's room, the nice nurse with the sing-song West Indian accent was checking his father's vitals. When she heard Troy enter the room she turned to him and offered a smile that warmed Troy's heart.

"Good afternoon Mr. Alexander." Her voice was music to Troy's ears. He could sit and listen to her soothing lilt all day.

"Fine, thank you. And you?"

"Wonderful," she sang and widened her smile, which reminded Troy of the sun's rays. "Mr. A, your boy here to see you. I leave you two alone now." She turned her attention to Troy, "You take care now, ya hear?"

"Yes, ma'am." Troy smiled back then approached his father's bedside. "Hey, Pop. How you feeling today?"

Mr. Alexander's white-washed lips were in desperate need of moisture, and it appeared that his presence had diminished even more since Troy's last visit just a week ago. Mr. Alexander made a weak attempt to lift his hand. Troy grasped it and shook it gently.

"Trying to make it, son." His breathing was labored, causing him to pause between each word.

"Yeah," was all Troy could manage to say as he held back tears. He hated to cry in front of his father. He hated to cry period. His dad always preached to him that real men didn't cry. That rule went out the window for him the first time his saw his father in the hospital once the cancer had prevailed over his health.

Mr. Alexander grimaced and then attempted a weak smile. Troy slightly recognized the difference between the two.

"How are things with your mama?"

"She's still going on about me wanting to marry Kennedy. She won't let up, Pop." Troy got up and walked over to the window. He stared at the skyscraper across from his father's room.

"Well, you know what you gotta do son. She always was one to let you know what's on her mind."

"I know, Pop."

"It's your life."

Troy remained at the window until he heard his father's

light snores. He didn't speak again and wouldn't until he knew his father was awake again. At this point, Mr. Alexander didn't sleep well or for long periods of time. His best slumber was cat naps here and there. Quick naps that would end once a stroke of pain jarred him awake.

This one wasn't long at all. Mr. Alexander moaned and Troy stepped over to his father's bedside. His eyes were still closed, but the grimace he wore told Troy that he was no longer asleep. He winced once more, and fresh tears remoistened the dried pathway to his ears. Troy closed his eyes and fought the urge to let down his own tears once again.

"I'd like to see her," his father said.

Troy smiled, his eyes still closed. "I'll bring her." He was going to see Kennedy and Evan when he left the hospice.

Troy envisioned a perfect scene with Kennedy, Evan and himself in their backyard. He would be at the grill while Kennedy relaxed in a soft lounge chair. Evan would be in the pool splashing around having the time of his life. Troy wanted to make it a reality. He decided then that he wanted to solidify their union as soon as possible. Even though Kennedy tended to skirt around the issue, he was determined to set a date for their wedding immediately. This would be one time he wouldn't give in to Kennedy's strong will. He loved her for it and knew that his willingness to give her what she wanted all of the time did nothing more than spoil her. Part of the problem was that he loved to spoil her. He's do anything possible to make Kennedy happy. If she was happy, he was happy.

The thought of talking about wedding plans with Kennedy energized Troy. The sullen mood begot by his father's condition and the load from his recent bouts with his mother gave way to the contentment that filled him when he thought about making arrangements to marry the love of his life.

He decided that it was time to go. Troy kissed his father's forehead and told him bye. On his way out of the city, he stopped for a bouquet of roses. He knew he had to butter Kennedy up a little in order to get her cooperation when it came to issues that she usually tried to avoid. Troy figured Kennedy needed time to absorb the whole idea of marriage since he sort of sprung the proposal on her. He intended to surprise her. Once she adjusted to the notion of marriage, Troy knew she'd look forward to making all the plans. She was good at that type of stuff, and it would give her an opportunity to shop. What could make her happier?

Chapter 20

When Kennedy heard the doorbell ring, she sighed. She really didn't feel like being bothered. Dina had sucked up her last bit of energy. She couldn't fully blame Dina, though, since she had already begun to wear herself out mulling over the baby growing inside of her belly. Kennedy had set Dina up in the spare room. She'd have to deal with her for a while but would be sure to aid her in the search for a new place. Otherwise it would be no telling how long she would have to put up with her living there. Dina was asleep, and Kennedy didn't expect to see any more of her for the night.

Kennedy made her way to the door. It wasn't until she saw Troy through the peephole that she remembered he was coming by after visiting his father. It was not a good time. After taking the pregnancy test, the last person she wanted to see was Troy, particularly because she wasn't ready to discuss her pregnancy with him or anyone else until she was sure who the father was. Just thinking of the possibility that Andre had planted that seed when he violated her infuriated her. She hated him. Or at least she wanted to believe she did.

Unfortunately, there was no way to tell who fathered her baby until the infant arrived. To Kennedy, all babies came out looking like wet birds. It took months before their features became more defined. By then Kennedy would find a discreet way of finding out just who the real father was.

Andre's sexual assault created an unwanted element of

surprise and now she felt more justified for blackmailing him. If it turned out to be his he would end up taking care of it whether he knew it or not and she'd surely get much more out of him than a quarter of a million dollars. Of course life would be simple if the baby turned out to be Troy's. Troy would be sure to take care of her and his kids for the rest of their lives, especially now that he was coming into an inheritance.

Kennedy finally opened the door to let Troy in. He stepped in and planted a big, sloppy, wet kiss right on her mouth. Kennedy wiped her mouth and Troy laughed. He was obviously in a great mood, which was peculiar after visiting his sick father.

"What are you so happy about?" Kennedy smirked.

Troy wrapped his arms around Kennedy's waist and smiled. Kennedy stared at him for a moment then he moved in for another kiss. This time she matched his intensity until the passionate kissed ended slowly with a finale of seductive, moist pecks.

111

"Did you visit your dad? How's he doing?" she asked with her back to him as she stole away from his embrace. Troy removed his shoes and followed her into the den.

"Okay. He'd like to see you." Kennedy rolled her eyes then turned to face Troy.

"Really? Why?" She tried to sound like she cared.

"He just asked." Troy picked up the remote and parked himself on the sofa. He looked around for a minute then asked, "Where's Evan?"

"Upstairs," Kennedy replied and sat next to him.

"Already? How did you manage that?"

Kennedy told him about Dina and the fact that she'd be

staying there for a while.

"How's she doing now?" Troy looked genuinely concerned.

"She's asleep in the spare room."

"How long is she staying?" Troy asked with raised brows.

"Not too long, I hope. I'm going to help her find a place."

Troy stopped talking and stared Kennedy directly in the face.

"What?" Kennedy questioned, knowing he was admiring her beauty. She knew the look well.

"Nothing. I can't look at my woman?"

"You're not looking, you're staring!"

Troy laughed and turned his attention to the television for a moment. Kennedy continued to ponder her situation since part of it was just staring in her face, literally. She hoped he wouldn't bring up the wedding thing just yet. She didn't feel like talking about that.

"Ken, we need to set a date." Kennedy's eyes rolled upwards. "We need to get this going. How do you want to do it?" Troy's face was serious, so Kennedy followed his lead. It's not like she didn't plan on marrying him. She just wasn't in a rush. She cared for Troy but certainly didn't love him the way he loved her. Kennedy wasn't sure she ever would, but the security that he offered was a very attractive perk.

"Let me get a calendar." Kennedy got up from the couch in search of the calendar. Troy was smiling from ear to ear.

"I'll run up and talk to Evan real quick." Troy took the steps two at a time.

The two met back in the den after a few minutes. Kennedy

settled in on the couch. Troy sat next to her and put his arms around her. Kennedy flipped into the calendar contemplating a potential date to become the better looking Mrs. Alexander. Kennedy figured if she gave herself a few months after the baby was born, she'd have time to get her body back in shape. With the baby probably being due sometime in March of the following year, Kennedy figured scheduling the wedding in the summer would give her plenty of time to prepare her body.

"What about next August?"

"Why so far away?" Troy asked incredulously. Kennedy smirked.

"Why not? Troy, we need time to make plans." Kennedy realized Troy had no clue about what went into planning a wedding.

"I'm sure we could plan it sooner than that."

"We can't, Troy. I'm pregnant and I have no intentions of sporting a maternity gown. Plus I'll need time to get my body back in shape."

Kennedy waited to witness the aftermath of the bomb she dropped. She read Troy's face as it hit him. He mouthed the word 'pregnant' then jumped up from the couch with his mouth hanging open. Troy lifted his chest, pounded it with one fist, and then thrust both fists in the air before sitting back beside Kennedy. He shook his head and smiled at her. For some reason that touched Kennedy and she smiled too.

"Baby? We're going to have a baby?"

"Yes, Troy."

Troy punched at the air a few times again and laughed. "Yeah," he shouted. He was truly elated. Kennedy couldn't help but enjoy his theatrics. If only he knew, she thought. She figured that now he wouldn't hassle her about setting a date so soon. Troy began to come down off of his high.

"Wow! When did you find out?" he asked and finally sat back down.

"Today. I took a test, but I still have to go to the doctor. I'm figuring the baby will be due around March. That's why I suggested August."

"August of next year won't do."

Kennedy was puzzled by Troy's response. Didn't she just spill the beans to justify her recommendation?

"What's wrong with August of next year?"

"My baby girl will be here by then."

"What makes you so sure it's a girl?" Kennedy asked.

"Because we already have a boy. We need a girl now and our family will be complete," Troy said as if he was totally convinced that saying they were having a girl would make it come to pass. "Now like I said, we need to do this now, not next August. I can't have you up in that hospital without my last name again."

"Troy, that won't be necessary. The baby will have your last name anyway."

"Yeah, but you won't. I want this done right this time."

Kennedy sat back and put her fingers to her temples. She'd let the cat out of the bag and it backfired on her.

"What are you saying, Troy?"

Troy faced her and took both hands in his. "Baby, let's just do it now. By the time the baby comes, we will be a married couple. I should have done this the first time around and we wouldn't have had all these wasted years behind us now. Let's do this. I know you are concerned about how you will look, so before you start showing, let's get it out the way. What's it going to take? We need a church, a hall and a honeymoon."

"Yeah, but what about a dress and bridesmaids, and limos, and flowers and tuxedos?" Kennedy could have gone on but stopped there. She wondered if Troy was losing his mind.

"Ken, you gonna tell me you can't pull all of that together? You, of all people?"

"I didn't say it couldn't be done. It's just that…"

"Well there you go. It can be done!"

"Troy, slow down. These things take time."

"It takes whatever amount of time you want it to take. What are you worried about? Money? I got that."

Money was the last thing Kennedy worried about. For once she was at a loss for words.

"Ken, all you have to tell me is how you want to do it. Do you want a big church wedding or what?"

Kennedy thought about all of their family members being in one place at one time and imagined disaster. Troy interrupted her thoughts with his questions.

"How far are you? When do you think you will start showing? What do you think about September?"

"Troy, September is only a little more than a month away!"

"So? You won't be showing by then, will you?"

Kennedy had to give this some thought. She had no clue what type of wedding she wanted or who she wanted to be there. Not to mention, she would have loved to ban Troy's mother from the festivities. Unfortunately Troy wouldn't let something like that pass. Kennedy had more on her mind now than she did before he came.

"Troy, go home. I'll call you tomorrow after I think all of this through." Kennedy stood up from the couch and marched to her bedroom.

Chapter 21

Dina hadn't seen the light of day since she came to Kennedy's house the other night. She hadn't even left the house to go to her job at the bank. When she wasn't crying herself to sleep she was calling Carl's cell phone. The best time to catch him was during work hours and she called often. Dina would let the phone ring long enough for the voicemail to pick up and then she'd hang up. He must have had over a hundred missed calls from her number. Yet Carl hadn't bothered to return any of her calls.

To make matters worse, the same night her life fell apart, Dina overheard Troy pressuring Kennedy about setting a date for the wedding. Kennedy, of course, had the nerve to try and brush him off. Dina hated the fact that Kennedy never felt the sting of rejection though she often administered it.

Dina went to the bathroom and took a long hot shower, hoping to wash away some of her pain. Angel had called to invite her out and for the first time in days she actually wanted to look and feel fresh. She picked out a charming little number, a soft yellow, linen halter dress and accessorized the look with a brown purse and sandals. Just as she put the finishing touches on her eyes, she heard Angel's horn blow. Dina raced downstairs to open the door. As soon as it opened Angel appeared, grabbed Dina, and held her in a tight embrace. Angel pulled back and looked at her and Dina suddenly felt naked. She lowered her eyes to stop what felt like a visual interrogation.

"Come on, honey, let's go get breakfast." Angel grabbed Dina by the hand then stopped. "Where's, Ken? She's not coming?" Angel asked as she looked around the house.

"There's more to that story. I'll tell you when we get to the restaurant." Dina chuckled.

Angel lavished Dina with attention, constantly asking her if she was okay and how she felt. Dina felt guilty for distancing herself from Angel and avoiding her calls earlier in the week. She knew that Angel would always be there for her, but Angel's bubbly demeanor annoyed her when she wasn't in the mood.

The girls ended up having breakfast at one of Dina's favorite diners. She hadn't eaten for days, so this meal was undoubtedly welcomed. At first the girls engaged in pure girl talk, shopping, the latest trends, and work.

"So what's up with Dr. Dentures?" Dina asked. Angel looked pensive. "It's okay Angel, I can handle it," Dina stated before shoving a large portion of pecan pancakes into her mouth.

"Well...things are fine for now." Angel smiled, giving light to what she really felt about her new man.

"Ah come on. Give me the juice. I can handle it. I'll be fine. This isn't the first man I've lost," Dina laughed "And I know it won't be the last." Both girls laughed this time. Dina knew Angel had held back for her sake.

"Okay. Where do I start? He's sweet. He's cute, and he went to church with me last week." Angel smiled again.

"Shut up! Girl, you found a God-fearing man." Angel blushed and the girls fell into a fit of laughter.

"I know. He seems too good to be true," Angel added.

"Then he probably, is so watch your back." Dina shook her head.

"Where is Kennedy? I tried to call her this morning, but she didn't answer."

"I don't know, but I do know she's up to something," Dina said and poked her lips out. "She has a secret. I think that's why she's been missing in action this morning. Think about it, it's Saturday. She would usually be home cleaning house or here having breakfast with us. By the time I got up this morning she and Evan were long gone. The house was empty."

"I'm going to try her cell again. Let me see if I can get her." Angel dialed Kennedy's number but received no answer. "She's still not answering…Wait missy, how do you know she has a secret?"

"I heard her say it." Forgetting about her intentions of keeping what she'd overheard a secret. Dina reveled in the opportunity to be the first to divulge the news of Kennedy's pregnancy. She knew Angel would be stunned, and it was the shock factor that motivated her.

"Dina, don't tell me you've been eavesdropping on her conversations." Angel looked disappointed.

Dina held her head down in mock embarrassment. "Well not exactly."

"Spill it, girl," Angel commanded. "Stop playing with me."

Dina perked up. She always did when gossip was involved. "I'm gonna tell you, but you can't say anything, all right?"

"All right! What's going on?"

"Girl, Kennedy is pregnant, and Troy wants to get married

119

yesterday."

Angel's mouth hit the table. "Are you kidding me? I wonder why she didn't say anything yet. Maybe she wants to wait until she reaches three months before she says anything."

Dina thought of how stupid Angel was to think that Kennedy had only remained tight-lipped for the sake of waiting until she reached three months.

"Believe that if you want. She only told Troy because he's been pushing her to set a date. She let the cat out of the bag the other night when he came by. He was shocked. But I think I know why she's holding out."

Angel looked at Dina with an accusatory glare.

"Why are you looking at me like that? I'm serious."

"Tell me."

"Well, a few weeks back, before the proposal disaster at Troy's house, I was at Kennedy's house. As I was leaving, Andre came by. Kennedy dismissed me and sent me on my way, girl."

"That's because you're nosy, Dina. Don't speculate," Angel warned.

"Why else would she hold out on her pregnancy? She didn't tell us. She didn't tell Troy at first. We are her girls. She told Troy the other day and still didn't mention anything to us. She usually tells us everything, right?" Dina confirmed. Angel looked at Dina and shook her head.

"Let's do some shopping." Angel dropped enough money on the table to cover the bill and a considerable tip, grabbed her bag, and slid out of the booth.

Regardless of what Angel wanted to believe, Dina knew Kennedy. There had to be a reason for her not to have said anything to them about being pregnant. Instead of going to the mall, Dina asked Angel to drop her back at Kennedy's house. She wasn't exactly in the mood to shop.

She hugged Angel and thanked her for breakfast. Once Angel drove out of sight, Dina got into her car and drove over to Carl's house. A thousand thoughts fluttered through her mind along the way. What would she say when she saw him? She wondered if he still loved her, if he ever loved her. Would he forgive her and take her back? Should she just get the rest of her things and forget about him? Dina swatted at the tears raining down her face, and then pulled the car over to get herself together. She knew she couldn't face Carl that way. She contemplated turning back then decided against it. She had to go through with this. She had to know if there was a chance left for them.

121

Just as Dina pulled up, a gorgeous woman with a little girl had just stepped onto the porch. Auburn-tinted hair cascaded down the woman's slender back. She wore a soft pink terry cloth sweat suit that matched the one the little girl wore. Dina could have mistaken her for Tyra Banks, only this woman was even more beautiful. The little girl was just as striking as her mother. Pretty pink bows held two long ponytails that gently teased the little girl's shoulders. Dina pulled the car pass the house, driving awfully close to the late-model Mercedes Benz coupe parked in front. Dina made a u-turn and parked a few houses down. Carl came to the door, opened it, and let the two in. Carl's ex-wife and daughter were supposed to come into town the night before. It was possible that Carl convinced them to come after Tamara said she would cancel. It had to be them. They came after all.

Dina slowly pulled off, not sure where she was going, but

driving nonetheless. She put on her windshield wipers to clear the window then realized it was her own tears that blurred her vision.

Chapter 22

Kennedy and her mother entered the crowded diner located on Sunrise Highway. This was one of their favorite meeting places when they had issues to discuss. Kennedy caught sight of her profile in a mirror and quietly appreciated what she saw in the reflection. Her fitted jeans hugged her shapely frame perfectly. Her keen haircut was styled to perfection. She was the spitting image of her mother at that age.

Mrs. Divine looked as dashing as ever herself with her long hair twisted into a smart-looking bun. She was still able to snag the attention of men in her vicinity, young and old copiously offering their admiration. Mrs. Divine sauntered alongside her equally beautiful daughter, taking note of the eyes of men and women surveying their every move. A short, plump hostess showed them to the first available booth. Before Mrs. Divine even sat, she told the tubby Latina to bring a cup of tea with cream and brown sugar to the table right away. Kennedy smirked at her mother's obtrusive demeanor.

"Your waitress will be right with you," the woman responded and left abruptly.

Kennedy had pondered the conversation she was about to have with her mother for some time now. Not because she wasn't certain that her mother would cooperate with her, but she wasn't sure if she wanted her mother to have so much access to her information, especially when it came to money.

A young black waitress approached their booth in a slapdash fashion with her pad in hand. Mrs. Divine turned up her nose. Kennedy imagined how her mother summed the young girl up, messy hair, neglected skin and nails that were long overdue for a refill. Three of her nails were broken down to the nail bed. When she spoke, her loud voice seemed to siphon the pretentiousness from their presence.

"Good morning, ladies, how are y'all doing?" Without waiting for a response she continued, "What can I get for you ladies today?" She ended with a huge smile, showing a mouth full of tan-colored teeth. Mrs. Divine reared her head back.

Kennedy chuckled and placed her order. Mrs. Divine also communicated her calculated order with very specific instructions on exactly how she'd like her steak and eggs prepared.

"Can I bring you anything to drink?" the waitress asked.

"Well I did ask for my tea when I first came, but that dreadfully chubby girl didn't even acknowledge my request."

"I'm sorry about that, ma'am. What would you like? I'll take care of it right away." She seemed honored to take Mrs. Divine's order.

"I want Lipton tea, with cream and brown sugar, please."

"Gladly. I'll be right back. And by the way ma'am, you have such pretty, long eyelashes."

Mrs. Divine blushed and batted her meticulously placed, fake eyelashes. Kennedy rolled her eyes. After Mrs. Divine fully absorbed the compliment, she finally spoke. "Thank you, honey. Listen, sweetie, I could help you out with that skin of yours."

The girl's eyes stretched wide, forming creases in her forehead. She touched her face and walked away.

"Ma, why did you say that? That girl could mess with your

food."

"Well, she obviously needs some help. The poor girl's skin looks like it was breathing bacon grease. Her pores are the size of dimes. Maybe if we start with her skin, it'll spark her to do something with that hair and those horrid nails."

"Whatever." Kennedy waved her mother's assessment of the girl away and thought of the reason she had invited her mother out to breakfast in the first place. "Troy is pushing for us to set a date."

The young waitress returned with Mrs. Divine's tea, placed it on the table and quickly walked away. Mrs. Divine carefully added three drops of cream into her teacup and stirred in two packages of brown sugar. She took a sip and closed her eyes momentarily, seeming pleased with the taste as if she had created a unique masterpiece. "Now that's how I like my tea." Finally, she turned her attention to Kennedy. "So, what's the problem? Wait...is his mother invited?"

"Anyway," Kennedy dismissed her comment., "I need you to do something for me."

"What would you like your mother to do for you, honey?" Mrs. Divine asked playfully.

"I need for you to open a joint account with me. I have some money coming in, plus I will need to make occasional deposits, and I don't want anyone to have access to this money."

"Like Troy." Mrs. Divine said. She gently placed her teacup on the table, leaned into Kennedy, and folded her arms across the table in front of her. "What's this about?"

"Protection and preservation."

"Enough said," Mrs. Kennedy responded with her hands

up to Kennedy, letting her know she need not go any further. "I taught you well," she added, visibly pleased. "When shall we get this going?"

"How about today? I have some checks I'd like to put in." Kennedy smiled as she thought about the money she'd received from Andre. She'd had him provide several checks, some made out to her name and some in her mother's name, all totaling two hundred and fifty thousand dollars. Each check was made out in different amounts not exceeding ten thousand dollars. Per her instructions, Andre had written 'gift' in the memo. Kennedy also instructed him to date the checks sporadically so that she can deposit the checks weekly until the full amount had been deposited into the account.

Her only reservation was having her mother be privy to the amount of money in the bank at any given time, but that was a small price to pay considering her plans for that account. Not only would all of the money she was due to receive from Andre go in to this account, but also the money she intended to stash away once she married Troy.

"Remember this is *my* money. Your name is only on the account so that no one else can make claim to the money at any time. I want all statements to go to your address and you are to tell no one anything about this account or the amount of money in it. Don't ask me any questions about the money, and don't look to get any of it."

Mrs. Divine narrowed her eyes towards Kennedy. She knew her mother wouldn't appreciate that comment, but she didn't care. She had to make it clear to Mrs. Divine that the money belonged to her. She earned it, deserved it, and literally

126

shed blood, sweat, and tears for it. Besides, Kennedy had lofty goals for the amount of money that would be in that account by the time she would be ready to access it.

"You have always been selfish," Mrs. Divine commented after a few moments.

Their food had finally arrived, and again the waitress quickly set their selections before them and walked away without saying a word. Mrs. Divine pushed her food around the plate with her fork while Kennedy enjoyed her meal.

"Anyway," Mrs. Divine finally said, breaking the silence. She waived her hand as if dismissing the previous comments. "What are you going to do about setting a date?"

Mrs. Divine had finally found her appetite and started to gracefully consume her breakfast.

"Well, since I told Troy I was pregnant, he wants to do it right away." A piece of steak caught in Mrs. Divine's throat in response to Kennedy's revelation. She coughed violently in an effort to dislodge the meat.

Kennedy took pleasure in the shock she saw in her mother's eyes. Mrs. Divine reached for a glass of water and cleared the congestion. When she regained her composure, she simply stared at Kennedy, cocking her head to the side.

"Did you plan this?"

"No, but I intend to use if for my advantage." Kennedy continued her meal as if nothing happened.

"So are you going to move the wedding up or what?"

"No."

"Smart girl. Besides, there's nothing more tacky that a haphazard, shot-gun wedding. No daughter of mine will be

127

caught dead in a mess like that. This must be a grand affair. We weren't blessed with a last name like Divine for nothing."

"You married into that name, remember?" Kennedy threw in.

"It doesn't matter. I was divine before my name was, and don't you ever forget it."

Kennedy believed she'd never meet a diva haughtier than her very own mother. Mrs. Divine wrote the handbook on mastering the art of living the 'diva life.'

"Now, about this wedding…no, first about this pregnancy, when are you due?"

"Well, I haven't gone to the doctor yet but I assume I must be around two months. That would make me due…" Kennedy paused as she counted on her fingers, "around March of next year."

"Plenty of time for you to get your body together for a summer wedding. How about August?"

"Fine with me," Kennedy said, getting excited about it for the first time. She knew that between her and her mother, this wedding was bound to be the event of the century. People would talk about this one for years to come.

"Wait!" Mrs. Divine yelled interrupting Kennedy's vision of the grand occasion.

"What?" Kennedy asked with a puzzled expression.

"Who's paying for this?"

"Oh, don't worry about that. Believe me, it will all be taken care of."

Mrs. Divine pushed her plate forward and motioned for the waitress to bring her the check. The waitress come over immediately, placed the check on the table, and again swiftly walked away. Mrs. Divine reached into her designer purse for her wallet.

"My treat," Kennedy offered. Mrs. Divine smiled and raised her brows.

"Well, hurry up and let's go," Mrs. Divine stated. "We've got a baby to get prepared for and a gala to plan."

Chapter 23

Troy held the keys to a grand home on the south shore of Long Island. He was energized about the surprise he had in store for Kennedy. Troy couldn't be happier. The love of his life agreed to be his wife, and now she was carrying another one of his seeds. Troy would finally have what he'd always wanted—a real family life with Kennedy.

Though Troy was already en route to Kennedy's place, he dialed her home number to make sure she was there. Even at four months pregnant, Kennedy never stayed put. Troy thought about how beautiful Kennedy looked pregnant. Her glow permeated his soul. As vain as Kennedy was, he was sure she'd stay active enough to keep her weight in tact. She had managed to stay fit and the only thing that seemed to grow on her was her belly. What a beautiful sight that was. He loved to rub her bare stomach and whisper to his unborn child. Visions of Evan and a little sister running around in the yard at their spacious home warmed his heart. He couldn't wait to show Kennedy the house.

Kennedy finally answered the phone after numerous rings. She sounded exasperated.

"You okay, baby?"

"Yeah, just working out. What's up?"

"Where's Evan?" Troy asked.

"In the den playing video games of course, why?"

"Turn the DVD off and get dressed. I have a surprise for you. I'll be at the house in less than five minutes."

"What's the surprise?"

"Can't tell you! It's a surprise, remember? Tell Evan to get ready and you just get dressed and hurry up."

"Okay, okay. Give me a few minutes. I'll leave the door open."

"If you just give me a key, you won't have to do that."

Kennedy hung up without responding.

All day, Troy tried to think of a nice, romantic way to give Kennedy the keys but was too anxious to collect his thoughts. After several failed attempts to come up with anything interesting, he just decided to come out with it.

Troy practically skipped to Kennedy's door and pushed it open. He called out to her and Evan but received no answer. Troy dropped his keys on the console and went searching for the two of them. As he's suspected, Evan was still in the den paying video games on the flat screen TV.

"Hey, boy," Troy said in a deep voice.

Evan paused his game and ran to his father screaming, "Hey, Daddy!" Troy picked him up and hugged his son, then nuzzled his nose into his neck. Evan giggled and squirmed out of Troy's embrace. Taking his father by the hand, Evan dragged Troy towards the TV. "Daddy come play this game with me."

"Not right now Ev, I have a surprise for you and mommy..."

"A surprise? What is it?" Evan asked jumping up and down. "Did you buy me a new game."

Troy laughed. "No, it's an even bigger surprise than that. Go get your shoes and let's get ready to go. I'm going to take you to the surprise right now?"

"Yeah," Evan yelled and ran off in the direction of his room. His excitement made Troy laugh.

Troy went upstairs to search for Kennedy. When he got to her room, she was just exiting the shower. Troy lay on Kennedy's bed and laced his fingers behind his head. The swell of Kennedy's exposed, pregnant belly made him smile. As she dried herself and rubbed cocoa butter oil over her body, Troy stood watch and admired her from head to toe.

"Stop staring at me," Kennedy said.

"Why? You look beautiful," Troy responded.

"That's fat, not beauty," she said and laughed. "You just like the bigger boobs."

Troy stood and made his way over to Kennedy in the adjoining bathroom. He placed his hands round her from behind and caressed her protruding belly.

"You're beautiful. This is a good look for you. Maybe we should do this again."

Kennedy looked at him as if he were crazy.

"Not unless you plan on carrying the next one. I'm done with this. I'm only half way through and I want my body back."

Troy laughed and continued rubbing her stomach. He complimented Kennedy on her radiant, lightly coated skin and moved his hands upward from her stomach to caress her breast. Kennedy leaned back until they met cheek to cheek and closed her eyes for a moment.

"Okay, stop! I thought you had a surprise for me. I know that's not it. There's nothing surprising about you feeling me up. I knew all you cared about was the boobs."

Troy laughed his lusting away, kissed the back of her neck,

and slapped her on the behind.

"Let's go before it gets too late." Troy took several deep breaths to contain his longing for her. If it weren't for the fact that he had to show Kennedy the house and return the keys to his father's real estate office by a certain time, he would have locked the door and taken Kennedy right then and there. "I'm going downstairs to get something to drink. Do you want anything?"

"Just put some water in the car for me. Thanks."

"Whatever you want, baby. I've got it," Troy teased.

Moments later Kennedy emerged from her room. Troy and Evan were waiting in the car and had set the temperature to make sure Kennedy would be comfortable when she got in. Kennedy looked adorable in her stylish maternity outfit. After making sure she was comfortable, Troy carefully pulled out and headed for the surprise. He drove most of the way in silence to avoid spilling the beans. The short ride brought them to a well manicured neighborhood with tree lined streets and handsome homes, each one set apart in style from the rest.

Kennedy had fallen into a light sleep, something that happened more frequently since she was with child. Evan was in the back playing with his Sony PSP and talking non-stop. Troy pulled in front of a grand split-level home bedecked with exotic landscaping and stunning flowers that lined the walkway. A huge picture window graciously offered a peek inside. Troy anxiously jumped out of the car, opened Kennedy's door and planted a firm kiss directly on her full lips to wake her. Kennedy awoke startled. She rubbed her eyes, stretched them wide, and examined her surroundings. Troy took her by the hand and led her out of the car. At the same time, Evan jumped out of the back seat.

133

"Daddy, whose house are we going to?" Evan asked anxiously.

"Troy, where are we?" Kennedy asked.

"Our new home, if you like it." Troy knew they would.

"Our new house, Daddy. Can I still have my own room?"

Troy smiled and knelt down so that Evan could jump on his back.

"Even bigger than the one you've got now."

"Yeah! Evan yelled with both hands in the air. He nearly tumbled off of Troy's back.

"Whoa! Hold on, Evan. I don't want you to fall."

"Okay, Daddy."

What was there not to like? The house was impressive,

the neighborhood was upscale, and the price was right. Troy took Kennedy by the hand and walked her to the double doors at the home's main entry with Evan secured on his back. Once inside, Evan jumped down and started scurrying through the house like a mouse, peeking into every room. He watched Kennedy take in the sights, hoping she loved the place as much as he did. Troy wanted Kennedy to come home to their new house when she left the hospital after having their baby, and this house was perfect for starting their new life together.

So far Kennedy didn't look impressed, but Troy knew there was more to see. He escorted her from room to room throughout the spacious house, pointing out all of the perks the house had to offer. He left the best part for last—the backyard. The back of the house opened out to a spacious yard that spilled into an amazing strip of tranquil water. The view was remarkable. Kennedy simply smiled when she entered the yard. Both Troy and

Evan were elated. Troy watched Kennedy's every expression waiting for a sign of approval. Her smiled filled his heart. He knew she loved the place as much as he.

"Baby, isn't it incredible? I can see us living here forever," Troy said.

"Whoa! Maybe not forever, but it's a good start," Kennedy said.

"Well! Tell me, do you want it? We can be in by the time the baby gets here," Troy acknowledged and raised his brows.

"Yes, daddy. Let's get it. Can I invite my friends over?"

Kennedy and Troy looked at each other, shook their heads and smiled.

"Yes, pudding, you can invite your friends over if we get it."

"Then what's going to happen to my place?"

Kennedy turned her attention back to Troy.

"We can sell it," Troy suggested.

"I'm not sure I want to do that," Kennedy said and stared out into the water.

Troy looked disheartened.

"Well, we can rent it if you don't want to sell it," Troy offered.

"Maybe that will work." Troy looked around one last time. He fell in love with the place all over again. "Just tell me the word, baby, and it's ours. I want you and our baby to come home in style. Look at Evan he loves it already. I even checked out the schools and they're excellent."

Evan was running the length of the yard making airplane sounds. Kennedy took another look around and tightened her lips. "It needs some work and a little decorating. How much are they asking?"

"I've got that covered. For me, it's a steal. For anyone else, it's top dollar, market value," Troy said.

"Well, what's your deal and what's market value?" Kennedy asked. Obviously Troy's answer wasn't sufficient.

"I can get it for about four hundred and fifty thousand. On the market it would be worth more than six hundred thousand."

Kennedy stretched her eyes.

"So, baby, do you like it?"

Kennedy paused. "Yeah, I can work with this? Let's go for it."

"Yes!" Troy yelled, jabbed a fist to the air, and lifted Kennedy off of her feet. "Come on, Evan," he yelled over his shoulder. Troy carried Kennedy over the threshold of the rear door. The sound of their laughter and Evan's happy feet rose and filled the empty space, bouncing against the vaulted ceilings, then echoed throughout the remainder of the spacious house.

Chapter 24

Pretending to be asleep, Dina overheard Kennedy and her snooty mother mulling over the baby's arrival, and the ridiculous details of the wedding.

"How amazing would the room look with white, silk fabric draped from the ceilings, lining the walls," Mrs. Divine said, with buoyancy in her voice. We can do it if we have the reception at one of those beautiful estates on the north shore. You know they rent their rooms, and even entire mansions out for all types of events. The wedding can be outside in one of those beautifully lush Tibetan-styled gardens. And, the reception could also be outside, or inside one of the luxuriously designed ballrooms. It will be just divine, almost like a fairy tale wedding, perfect for my princess."

Dina rolled her eyes to the heavens and shuddered. 'My little princess', she mouthed, mocking Mrs. Divine, and mimicking the snobbish expression that was sure to be painted on the woman's face.

"Now just how are we supposed to book a place like that?" Kennedy asked.

"Leave that to me. Can you just picture it; stately French doors leading to the ballroom, nothing less than cymbidium orchids for the beautiful bride, and striking white lilies for the girls! People will talk about this wedding for years to come," Mrs. Divine's jovial laugh wafted through the townhouse, stealing its way throughout the second floor bedrooms.

137

Dina rolled her eyes so long and so hard that her sockets hurt. Then she put her index finger in her mouth, pretending to gag. She stopped for a moment and thought, *the girls? What girls?* Other than her and Angel, Kennedy had no friends. Dina imagined a pathetic show about three rows of people on Kennedy's side of the church while Troy's side bustled with countless family and friends.

Speaking of Troy, Kennedy certainly didn't deserve a kind, honest and loving man like him. If Troy could capture the star's he'd suffer the burns if he thought it would put a spark in Kennedy's eyes. Could Dina ever be so lucky as to find a man that lived to see her happy?

When she heard Kennedy climb the stairs, she turned over so that her back would face the door, and pretended to breathe deeply as if she were asleep. After a few minutes she could hear the padded thump of Kennedy's feet once again as she descended the stairs. Dina kept up her front until she heard the front door close and the engine from Kennedy's Mercedes purr.

"Great they're gone," she said and flung her legs around the side of the bed. It' was time to get up, but for what?

The emptiness she felt inside seemed to seep out into the room, creating an eerie quietness. Suddenly, Carl came to mind, the source of her void. Months had past since he kicked Dina out, and still she yearned for him daily. Spying on him occasionally had helped her to stay abreast of his relationship status. She'd often park a few houses away and watch his comings and goings. A few times she did see that perfect looking Tamara woman come and go with their little girl. But lately she hadn't been around. Maybe she went back to wherever she came from.

She belly-flopped on the bed and spilled a fresh batch of tears into Kennedy's expensive down pillows. The pain had become physical. Her heart ached so badly, she thought it would pound right through her chest.

Dina decided that their breakup was not just her fault. Carl could have mentioned something to her about Tamara and their daughter. Maybe she wouldn't have acted so crazy when the woman started to call. It wasn't fair for her to take all the blame. She needed to get her man back, and decided that there was no better time than the present, so she jumped out of bed.

The sight of her reflection in the full-length mirror positioned in the corner of the room, gave her pause. The brutally honest image confirmed that she looked as bad on the outside as she felt on the inside. Dry, lifeless hair, bushy legs, and the old tattered night shirt were more than she could stomach. Dina couldn't ever remember the last time she dressed with meaning. As she prepared for work every morning, she'd just go through the motions, not really caring how she looked.

Dina tipped to the bedroom door, peeked out then rushed into Kennedy's bathroom to borrow bath foam, candles, and a disposable razor. From her own collections, she pulled out a body brush and filled the tub with hot, scented, bubbly water. Dina lit the candles, discarded the funky pajamas that she'd been lounging in since she left work on Friday afternoon, and sank into the silky, steamy bath. Almost immediately, she felt some of the tension ease from her body. Reveling in the soothing heat, Dina let the water wash away her depression, feeling rejuvenated. She shampooed her hair, then shaved her underarms and shapely legs. A simple bath had helped to renew her confidence and energize her spirit.

Once she emerged from the bath, she wrapped one of Kennedy's plush towels around her naked body. The delicate scent of the fragrant, mango body butter she used decorated the air. Dina carefully selected her attire, choosing to wear something cute and sexy but not over the top for the first time approaching Carl since their breakup. Dina opted for a flirty denim skirt, a bright white, cotton tank with a beaded trim around the collar, and a short tan blazer to ward off the crisp fall breeze. She curled her hair, letting the soft twirls tease her shoulders, then placed a whimsical applejack hat atop her head, allowing the bushel of silky curls to cascade out from under the hat. She finished off her outfit with crisp white sneakers and amber-tinted, rimless shades.

Dina stopped at her favorite local salon for a quick manicure before heading over to Carl's house. The closer she got, the more nervous she became. Dina fought the urge to turn back, encouraging herself to forge forward with pep talks. It seemed strange to pull up directly in front of his house instead of parking inconspicuously and spying like she'd been doing for the past few weeks. Dina continued to encourage herself to follow through with her intentions. Finally, she stepped out of the car, cautiously headed up the walkway to Carl's front door, and tapped on the door so lightly that she knew Carl couldn't have heard it. Then she pondered whether or not she should knock again or just go home. Tossing the thought back and forth in her mind, she decided to abort her mission just as the front door eased open. Carl stood in the crack looking as fine as ever in sweat pants and a crisp, white muscle shirt. Dina lost her words, thoughts, and composure. Not sure what to say, she decided to lean on the stability of honesty.

"Hi, Carl, I just wanted to see you."

"What's up?" Carl asked but still hadn't opened the door. Dina wondered if he had company. She also thought it was funny that Carl was even home on a Saturday evening. From the looks of his attire, he didn't seem to have any other plans.

"Can I come in?"

"Come on," Carl offered and stepped back from the door. Dina's heart leaped.

She followed Carl into the living room where he took a seat and silenced the TV with the remote, but kept his eyes on the images moving on the screen. Dina felt troubled because Carl hadn't made eye contact, but she took that as a sign that he still cared.

141

"How have you been?" she asked.

"I'm good. What about you?"

"All right I guess." Dina continued to lean on honesty. "I really miss you, Carl. And you have to admit, it's not all my fault. You could have told me about Tamara and your daughter. Maybe I wouldn't have acted out so badly."

Carl stared. She read the expression. They both knew better.

"Dina, it wouldn't have mattered who it was. If you didn't know my mother, you'd get pissed if I talked to her on the street."

She was at a loss again because what he said was true.

"Listen Carl, I realize I had issues. I have worked them out." She wasn't sure if she could continue and felt a need to lighten the tension in the room. "You eat yet?"

"Nah, I haven't eaten since earlier today."

"I'm hungry myself. I can make us something." Dina got up and went into the kitchen then called out, "What do you have?"

She heard Carl laugh then laughed herself knowing that Carl probably had nothing but water and beer in the fridge. He didn't exactly know his way around a kitchen or a supermarket.

Dina looked through the scarcely stocked fridge and decided on the old pizza. She checked the cabinets. Most of the seasonings were what she had bought. She tried her best to jazz up the pizza, heating it in the oven so the crust would remain crispy. She poured two large cups of soda while the pizza heated. Dina dressed a tray to make the meal look more appealing. When she returned to the living room and placed the pizza on the coffee table, Carl looked at it questionably. Dina was alarmed.

"Carl, how long have you had this pizza in there?"

"I ordered it earlier."

"Then why are you looking at it like that?"

"You made it look like it was just delivered. How'd you do that? It never looks like that when I reheat it." Carl leaned in and started in on his first slice.

"That's because you don't do it right." The two laughed.

They were silent while they ate. Carl shoveled in two slices in no time and washed the remnants down with the ice-cold soda. Dina took her time, properly eating her pizza with a knife and fork as she studied Carl. When Carl was done, he picked up a napkin and roughly wiped his face. Dina leaned over and gently swabbed sauce from the corner of his lips.

"You missed a spot." Touching his face sent a chill through Dina's fingers and straight to her core.

Carl finally faced Dina. His eyes roamed her entirely then rested on her breast. Dina straightened her back, offering a clearer view of her cleavage. She was thankful that she decided to wear her minimizer bra because it enhanced the roundness of her breasts while adding depth to her crease. Carl's gaze rose to her lips. Dina took the initiative and leaned in to kiss him. Carl's open mouth accepted her advance. The kiss was long and deep. A spark had been ignited, and Carl's hands began to roam her mounds, caressing and squeezing.

Carl leaned Dina back on the couch, covering her with his body and warm mouth. Dina wrapped her arms around him and caressed his back. The heat of their passion increased tenfold and soft moans turned to hungry pants. With unbridled intensity, they undressed one another, drinking each other's essence. Their bodies entwined and Carl entered Dina with fervor. They rode together to the brink of passion, slowed just enough to contain the raging fires, and then stirred up the flames once more before going over the edge. Carl's emerging climax riddled his face with a look of painful bliss and hastened his breath to short gasps. Dina sang his name in fanatical pleas as he reached the depths of her soul with each thrust. She could feel the swell of his manhood as he reached his breaking point. Tears sprang in her eyes as she held on tighter, burrowing her nails into the flesh of his back until her body convulsed in violent waves. The rush of Dina's juices drove Carl wild. At his attempt to withdraw, Dina forcefully wrapped her legs around his backside and pulled her center to him. She squeezed the walls of her vagina and suctioned the flow

143

from his erectness, receiving every drop of his life-giving fluids. Only when she was sure that she'd drained him completely, did she release her hold on him. Too spent to dispute, Carl's limp, naked body fell on top of hers as he worked to steady his breath.

Carl languidly pulled himself off of Dina and headed to the bath to clean up. When Dina heard the bathroom door close, she raised her legs over her head, hoping to guide his semen through her canal. She reveled in the knowledge that the timing was just right. Dina had stopped taking her birth control pills weeks before and had already purchased two packages of pregnancy tests from the nearby drugstore. Now all she had to do was wait patiently for the outcome. Whether he knew it or not, Carl would be in her life, one way or another.

Chapter 25

Kennedy tried everything she could to get out of going to the hospice with Troy to visit his father. Troy was insistent, so she finally gave in and sent Evan to her mother's house. Besides, the man was extremely ill—who was she to deny him a wish before his eminent death.

Begrudgingly, she prepared for the visit even though it wasn't a good morning for her. Morning sickness had begun to take its toll. Kennedy assumed that she would be passed the morning sickness stage since she was officially in her second trimester. Unfortunately for her, morning sickness hadn't begun until now. Preparing for work in the mornings had become a daunting task. Kennedy often had to take several breaks while getting dressed just to steady her head and balance her nausea. Tea and dry toast or crackers had become a habitual morning meal. Her stomach couldn't handle much more than that light fare until at least noon. Saturdays, she spent the entire day in her loungewear, hanging out in the den watching movies with Dina. As she prepared her new midday staple, decaffeinated tea with no sugar, she thought about Dina acting more strange than usual. Kennedy made a mental note to talk to her about that when she returned from visiting Troy's dad.

This Sunday morning Troy had accompanied his mother to church, but it was near two in the afternoon and Kennedy had expected him to be at her house by now. Visiting hours didn't last as long on Sundays, she assumed. But then again, what did she know. She'd never visited anyone in a hospice before. Just then she heard Troy's truck pull up. One thing she did enjoy about being pregnant was her heightened senses. Each one operated in overdrive, especially her hearing and her sense of smell, both of which she used to her advantage. Troy had just reached the door and rang the bell as Kennedy entered the living room. She took her time getting to the door and opened it slowly.

Troy gave a timid smile then sighed instead of offering an appropriate greeting.

"What's wrong Troy? I know that look."

"Ah...nothing, babe. Are you ready?" Troy asked as he rubbed his palms together then wiped them against his slacks.

Kennedy eyed him with a raised brow. Lucky for him she didn't feel like going into whatever his problem was right then. She didn't fail to notice how handsome he looked in his button-down navy blue, French-cuffed shirt and matching navy slacks. His hair was freshly cut and his dimples seemed to reflect the sun's rays even in the midst of his awkward smile. Kennedy rolled her eyes and turned to get her things.

"Let me get my bag. I'll be right there."

"Okay, babe. Um, I'll wait in the car."

What is his problem? Kennedy thought then dismissed the issue. She picked up her purse and took a final look around to make sure she didn't forget anything.

"Hey, Dee. I'll see you later, okay," she yelled upstairs to Dina.

"Have fun!" Dina teased.

"Yeah right. Why don't you fix us some dinner while I'm out? Do something creative with yourself instead of sitting up in that room all day," Kennedy teased back.

"Ha! Girl, you are so funny," Dina's laugh infiltrated the entire home.

"Whatever. I'll call you when I'm on my way back. Come lock the door," Kennedy said.

"Go ahead, I'm coming right now. See you later."

Kennedy slid her small designer purse under her arm and pulled the door closed, then she placed her ear against the door to make sure she heard Dina come down the steps. Kennedy turned and started down the walkway, assessing her attire as she walked. She brushed away some imaginary lint from the front of her maternity wrap dress and took a side look at her low-heeled, Via Spiga sling backs. Pleased with her look, she continued down the walk but halted when she noticed Troy's chunky mother seated in the front passenger seat of his truck.

Kennedy's insides ran hot. That's why Troy had acted so strangely at the door. Her eyes narrowed into tight slits as she glared at Troy. His eyes pleaded with her. She stood wondering whether or not she should turn back. Determined not to let that woman get the best of her, she continued forward, her eyes locked on Troy as she looked passed Mrs. Alexander in the front seat. Kennedy approached the car and opened the front passenger door wondering why his mother hadn't already leaped into her rightful place in the backseat. She was Troy's pregnant fiancée, so why would his mother think she had any intention of riding in the back? When Kennedy opened the door, Mrs. Alexander stared her up and down as if she was crazy then pulled the door closed.

Troy jumped out of the driver's seat and ran to Kennedy's side just as she was about to grab the door handle once more.

147

"Babe!"

Flames appeared to shoot from Kennedy's eyes. Troy looked distressed.

"I'm sorry, baby. My dad wanted to see her and when she found out I was going to see him today, she wanted to come."

"Then why didn't you tell me? I could just go another day," Kennedy managed through clenched teeth.

"Baby, please. You are going to be my wife. And she's my mother. That's not going to change. At some point you two are going to have to learn to coexist. Please, baby. Do this for me, please!"

Kennedy didn't budge. Her narrowed eyes stared passed Troy as her foot tapped rapidly against the ground.

"Ken, come on," Troy pleaded.

"Take her, drop her off, then come back and get me," she ordered.

Troy sighed. "By then visiting hours will be over. Dad wants to see both of you. It won't be that bad. Come on now, baby. I promise I'll make it up to you!"

Kennedy's lips slid into an evil smirk.

"Fine. I'll go," she agreed nonchalantly.

Troy raised his brow. Kennedy smiled and winked her eye. She knew Troy was puzzled, but she was determined not to let that chubby little woman get the best of her. Kennedy spun on her elegant little heel, sauntered toward the truck, and threw Troy's mother a wry smile. Mrs. Alexander's brows furrowed.

The ride to the hospice was completely silent. Kennedy and Mrs. Alexander never exchanged a word. Troy's forehead was dotted with beads of perspiration, and he spent more of his drive viewing Kennedy through the rearview mirror than he spent watching the road. Kennedy smirked at him every time she caught him looking.

When they arrived at the hospice, Kennedy hopped out of the car and headed toward the entrance before Troy could get to her. Troy helped his mother out of the car and jogged to catch up to Kennedy.

"Are you all right?" Troy questioned.

"Just fine," Kennedy responded without looking at Troy. She had every intention of making him pay a hefty price for this later.

Mr. Alexander appeared to be happy to see both Kennedy and his wife. Kennedy was astounded by his infirmity and labored speech. The sight of Mr. Alexander rocked even her hard demeanor. It took all of her strength to keep the tears from bursting out of her eyes. Until she was able to swallow the lump in her throat, she refrained from speaking. She could hardly believe that this was the same brawny man she had known for many years, and she wasn't prepared for the way he looked.

"Ah...look at here...two beautiful ladies." Mr. Alexander sputtered between coughs.

Kennedy's eyes stretched to the size of saucers when she witnessed his entire body quake as he coughed. She looked at Mrs. Alexander to see how she was taking everything. Mrs. Alexander silently stood at her husband's feet, her head held high as a single tear rolled down her cheek.

"Come on over...here...a...let me see...you."

Mr. Alexander attempted to lift his hand and wave Kennedy over with a limp gesture. Kennedy took small, unsteady

149

steps until she reached his bedside. She held her hand down in front of her to keep from covering her mouth. Unchecked tears slid down her cheeks.

"Hi, Mr. Alexander." She couldn't think of anything more to say.

"You look beautiful. You take good care of my grands, you hear me...I've..."

Kennedy leaned forward, unsure of why he stopped speaking. Her lower lip quivered as she watched his body writhe in pain. His chest rose and fell rapidly as he tried to steady his breathing. Mr. Alexander rolled his head from side to side as tears scurried down the side of his face, filling his ears and wetting the pillow below him. Finally his breathing regained a more tranquil rhythm, and he opened his eyes to find Kennedy looking down on him with her lips parted and tears streaming down her cheeks.

"Are you okay?"

"Yes. This old guy's just fine," he whispered. "That's just the way this thing goes. I've put a little something aside for my grandchildren. You make sure to tell them grandpa loved them very much, ya hear?"

"Yes sir, I will."

For the first time since Kennedy entered the hospital room, she noticed the earthy scent that filled the air. As the scent filtered through her and settled in the pit of her stomach, she was overcome with the urge to regurgitate. Kennedy whipped her hand to her mouth to fight the onslaught of emotions and bile rising inside and raced into the nearby bathroom. The mixture of the cleaning chemicals and the scent of sickness filled her and made her purge until there was nothing left. Though she felt empty her muscles continued to spasm, causing her to gag and cramp with no results.

Kennedy felt Troy's large, strong hands rubbing loving circles on her back. The circles ceased and Troy returned with a cup of water. Kennedy rinsed her mouth then cleansed her face. Troy held her the entire time

"Let's go outside and get some fresh air. We'll wait for my mother down there."

As Troy walked Kennedy out of the hospice, Kennedy recalled the image of his ailing father's scant frame. She decided that she needed to marry Troy sooner rather than later.

Chapter 26

Troy could hardly contain his excitement as the aircraft taxied toward the gate at the Belize City Airport. Three weeks before, after their visit to see his father, Kennedy had suggested they get married right away. Troy was ecstatic and credited Kennedy's sudden change of heart to her realizing the frailty of life. The very day she mentioned it, Troy searched the Internet travel sites for last minute deals and came up with a four-day three-night trip to Belize. The next day, he and Kennedy got on the phone and began making arrangements for their nuptials. Within forty-eight hours they had arranged all the necessary documents and secured a chaplain, photographer, and personal assistant for Kennedy for the day of the wedding. By the end of that week, with the help of her mother and two best friends, Kennedy had her dress, shoes, and accessories picked out. Mrs. Divine offered to care for Evan while they were away.

It saddened Troy a little that his mother and sister wouldn't be present but at least he wouldn't have to deal with the tension between Kennedy and his mother during the ceremony. Kennedy had also expressed concern that none of her family or friends would be there, so they decided to redo their vows and hold a huge reception back home on their first anniversary.

The moment the captain turned off the seat belt sign, Troy leaped to his feet to retrieve their bags. His sudden movement startled Kennedy awake. She had managed to snooze most of the way since staying awake made her incredibly nauseous.

Troy secretly admired her as he watched her rub the sleepiness from her eyes. He leaned to her and covered her cheek with his full, sensual lips. Troy laughed knowing Kennedy would be disgusted by the big, sloppy, wet imprint.

"Ewe, Troy! Stop that."

Troy laughed hard. Kennedy sucked her teeth and continued to fuss as she searched for something to wipe the moisture from her face.

"We're in Belize, baby! And you're about to be my wife. There's more where that came from."

"Troy, if you do that again, I swear I'll hurt you."

"Now that's what I'm talkin' about! Hurt me, baby!"

Troy's laughter filled the first-class cabin. Nearby passengers giggled at his delight. Kennedy had to laugh too. As they parted the aircraft, a few passengers within earshot congratulated them on their upcoming nuptials.

A white stretch limo served as a pleasant surprise, compliments of their hotel. Troy relished in the striking scenery beckoning him. The flora seemed to welcome them as it danced along the roadside to the rhythm of the gentle tropical breeze. Zest was in the air. Troy took a deep breath, allowing the infectious atmosphere to saturate him. Kennedy was nestled in the crook of his arm. Troy felt sorry that she couldn't completely appreciate the atmosphere due to her delicate condition. He beamed again as he pondered the arrival of his daughter. No one knew the baby's sex, yet he was certain that the Lord had smiled upon them and blessed them with a baby girl. Their family would be complete. What more could he ask?

Kennedy stirred beneath him.

"Feeling better, babe?"

"A little. That was a rough ride. I'll get some tea when we get to the hotel. Those crackers I had did nothing for me."

"Well, continue to rest until we get there," Troy said and tenderly nudged her back into the crook of his arm, where she remained until they arrived at the hotel.

The entire staff catered to their every need. Kennedy drank her tea and took a short nap while Troy changed into a pair of swimming trunks and jumped into the pool. After a few laps, Troy found a comfortable lounge chair in a shaded area. He laid back and took in the scenery. The hotel grounds were picturesque. Colorful, large-leafed plants encircled the area. Lofty, handsome palm trees offered protection from the powerful sun rays and illustrated the essence of paradise. The earth receded into a serene procession adjoining the clear blue sky with the aqua tinted waters. The soothing resonance of the cascading waters worked to lull Troy into a peaceful resting state.

From the corner of his eye, Troy spotted Kennedy as she emerged from the confines of their bungalow. Reminiscent of a goddess in her all-white flowing halter dress and white thong sandals adorned with brilliant crystals. Kennedy seemed to glide towards him. Troy breathed deeply and released the air slowly as he watched his bride-to-be. He was glad to see that she was obviously feeling better. The radiant glow had returned to her flawless peanut-colored skin. Her closely cropped hair shined healthily as it framed her pretty face.

Troy stood leisurely and washed his eyes over his own frame in contest. With his slightly thin but taut build, six-pack abs, and smooth, milk-chocolate brown skin, they complimented one another extremely well. Troy offered Kennedy his lounge chair and retrieved another from close by.

"How you feeling, babe?"

"Much better," Kennedy said as Troy helped her into her chair.

Troy noticed that her demeanor was much lighter than before. Once she sat, he began to gaze at her.

"So, baby, you ready?" Troy asked, smiling.

"As ready as I'm ever going to be," Kennedy said.

"Do you even realize how beautiful you are?" Troy complimented. Kennedy smiled and as always Troy felt complete.

Troy's lips curled into an adoring smile, happy to know that he put that smile on her face. He was simply happy to be anywhere with her. They had spent too many years apart. Troy laid his head back, and they enjoyed a relaxing evening together.

155

Before dawn, the next morning Kennedy was whisked away by her bridal assistant to prepare for their beachfront ceremony. Troy was left to himself to get ready. Smooth R&B filled the bungalow as Troy danced in the mirror as he prepared for his big day. He and Kennedy had chosen to allow the tropical vibe to guide them in their selection of apparel for their ceremony.

Troy donned an eggshell-colored linen pant suit with loose-fitting drawstring bottoms and a collarless, short-sleeved, button-down shirt. He let the shirt fall freely to reveal his hairless, chiseled chest. On his feet he wore tan woven sandals. He pulled Kennedy's wedding band from his pocket and looked it over. It was time to go, and Troy could hardly wait. Soon, Kennedy would be his wife.

Troy went to search for Sherri, their assigned wedding coordinator, to let her know he was ready to go. Just as he closed the door to the bungalow, the petite, nut-brown woman greeted him with a warm smile.

"Ready, Mr. Alexander?" Sherri sang in the rhythm of her native tongue.

"Yes I am," Troy said with a smile.

Sherri led Troy through the grounds to the hotel's designated location for beachfront weddings. Troy looked up to take in the beauty of the striking blue sky, which was dotted with a few friendly clouds. The pathway leading to the wedding site was lined with vibrant, picturesque plant life. When they reached the white coral beach, Troy took his sandals off to allow his feet to sink into the warm, alluring sand. Just a few feet ahead stood an all-white gazebo decorated with ceremonial white chiffon. In the center stood the chaplain dressed in a long, ivory robe. Beside him was a tall, dark gentleman, wearing a colorful shirt with white shorts. Troy greeted the Chaplain, nodded at the flutist then closed his eyes to feast on the soothing melody stirring in the wind, compliments of the flutist.

When the music stopped, Troy opened his eyes to witness his wife-to-be walking towards him. He sighed and closed his eyes again for just a moment, as if to capture and record her enchanting image. Could he remember ever feeling this much joy? The dark man continued to release gentle sounds into the atmosphere, massaging Troy into a state of euphoric bliss.

As Kennedy drew closer, Troy found it impossible to take his eyes off of her. The space around her seemed to glow. Her gown was an elegantly understated strapless flow of shimmering soft silk that ended just before the center of her foot. The back hung slightly longer than the front, giving the appearance of a petite train. Her closely cropped hair was neatly primed and topped with an exquisite white lily, and she carried an array of exotic flowers for a bouquet. Refined ivory-colored pearls adorned her ears and neckline. Troy held his hand to Kennedy and assisted her up the two short steps onto the gazebo. It was then that he noticed her freshly French manicured fingers and toes and her stylish beaded sandals. If there was ever a time that the mere sight of his lovely Kennedy could bring him to tears, this was it.

Troy had yet to release Kennedy's hand and didn't intend to. The chaplain nodded at both of them to signal the start of the ceremony. The flutist ceased for the vows as Troy and Kennedy faced each other and pledged their allegiances to one another till death did them part. The brief rite went quickly as the photographer captured the entire ritual on film. A few more shots were taken with pristine waters and a clear blue sky as a breathtaking backdrop. The newlyweds were whisked away to set sail to a nearby private island for a few more snapshots and a romantic seaside dinner where the sunset presented a perfect finale to a special day.

After dinner, the two returned to their bungalow to change and join the other patrons for a Belize-style beach celebration in honor of their big day. Kennedy wore a comfortable, light pink maternity halter dress with beaded flip-flops and Troy donned a light blue linen short set with sandals. Together they danced to the sounds of the tropics and feasted on exotic fruit juices and island finger foods until Kennedy was too tired and too full to continue.

When they got back to the room, Troy was eager to consummate their marriage before all of Kennedy's energy was depleted. The cool night breeze, the swish of the ocean, and the flicker of the moonlight against the navy blue water highlighted their love-making then coerced Kennedy into a peaceful slumber. Troy stayed up a little longer, basking in the afterglow and contemplating how wonderful their life together would be. He was happy and hoped that Kennedy, his wife, Mrs. Kennedy Alexander, was just as happy.

Chapter 27

Dina helped Kennedy and her mother prepare for the Thanksgiving Day festivities while Evan watched movies in the den. There was the traditional turkey, stuffing, and cranberry sauce along with many other appealing side dishes. She actually enjoyed working in the kitchen with the ladies this morning. She just wondered how the rest of the day would turn out since both Kennedy's and Troy's families would be present. The last time they were all together, all hell broke loose.

"Okay, Mrs. Divine. Try to behave when Troy's family arrives," Dina said and chuckled as she prepared a salad for dinner.

Kennedy shot her a look and Mrs. Divine simply laughed.

"Sweetie, don't worry about me. I don't have much to say to the little fat ass woman."

The three cracked up with laughter.

"Let's hope so," Kennedy added. "But you know she's not necessarily fat. She's just short and that makes her look plump."

"Plump, chubby, fat—hell, it's all the same. And she's got the nerve to try and be snooty on top of that. I know she's just one step away from the backwoods of Mississippi," Mrs. Divine said.

Dina almost spit out the carrot she'd stolen from the colorful salad she had just prepared.

Kennedy rolled her eyes and shook her head at her mother. "Weren't you born in a little ole town in Georgia?"

"Yes, but I'm refined," Mrs. Divine retorted as she straightened her back and lifted her chin.

After that, all three women shared a hearty laugh one more time.

"So I guess you'll be moving out soon and I'll be here all by myself," Dina said with a mock expression of sadness on her face. She placed her index finger on her bottom lips, resembling a little girl. Dina wondered why she hadn't seen Kennedy pack a single box.

"I'm not going anywhere, at least not until we close on the house."

Dina's head jerked in shock. She couldn't believe her ears.

"You mean you are not going to live with your own husband?" Dina asked rounding the counter as if it would help her hear what Kennedy was saying.

"I will, in the new house. I don't want to move into his place, especially when I like mine better," Kennedy said nonchalantly as she reached into the refrigerator to retrieve butter for the corn she had just boiled.

Dina had a plethora of questions, but decided against asking any of them, knowing it wouldn't make a difference anyway. Kennedy had audacity, but who was she to complain if Troy was okay with it all.

"Troy's okay with this?" Dina just had to ask.

Kennedy cocked her head to the side and looked at Dina for a moment, and then continued preparing her dish.

Dina surrendered both hands to the air and shrugged her shoulders.

"If it's okay with him, then who am I to complain," she said.

"So can we expect to see Carl today?"

"Actually, yes. Things are looking up. He'll be late because he has some family to visit first." Dina wished she could have retracted that last sentence because it made her feel inadequate.

Dina hoped Kennedy didn't ask her the very question that was in her own head, *'Why didn't Carl invite her to join him for dinner with his family?'* One day at a time, Dina reminded herself. Things will be back on track soon enough. Even though the pregnancy test she took earlier during the week came up negative, Dina knew that if she stuck to her plans, she'd be pregnant in no time. Then she'll be on her way to having a family too, just like Kennedy.

"I'd better get changed before people start to get here," Dina said as she removed her apron and placed it on the counter before heading upstairs.

The first to show was Lacey, Troy's big-mouth cousin, his sister, Courtney, and her son, Dylan. When Evan heard Dylan, he ran to him. The two energetic boys loudly shared info on their latest electronic games and shot up to Evan's room to try them out. Courtney was cool as far as Dina was concerned, but that Lacey, humph! Dina couldn't imagine a bigger gossip, and it sickened her the way she hovered around Kennedy. When Dina came back downstairs, she heard the women approaching the kitchen, so she slipped into the formal dining room to check the table settings. She'd rather listen to their conversation from there.

"Hey, girl! Oh, look at you. I can't believe you are having another baby. You look so adorable," Lacey commented as she enveloped Kennedy in a warm, tight hug.

"Thanks," Kennedy said, smiling.

"Hello, everyone. Happy Thanksgiving," Courtney offered a cordial, generic greeting.

"Do you need any help? Here I brought a peach cobbler and some sweet potato pie," Lacey said. "This pie is to die for."

Dina stayed in the dining room toying with the flatware and wondering why Lacey talked so darn loud.

"Thanks, honey, I'll take that over here," Mrs. Divine said. "Go on out to the living room and make yourself comfortable. In a moment we'll bring out some mimosas to start until all the guests have arrived."

"Mimosas? Wow, now that's what I'm talking about. You always do things real classy, Mrs. Divine. I guess that's why Kennedy is the way she is." Lacey said.

"Oh, please. Give it a break," Dina said under her breath. She waited until Lacey was out of the kitchen before she returned. "That Lacey..." Dina started.

"I know, I know, just leave it alone for now, Dina," Kennedy said rolling her eyes. "It's going to be a long night."

Just as the ladies finished in the kitchen, the rest of the guests arrived starting with Troy and his mother. Dina's mother also came with her boyfriend. Dina was pleased yet somewhat surprised that she actually showed up.

Everyone settled into the living room for pre dinner cocktails until Mrs. Divine made the finishing touches on the meal in the formal dining room. Despite the fact that Mrs. Divine was a diva, not many could match her abilities in the kitchen. She was indeed a phenomenal cook, often adding gourmet spins to traditional southern dishes.

Dina watched Lacey as she walked around the room checking everything out, from the floral arrangements on the console and coffee tables to the art on the walls and the window treatments.

"Oh my God, these are so nice, Ken," she said as she felt the honeycomb blinds at Kennedy's picture window. "And that painting, girl, who is that by?"

No one you could afford, Dina thought. Damn, didn't the girl have any pride? Lacey was really getting on her nerves.

"Those are by a black artist by the name of A. Gockel. I love abstract, and I particularly love his work," Kennedy answered.

"You did such a great job decorating this place. I can't wait to see what you do to the new house. You are going to have to help me with my place when I get it."

"Oh, are you about to move out?" Dina asked.

"Not right now. I just did some work. Girl, you should see my room. I just had it painted crimson red and bought an ivory, leather bed and put in brand new carpet. It's just beautiful. Ken, you've got to come over and see it."

"Wow!" Dina said, feigning interest. "It must look like MTV Cribs up in that room."

"Girl..." Lacey stopped mid-sentence and rolled her eyes at Dina.

It obviously took a few seconds for Lacey to realize that Dina was actually mocking her.

Dina turned to notice that her mother had just downed yet another flute of mimosa. It had to be at least her third. By now she was giddy and practically on top of her friend. Dina hoped that her mom wouldn't get too carried away in front of everyone.

Seeing her mother all over her guest made her think about Carl and she wondered when he would get there.

Courtney and her mother engaged in small talk as they waited. Mrs. Alexander looked confident as she secretly gazed around Kennedy's home. Dina could tell she approved of what she saw. No matter what, Kennedy and her mom were very stylish people, and that was reflected throughout their homes.

Mrs. Divine garnered the guests attention when she removed her apron and snapped it as she announced, "Dinner is served." She spun on her stilettos and yelled upstairs for the boys to join the adults in the dining room. Several flattering remarks rang out as everyone entered the beautifully decorated dining room. Mrs. Alexander remained tight-lipped.

After a quick, thankful prayer, it was time to indulge. The food was delicious, and the meal was complimented with fine South-African white and red wines. At first, hardly anyone spoke as they enjoyed their meals. After a short while, light conversation began.

Dina noticed that her mother had just finished another glass of wine even though she was only halfway through with her meal. She smiled at her date so hard that Dina swore the muscles in her face would eventually get stuck, forcing her to forever sport a grin like the Joker. No one existed besides the two of them. Lacey drew Dina's attention away from her mother when she asked Kennedy and Troy about their trip to Belize and the wedding.

"It was beautiful. I'll get the pictures after dinner," Kennedy said.

"Oh, I can't wait," Lacey squealed.

"Yeah," Dina's mother said, and the entire table turned to face her. It was the first time she'd taken her eyes off her boyfriend and directed a statement to anyone else since she arrived. "When you gone...get hitched, Dina? It's about time for you." A hiccup parted her sentence.

Dina had hoped that her mother wouldn't go too far. Mrs. Jacobs had obviously had more than her fill of drinks for the evening. Too bad the drinking had only just begun.

"When my time comes," Dina snapped. *Please don't start,* she prayed silently.

"I was just asking," Mrs. Jacobs slurred.

Mrs. Alexander shook her head.

The doorbell rang. "I'll get it," Dina sang and leaped out of her chair. She hoped it was Carl. Instead it was Angel and Dr. Dentures.

"Hi, everyone. Sorry I'm late. We had to make a few other appearances. Oh, it smells great in here. Mother Divine this is definitely your work here, isn't it?"

"Of course, baby girl," Mrs. Divine chimed.

"You all know Patrick," Dina said as a general introduction.

Patrick said hello and everyone responded cordially.

"Come on honey, grab a seat and dig in," Mrs. Divine said.

"Thanks, Mrs. Divine. I'll just have a little. We already had a little something, and we still have one more stop to make," Angel said.

Angel and Patrick squeezed in and the conversation continued from there. All was well until Mrs. Jacobs started again.

"You know, Ken, this is a nice place you have here. Dina, when you gonna get you someplace to stay like this?"

"Ma, don't start please, I'm begging you." Dina put her head down and massaged her temples.

"What? All you need to do is get you a man you can keep around for a while and maybe you could be doing some of the nice things that Kennedy is doing. It's about time you get married, have some kids, and get you a nice place. I know Kennedy must be tired of you staying here."

The room fell silent.

"Really, it's not a problem, Mrs. Jacobs," Kennedy said. "Besides, I won't even be here long. We'll be moving into our house soon. This place will practically be Dina's."

Mrs. Jacobs raised her eyebrows. "Oh, so you bought a house? How nice!" she said to Kennedy, but looked at Dina.

"Troy, do you have a brother for Dina?"

"Ma! I don't need you of all people hooking me up." Dina said.

"Not with someone from my family, that's for sure," Mrs. Alexander interjected.

"Ma! Don't," Troy stated firmly.

"What did I say?" Mrs. Alexander asked with faux innocence.

"I was just asking that's all," Mrs. Jacobs said.

Dina wondered what was wrong with her mother and Troy's.

"Well, don't worry about it. I have someone and my time will come," Dina said.

"Well, where is he?" Mrs. Jacobs looked around as if she

was looking for him. "I don't see him. Everyone here has a man, except you. What happened to that boy who put you out a few months back?"

"Oh, you mean when I called you and you were too busy to be bothered with me?" Dina said snidely. She'd had enough of her mother's antics. Why did she always have to make a spectacle of herself?

Courtney got up and sent the boys to Evan's room to play more games.

"I don't know what you're talking about. I just want the best for you. A family, nice house, you know," Mrs. Jacobs said.

"Sure. Right! Don't pretend you care. All you ever wanted was for me to be out of your way. You know what? I've just lost my appetite," Dina said and pushed her chair back to get up.

Mrs. Divine put her hand on Dina's and stopped her. She pleaded with her eyes. Dina wanted to say that Carl would be there but didn't want to be embarrassed if he didn't show.

Mrs. Jacobs' eyes stretched as wide as saucers. Then her face turned into an evil scowl. "You see, that's your problem. You're too damn needy."

"Enjoy your dinner, honey. You know how your mother gets," Mrs. Divine said softly to Dina.

Dina slowly pushed her chair back to the table, hoping her mother would stop there.

"All right, Judy, that's enough. We all came here to enjoy a nice dinner with friends and family. Let it go for now," Mrs. Divine said.

"I'm talking to my daughter. This has nothing to do with you. You've already got everything. What's the matter? You don't want anyone else to have the nice things you have? I want my daughter to find a nice man too," Mrs. Jacobs snapped.

"Judy, you have obviously had too much to drink, and I won't entertain your chatter tonight. Now this is my daughter's house, and if you can't respect it, then you can leave," Mrs. Divine retorted.

Mrs. Jacobs jumped to her feet. "Oh, now you gonna kick me out? Me, of all people? The only reason you and your daughter have half the nice stuff you got is because of what you get from men. So don't sit here and act like you're any better than us. I know you, woman!" Mrs. Jacobs was now spitting as she spoke. A few random drops landed on Dina's face.

Mrs. Alexander seemed to be enjoying the show. Courtney and Troy just sat with their heads down. Lacey stuffed her mouth as her eyes darted back and forth as if she was watching a tennis match. Kennedy's face twisted with anger. Angel and Patrick didn't know what to do with themselves.

"Ma! I can't believe you. You need to stop," Dina said firmly.

"Listen, I think you all need to calm down," Kennedy said.

"I'm not going to sit here and let her speak to me any kind of way. Look at you. They got you all wrapped up in their shit. What do you get, the leftovers?" Mrs. Jacobs turned her attention back to Kennedy and Mrs. Divine. "I guess if I handled men the way you do, my daughter and I would have these things too."

Both Kennedy and Mrs. Divine were now seething.

"Well, I'm glad someone else knows besides me," Mrs.

Alexander threw in.

Mrs. Divine transferred her look of fury to Mrs. Alexander.

"Now, I know you're not starting. Judy is drunk. She has an excuse for acting ill-bred," Mrs. Divine snapped.

Troy's arms flew in the air. Mrs. Jacobs scowled and drool dripped from her bottom lip. Her male friend just sat back and watched, sneaking glances at Mrs. Divine as he had since he'd arrived.

"Ill-bred?" Mrs. Jacobs yelled.

Mrs. Alexander placed both hands on the table and lifted her plump frame slowly. "You're calling *me*, ill-bred? I don't care how fancy you cook or dress. You don't fool me. I know your type," Mrs. Alexander added.

169

Mrs. Divine's chest heaved like she was gasping for air.

"How dare you ruin my daughter's gathering? OUT! All of you! Get out!

"That's fine with me. Come on, Courtney. Let's go, Troy," Mrs. Alexander said and began making her way out of the dining room.

"I'm not going anywhere. I'm staying right here with my wife," Troy asserted. Kennedy revealed a slight smile.

Mrs. Alexander shot him a smoldering glare. Judy Jacobs continued ranting and slinging insults. Her friend followed Mrs. Divine to the door. Mrs. Divine continued yelling as she marched through the living room to open the door for everyone to leave. When she opened the front door, Carl stepped in. Dina was elated to see him. She wanted to get away fast. In the midst of the pandemonium, Troy's cell phone rang loudly. He listened intently for a few minutes with the phone on one ear and his finger posted in the other. Then he snapped the phone closed.

"Daddy's dead," he said deadpan.

All movement ceased. The entire house fell silent.

Chapter 28

The funeral service for Mr. Alexander was nearing its end. Kennedy was happy that this sad occasion was almost over. The smell of the floral arrangements caused a slight wave of nausea. She'd have to tell Troy that she would meet him outside so that she could breathe more easily. If she took in the aroma any longer, she'd be sure to christen the parlor's carpet with her breakfast.

Troy had been immersed in paperwork and preparations for his father's burial since the day he received that dreaded call. Mrs. Alexander was civil during the entire ordeal but had taken the actual death much harder than Kennedy expected. Despite the years of separation, she truly loved her husband. Lela, his long-time mistress, appeared to be completely distraught but kept her distance during the services and slipped out before anyone could really notice.

Kennedy stood in the rear of the funeral parlor watching as family and friends viewed the body of Mr. Alexander and offered their condolences to Troy, his sister, and his mom. Angel and Dina stood by Kennedy's side. One particular man approached Troy and embraced him. There was something familiar about him, but Kennedy couldn't quite put her finger on what it was. His back was to her as he spoke with Troy and acknowledged the rest of the family. The gentleman turned slightly towards Mrs. Alexander, smiled, and nodded with understanding. Kennedy's eyes bulged and her jaw dropped. Dina had also recognized the man.

"Isn't that Andre? What the hell is he doing here? He knows Troy?"

Kennedy wanted to disappear. She hadn't seen Andre since spying on him a few months back. He'd called numerous times to apologize, ask Kennedy to reconsider or simply try and work his way back into the picture. All attempts failed.

Kennedy never expected to see him here. She had no idea that he and Troy were acquainted in any way.

"I don't know what he's doing here," she finally answered. "I didn't even know he knew Troy."

"I can not believe your luck, Kennedy," Dina probed.

"Not now," Angel interjected.

"What?" Dina asked innocently.

"Because he and Troy are on their way over here right now," Angel said. "Come on Kennedy, let's start walking. We can act like we didn't realize they were coming."

Kennedy exhaled. She didn't feel like dealing with Andre. Her body temperature was higher than normal, causing her to perspire profusely despite the cool, fall weather. Her stomach was threatening a protest to the aroma of the carnations floating in the air and her gorgeous sling backs were cutting into her swollen feet. She just wanted to go home, take a shower, and get in the bed with a nice, hot cup of chamomile tea. The girls started walking towards the exit. Kennedy became annoyed because Dina kept looking back to see where Troy and Andre were.

"Stop doing that. They are going to think something is up," Kennedy scolded through clenched teeth.

"Okay, but they are getting closer, and as crowded as this

place is, I don't think we are going to make it outside in time." Dina looked back one more time. "Oh damn Ken, they've sped up. Troy is calling out to you. Don't you hear him?"

The girls picked up their pace, trying to maneuver through the crowd. Kennedy tried to ignore Troy as he called her name several times.

"Kennedy!" Troy called out again much louder.

Each girl froze.

Kennedy stopped and exhaled once again, then turned slowly. Uncertainty spread across Angel's and Dina's faces. Dina began gnawing at her acrylic tips, and Angel shifted her weight from one leg to the other.

Troy trotted through the crowd with Andre in tow.

"Wait, baby. I want you to meet someone."

Angel's and Dina's eyes stretched simultaneously. Each friend stood on either side of Kennedy.

"Whew! You all right, babe. I almost had to run after you."

Kennedy looked passed Troy. Her eyes locked with Andre's.

"I just needed some air," she said

"Are you feeling okay?" Troy followed Kennedy's gaze. "Oh, this is why I called you. I wanted you to meet Andre. His father-in-law and my dad did a lot of business together. He's assisting us with the mortgage process with our house. Andre, this is my wife, Kennedy."

Andre raised a brow and his eyes traveled towards Kennedy's protruding belly. He extended his hand to Kennedy and frowned.

"Congratulations. How far are you?"

"I'm due in March. Thank you."

Kennedy spun quickly and marched out the chapel door into the lobby. Dina and Angel were right on her heels. Kennedy could feel the eyes of both Troy and Andre burning a hole in her back. Andre was sizing her up, and she knew it. His probing about the baby's due date meant one thing. He was trying to figure out if the baby could be his. Kennedy was pissed because she knew there was a chance that Andre could be the father of her child. She didn't want to deal with it and hoped to avoid the entire subject. Now it would be hard because Andre had seen her pregnant.

Kennedy wiped her forehead with the back of her hand and noticed sweat pool in the crevices between her knuckles.

"Kennedy, honey, are you all right? You're panting like a pig in heat. Let's get you out of here. You need air now!" Angel said.

"I can hardly believe what happened back there. Who would have ever thought you would run into Andre here?" Dina said. "Did you hear Troy say that he's working on your mortgage? I just can't believe this."

"All right already, Dina. We were all there," Kennedy snapped.

Dina frowned. "Sorry, it was just surprising. That's all."

Kennedy was about to retort when she saw Troy headed her way, Andre was not far behind talking to other guests. Why was Andre still around? she wondered. He should have disappeared a long time ago. Was he trying to torture her?

"Ken, babe. You all right?"

Kennedy turned her back to hide her angry expression from Troy.

"Yes, I just needed air. I was getting a little too stuffy in there, and the scent of the flowers was getting to me."

Troy moved around to face Kennedy. He studied her expression, lifted her chin with his forefinger, and kissed her lips gently. "You want to go home?"

"That's a great idea. I think I've had enough excitement for one day. You go back in with the rest of your family. I'll have Angel drive me home. See you later."

"Okay, I'll be there as soon as I get out of here. You sure you're gonna be all right?"

Kennedy forced a smile. "I'll be fine."

Troy kissed Kennedy once more then bent over and kissed her belly. Kennedy placed her hand over his head when he bent down. A habit that she's developed since her belly grew.

"I'll see you later, babe. I need to stop by my mom's after this, so just call if you need me, okay," Troy said with pleading eyes.

"Will do. See you later," Kennedy said before leaning forward to plant a quick kiss on Troy's full chocolate lips.

Kennedy watched Troy turn and re-enter the funeral home before she descended the steep concrete stairs with her girlfriends in tow.

"Come on, Ken. I've got you. Are you hungry? Maybe we can stop for a bite to eat and then I'll take you home," Angel offered.

"Well, I do have a taste for dim sum. Let's go to our spot on Union Turnpike for Chinese."

"Um, that sounds good. We haven't been there in such a long time. Count me in," Dina said.

As the girls were headed for Angel's car, Andre called out to Kennedy. Kennedy stopped, took a deep breath, and sighed before turning slowly.

Angel and Dina looked at each other.

"I'll go get the car. You stay here with Ken to make sure she's okay. But stay out of her business, Miss Busybody."

"What?" Dina inquired innocently.

Angel shot her a knowing look that made Kennedy chuckle. Everyone knew how Dina lived for other people's business. Within minutes, Andre was standing face to face with Kennedy.

"So you married him and now you are going to have his baby!"

"You're questioning me? What do you want, Andre?"

"How are you, Ken? I didn't know you were pregnant. When did this happen?"

"I already told you I'm due in March. What do you want from me?"

"Is there a chance that the baby is mine?"

Kennedy grunted loudly and stepped in closer to Andre to speak. The last thing she wanted was for Dina to get wind of what they were discussing.

"You know what? This is not the time, nor the place."

"Just answer my question. Please!"

"My baby belongs to my husband, just like yours belongs to your wife. By the way, how is Indira?" Kennedy asked, dripping with sarcasm. "Oh, yeah! Your father-in-law must be sad to lose such a longtime friend."

Andre's eyes narrowed, and Kennedy reveled in the fact that she was getting to him.

"No wonder it took so much effort for you to get my money together. I guess you needed to consult with your partner. Or should I say, your father-in-law. All the more reason to keep the wife around, huh, Andre?"

Andre looked around before leaning closer to Kennedy.

"It's not like that Kennedy."

"I'm sure, Andre."

"I can find out if the baby is mine."

"Oh yeah. I'd like to see you try. What makes you think it could be yours." Kennedy enjoyed taunting him.

"Because we…"

"Because we what? Had sex? No, from what I remember, you raped me." Kennedy moved in even closer and clenched her lips as she spoke. "Call it what it was. If you interfere with this, I'll make sure your wife, your father-in-law and the police find out. Now leave me and my family alone," Kennedy asserted, now visibly shaken.

Andre lowered his head and gnawed at his bottom lip. Kennedy could tell she hit several soft spots, the rape, the threat of an arrest, and his wife finding out.

"Now if you'll excuse me, I have a life to live that has nothing to do with you."

With that Kennedy stormed off and walked right passed Dina, who was waiting a few feet away. She hoped Dina didn't hear the exchange. Whatever appetite she had was now gone. Instead of dim sum with the girls, Kennedy just wanted to be alone. Even if this baby did belong to Andre, she'd never tell. It would be one secret that she would take to her grave.

Chapter 29

Kennedy called out to Troy just as she and her interior designer, Rachel, completed the finishing touches in the newly decorated living room. She had finally moved into their new home with Troy, but only after she had nearly the entire home remodeled to her liking. The décor was an eclectic mix of African and Asian-inspired style. The amber-colored walls glowed and provided the perfect backdrop for the beautifully stark black, crimson, and ivory furniture and accents. The completion of the living room marked the end of the extreme makeover.

Kennedy's favorite room was, by far, the new master bedroom suite. The sleeping area was painted a deep chocolate brown with ultra-white trim and crown molding. A white, upholstered California king-sized bed and white carpet added an impressive finishing touch to the space. The sitting area boasted a white, oversized chaise lounge large enough for both Kennedy and Troy to fit, a mahogany accent table, and a wood-burning fireplace surrounded by beautiful multicolored travertine tile. The new marble master bath consisted of his and her sinks, a private commode, a whirlpool tub, and a frosted glass shower that was large enough for three people. The walk-in closet was accessible by both the master bath and the bedroom. It was larger than the bedroom Kennedy grew up in.

"Rachel, this is beautiful. I love it. I just love it," Kennedy said as she admired Rachel's handy work.

Truthfully, Kennedy was a handful to work with, and she

knew it. She wanted only the best of everything and shunned anything that looked like it was manufactured in bulk. She treasured rare and custom-made items that were sure to serve as interesting conversation starters, like the original artwork she had commissioned a local artist to create. The abstract piece in the living room was stunning and included all of the tones in her color scheme. She also had him make a sensual piece of artwork using images of her and Troy. She hung it above their massive bed.

"I'm glad you like it, Kennedy. This wasn't easy; but I must say, with your input, this has to be my best work yet."

"I'd say so. Let me get Troy so he can see it."

Kennedy ran and opened the basement door then called out Troy's name. She wondered if he could hear her over the loud music he was playing. The basement was their recreation area. Troy endearingly called it the playhouse. It was a fully operational media room complete with large projection TV, comfortable over-sized seating, a very intense sound system, a bar, and an adult play area, which included air hockey and pool tables. It was the only area in the house for which Troy had been given an opportunity to provide input. On weekends it was hard to get him out of the room.

"TROY!" Kennedy tried to yell over the deafening music. "Sorry, Rachel, sometimes I think he loves this room more than me. He's like a kid in a candy store when he's in there. I'll have to go down and get him. Just give me a sec."

"No problem. I understand. I have one of those at home."

"What? A boom-boom room?"

"No. A husband." The women shared a knowing laugh.

Kennedy disappeared down the steps and returned seconds later with Troy on her heels.

"Look at it, Troy. Isn't it beautiful?"

Troy's eyes stretched as he agreed. It was obvious that he was impressed. "This is hot. You ladies outdid yourselves. This looks like it belongs in one of those home decorating magazines you're always looking at. Maybe you should take some pictures and send them in."

"You know, that's not a bad idea, Kennedy," Rachel said.

"Maybe I will. Maybe we should, Troy."

"Whatever you want, babe! I'm going back downstairs." Troy trotted off to his preferred domain.

"If this room shows up in one of those magazines, I'll have a client list a mile long."

"You already have a client list a mile long. Look how long it took you to fit me in," Kennedy joked and they both laughed.

"Well, I have to get going. Enjoy your new space. I'm so happy you're pleased."

"After all of this work, would you at least like a cup of tea in the new room before you go?" Kennedy asked.

"You wouldn't happen to have cranberry apple?" Rachel asked.

"I have everything. I only do gourmet teas. Have a seat, I'll be right…" The ringing telephone stole their attention. "Excuse me, Rachel." Kennedy ran into the spacious kitchen to retrieve the telephone. "Hello."

Just as she finished her greeting, Troy entered the kitchen and pulled the refrigerator door open. The caller spoke and Kennedy's eyes traced Troy's every move as he leaned in the fridge searching for a snack.

"Kennedy, I know you know who this is," the caller insisted.

Kennedy kept quiet. She needed time to think of how to respond with her husband standing no more than three feet away from her. She tried to stay calm.

"Hello? Who would you like to speak to?" Kennedy feigned confusion.

"Stop playing games with me, Ken. Is the baby mine?"

She wondered how he got her home number and why he thought it was okay to call her on it. The nerve of this man! Now she was seething but had to control her anger in front of Troy.

"Oh, girl, I can hardly hear you. I was just about to hang up the phone."

Troy emerged from the fridge with a Granny Smith apple and leaned on the granite topped peninsula making seductive gestures at Kennedy with his tongue. Kennedy tried to ignore Troy. Andre was on the other end of the phone asking the same question over and over again, and her husband was in her face making suggestive movements with his tongue.

"Kennedy, is it mines? Just tell me, is it mines?" She listened to Andre's urgent questioning. *What an idiot*, she thought. He should have known better than to put an s on the end of mine.

Now! Right now! Ah man, Dina. This really isn't a good time…Okay, don't worry, I'm on my way. I'll call you back in the car."

Troy creased his forehead and held his hand up, gesturing his question about what was going on with Dina. Kennedy shrugged her shoulders as if she wasn't quite sure.

"Okay, okay. I'll be right there." With that she ended her charade and hung up the phone just as Andre warned her not to hang up on him.

"Troy, sweetie, I have to run over to the condo. Dina is having some kind of issue. You know how she gets. It shouldn't take long. I'll be right back."

Kennedy ran off before giving Troy an opportunity to ask any questions that she wasn't prepared to answer. She rattled off an apology and a few excuses to Rachel, explaining that she had an emergency to tend to and she would call her soon. Kennedy ran upstairs to her bedroom to retrieve her Gucci bag and cell phone and was out of the door in a breeze. Moment's later she was inside of her brand new Cadillac Escalade driving in the direction of her townhouse, while dialing Andre on his cell phone. He picked up on the first ring.

"How dare you call my house? What the hell is wrong with you? And how the hell did you get my number? You're obviously having a hard time understanding how serious I am about reporting you to the authorities if you don't leave me alone."

"Kennedy, tell me there's no way the baby is mine and I'll leave you alone."

"Fuck you, Andre!"

Kennedy hung up the phone. She had to pull the car over now because her anger had her swearing and trembling. She needed to calm herself before she put herself and the baby in danger. Why couldn't he just leave her alone? And how the hell did she get their home number. She had requested an unlisted number just to keep people like him from getting it. What if Troy had answered the phone? The baby kicked, and Kennedy placed her hand on the spot where the baby was. She wanted to know who the father was also. She was guilty of a lot of things, but deceiving her baby for a lifetime was not something she looked forward to. But how would she find out without alarming Troy. She couldn't let him know there was a possibility that the baby wasn't his. That would only succeed in opening up a can of worms and ruining her plans of getting Troy to serve as her lifetime sponsor. First and foremost, she didn't want to have to reveal any of the details about the rape or the money she gained as a result of it to anyone. The only people that knew anything about it were, Andre, and her mother and she had every intention of keeping it that way. There was too much at stake. Yet even she felt the need to know the truth, even if she planned on keeping it to herself.

Kennedy thoughts kept going back to the fact that Andre had called her on her home number. She had managed to avoid him for months, ignoring all of his calls to her cell phone and deleting his messages without ever listening to them. It was getting close to her delivery date; and the closer she got the more Andre harassed her. But calling her house was the last draw. She needed to do something about him soon.

The cell phone danced across the passenger seat as it rang for the umpteenth time. Kennedy picked it up to check the display. Andre's number appeared across the screen. Kennedy threw the phone into the backseat and rested her head on the headrest. She needed to think. Seconds later, the mechanical voice emanated from the phone advising her that she had a message, again. Kennedy screamed to release some of her frustrations. A passerby leaned over and gave her a questionable look as if to ask if everything was okay. Kennedy snarled and rolled her eyes at the concerned stranger. The person waved his hand to dismiss her rudeness and kept walking.

Kennedy turned on the radio hoping music would help her get herself together. She was tired after working with her interior designer all day and just wanted to go home and rest. Andre was making that impossible. She would have to figure out something to tell him, or he'd continue to harass her. Kennedy flipped past a few stations trying to find something light to ease her mind but stopped when she heard an advertisement from some company that offered confidential mail-in DNA testing. She quickly turned up the radio to catch what the announcer was saying, but it was too late. She did, however, catch the number.

Kennedy looked around the car for her cell phone and remembered that she had tossed it in the back. She leaned over the seat but didn't see it. Repeating the number in her head over and over again in an attempt to instill it in her memory, she searched frantically for her phone. Her large belly prevented her from feeling the floor in the backseat, so she had to get out and look for her phone from the back. All the while she continued reciting the number aloud until she was able to retrieve the phone from way under the passenger's front seat. Kennedy punched in the digits and saved the number. First thing Monday morning she would find out more about this confidential mail-in DNA testing.

The phone rang again. Andre's number appeared on the display. Kennedy pressed the button on the side of the phone to silence the ringing and cease the vibration. Then she went into her voicemail, deleted the messages Andre had left, and drove home.

Chapter 30

"Dina! Dina! Can you hear me now?"

Dina chuckled and answered Angel's frenetic yells. "Yes already. I hear you. What's up? Is everything okay?"

"It's Kennedy. She's in labor."

Dina frowned. "She called you?" Dina was peeved by the fact that Angel knew before she did.

"No. I called her cell phone and Troy picked up, and said he was taking her to Mercy Hospital. I'll swing by and pick you up and we can meet them there."

Dina paused. "Okay, come get me. Let me get off of this phone because I'm sure she's probably going to call me soon. I'll be ready." Dina wondered why Kennedy hadn't called her. She had just pulled up to Carl's house to spend the evening with him, but hadn't mentioned that to her friend. "Angel! Angel! Wait!"

"What is it?"

"I'm not home. I'll meet you there in about a half hour."

"Okay, sweetie. See you soon."

Dina hurried out of the car to let Carl know that she would be leaving for the hospital. She wanted to get there before Angel or anyone else for that matter. Kennedy was her friend first. How would it look if everyone showed up at the hospital before her?

Dina's stick-thin heels clacked against the concrete as she raced towards Carl's door. Carl opened the door just as she hit the top step, panting like a dog in need of water. White smoke-like curls escaped her mouth with every breath due to the frosty air.

"Hurry up. It's cold out there," Carl said and ushered her in. "What took you so long to get out of the car?"

Dina rubbed her hands back and forth to ward off the cold. She had taken her gloves off in the car when she answered Angel's frantic call. Carl closed the door and turned to walk back into the living room.

"Wait, babe," Dina said.

"What?"

"I've got to go," Dina said, hoping Carl didn't get upset.

"Where? What about our plans?"

It was Valentine's Day, and Dina and Carl had planned to spend a quiet evening at Carl's place away from the bustle of the many overcrowded restaurants. She told him about the call and having to meet Angel at the hospital.

"I promise, I'll be quick, babe. I have to go. She's my best friend."

"I guess it's a good thing I didn't make reservations anywhere. Call me when you get there. I'm not going to sit here and wait all night."

Dina raced to the hospital to find Angel in the waiting area. She frowned, upset that Angel had gotten there before her. She had wanted to be able to say that she was the first one at the hospital. Angel came running up to greet her, hardly able to contain her excitement.

"Did she have the baby yet?" Dina asked.

"No. She's in delivery now. They were already inside by the time I got here. Troy came out once and told me she was doing fine. Her water had broken, and she didn't even know it.

Guess how her water broke?"

"How?" Dina asked.

"Well from what Troy said, they were getting into it—if you know what I mean—and water just started gushing from between her legs. Then the pains started."

"You mean to tell me her water broke while they were screwing?"

Angel chuckled like a young, embarrassed girl.

"Wow!" Dina said.

Just then Troy reentered the waiting area wearing a huge smile. The girls ran up to meet him.

"It's a girl, ladies!"

Dina and Angel screamed.

"A little princess! And on Valentine's Day. Can we see her?"

"You mean a little diva. This is Kennedy's baby we're talking about. Wait a minute Troy, I just thought about this. Isn't she a little early?" Dina asked.

"Yes. About three weeks. But the baby's fine."

"Can we see her?" Angel asked again.

"Just as soon as they clean her up, I'll come out and get you so you can come in."

Troy disappeared beyond the sterile, white double doors. The girls talked about how they were going to spoil their little niece. Shortly after Troy came back to tell them they could come in to see Kennedy, but the baby had been taken to the nursery. After they visited with Kennedy, he would take them down to see the baby.

Dina stepped up to enter the room before Angel. Kennedy

looked completely spent with wild hair and dark eyes.

"Whoa, look at you. You sure are a sight for sore eyes," Dina said sarcastically.

"I just had a baby, fool. What did you expect?"

"Dina! We can always count on you to say something crazy. Kennedy, sweetie, how are you feeling?" Angel asked.

"If you feel anywhere near how you look, then I feel for you myself, girl," Dina said and chuckled.

Kennedy threw her pillow at Dina, and they all laughed.

"You know I love you, girl. How was it?" Dina asked.

"Not too bad. I can't complain. She came out on the third push. It went so fast. Giving birth to Evan was nothing like this. I was in labor for hours with him. It took forever for him to come out," Kennedy said.

"I can't believe that. I hope it's that easy for me when I have mine," Dina said.

"Oh my God, Kennedy! This is so exciting. What's her name?" Angel asked

"Zola Christine."

"That's beautiful," Angel said.

Dina fantasized about how things would be when she finally became pregnant by Carl. She would finally have a family and be happy. Maybe Carl would even marry her once he found out she was carrying his child. She decided it was time to get back to her man.

"Perfect name, Ken. My little niece is going to be a true diva. I need to go shopping for her tomorrow. She told me she wanted those new boots by Michael..."

"Who told you what?" Kennedy asked.

"That nut is talking about the baby, girl," Angel said.

"That's right, we communicate. She's a shop-a-holic already," Dina joked.

"You are a mess," Angel said.

"I need to go take a peek at my little girl before I run back home. Carl's waiting for me. We have some celebrating to do for Valentine's Day and now the arrival of baby girl Zola. Maybe I'll make a baby myself tonight."

Kennedy and Angel looked at each other and then at Dina, who simply waved their questionable stares away. The girls kissed Kennedy goodnight and went off to check out the baby in the nursery.

"She's beautiful," Angel said as she peered through the glass separating the spectators from the infants.

"She sure is. She doesn't look like a wet bird like most babies do when they are first born. She's going to be a force to be reckoned with, just like her mama," Dina said and laughed. She was genuinely happy and excited to see Zola. "Well, I need to run. My man is waiting for me." She gave Angel the usual air kiss and click-clacked down the corridor to the exit.

As Dina drove, she pictured her family setting, complete with herself, Carl, a young son, and a baby girl. She wanted that baby more than ever now. When she got back to Carl's house, she was giddy. They shared a nice dinner that he ordered along with a bottle of Chardonnay. Dina encouraged Carl to continue drinking along with her to spice up the mood. She selected Maxwell's debut CD, popped it into the player, then commenced to perform a little strip tease for him. Slowly Dina peeled off piece by piece of her clothing until she was down to a red lace demi-cut bra, matching thongs, and stiletto boots. Her smooth caramel legs were well toned for someone who didn't exercise regularly. Dina seductively slid to her knees and crawled towards Carl like a fox charming its prey. She toyed with his chin using the tip of her tongue before turning and giving Carl a slow and sensual lap dance.

Carl's head rolled back as he released a satisfied sigh. Dina faced him and pulled his mouth to her center. Carl took in the sweet scent of her mango body oil and nuzzled his face between her legs, smelling the sugary oil that Dina always rubbed into her neatly trimmed pubic hairs. Dina climbed onto Carl's lap facing him and gracefully stroked Carl's erectness with her kitten. When Carl neared his breaking point, he slid Dina's lace panty aside and inserted his finger into her moist and warm passageway. She muttered incoherently. Carl penetrated her and Dina closed the walls of her canal snugly around his thick manhood, riding him until he exploded and filled her inner walls with his juices.

Dina leaned back to allow the juices to flow deeper into her, hoping that this time would prove to be a success.

Chapter 31

Troy dropped Evan off to school and stopped to pick up several bouquets of pink and yellow roses to help welcome two of the most important women in his life. Evan tried everything he could think of to get out of going to school so that he could accompany Troy to the hospital to pick up his baby sister, but Troy figured Kennedy could use a few hours of rest before Evan came barreling through the house to be with her and the baby. Troy thought about picking up a bottle of champagne but remembered that Kennedy wouldn't be able to indulge since she was nursing. He set the flowers around the bedroom and their sweet aroma wafted through the air lightly scenting the entire space. His special gift to Kennedy as a thank you for giving him two beautiful children, was sprawled across their white chaise. The lavish, full-length white mink covered the entire chair, and gracefully swept the floor. A single, deep-red rose was settled in the soft folds of the fur. Troy placed another red rose inside the white, lacy bassinet next to their bed. Although Kennedy had meticulously designed a nursery fit for a real princess, Zola would remain in the bedroom with them for her first few months. Troy took a final look around the spacious master suite to ensure that it was perfect, and it was. Then he set off to the hospital to bring his family home.

Troy carried one bouquet of roses to the hospital with him to present to his lovely wife. When he stepped off the elevator it seemed as though he never left. He'd only been away from her a few hours, leaving in the middle of the night to get some rest in his own bed. Smiling all the way, Troy practically galloped to Kennedy's room. He stopped a time or two to thank a few of the nurses for being so accommodating. He really appreciated their kindness. After spending so much time at the hospital with his father, he knew that being polite went a long way. The staff was very fond of Troy, but Kennedy was a different story. The nurses only kept their cool because of him.

Troy slowed down as he approached the room. He wanted to surprise Kennedy with the bouquet, so he tipped in. He could hear Kennedy on the telephone. At first he couldn't make out what she was saying though it sounded as though she said something about DNA. Then he heard her question how long it would take to get results. This piqued his curiosity, and he made his presence known, startling Kennedy. She stammered quickly, thanked the person on the other end and abruptly hung up.

"Hey! I didn't realize you were here already. You're early. The baby is still with the pediatrician," Kennedy said. She got up and began fumbling with her overnight bag.

"I know. Who was that you were speaking to?"

"Oh, that was my doctor," Kennedy said without hesitating.

"You were talking about DNA?"

"She was just telling me about all of the different tests and things they perform on the newborns now, like HIV, DNA testing etc."

"I can understand HIV and all, but why would there be a DNA test?"

"Not sure, maybe it's something new. I remember getting a child safety kit from Evan's school, and it suggested that you provide some type of DNA sample, like a strand of hair, along with a picture of the child and other pertinent information in case the child is ever missing or abducted or something like that. I don't know, maybe it's some new law or something. Why are you asking me so many questions?"

"I'm sorry, baby. That just threw me off—unless you have something you want to tell me," Troy joked and raised his brows.

"That's not funny, Troy." Kennedy said and glared at him.

"I'm just kidding, babe." Troy threw his hands up in mock surrender and tried to loosen the tension the moment created. He didn't want to get Kennedy upset right then. He'd address his curiosity later. "These are for you." He handed her the roses.

Kennedy took the roses, closed her eyes, and buried her face in their freshness.

"They're beautiful, thanks."

Kennedy turned away from Troy to finish packing her bags. Even with her puffy stomach and not-so-perfect hairdo she was still a sight to behold. Troy walked up behind her and wrapped his arms around her waist from behind.

"No. Thank *you*. You gave me a handsome son and now a beautiful baby girl. I have a beautiful family, from my wife right down to my brand new baby. I hope she grows up to look just like you. I'm going to have to beat the boys off with a bat," Troy said, then snuggled and kissed Kennedy's neck.

"Troy! Stop! You know I'm ticklish on my neck." Kennedy smiled and pushed Troy off of her with her elbows. "Let me find out when Zola will be ready. Did you bring the car seat?"

"Ah damn! I forgot it. I'll run down and get it right now!

Try to be ready to go when I get back. I want to hurry up and get you two home!"

When Troy returned with the car seat, Kennedy and Zola were all ready to go. He couldn't wait to get them to the house and surprise Kennedy. He loved to see her smile and thought about one day bringing smiles to Zola's face.

When they reached home, Troy led Kennedy to their master suite to show her his surprise. Troy could tell that Kennedy loved the flowers and most of all her new fur coat. Though Kennedy was never one to ever show her excitement, Troy knew by the way she modeled her coat in their full-length mirror that she was in love.

"Oh thank you, Troy. It's beautiful," she said, still admiring herself in the mirror.

Kennedy let the coat hang open and began a sexy swagger in Troy's direction. Her wicked smile gave Troy and idea of how happy she was. Kennedy closed the space between her and Troy, wrapped her arms around him and seductively slid her tongue in his mouth. When they finally unlocked their passionate embrace Troy traced a line across Kennedy's bottom lip. Kennedy pulled back from him maintaining eye contact.

"There's more where that came from. I'd be happy to show you in about four to six weeks," Kennedy said and chuckled as Troy smiled and shook his head from side to side. "Oh, babe, I need for you to run to the store to pick up a few things, could you do that for me?"

The end of that sentence sounded like she was purring. That was one of her ways of getting what she wanted from Troy. He ate it up every single time. Troy smiled because he knew that no matter what the request, he was going to honor it.

"I need pads and plenty of water."

"Yuck, pads?" Troy scrunched up his nose. Kennedy looked at him, rolled her eyes, and laughed.

"Trust me, Troy. They are not going to think they're for you."

"I'm just kidding. It's not a problem. Is there anything we need for the baby while I'm out?"

"Not at all! After that huge shower my mother, Angel, and Dina threw for us, we won't need anything for this child for at least six months. Speaking of which, my Mom will probably stop by after work today."

"Okay, I'll be right back," Troy said.

Troy trotted down the steps at lightning speed and headed for the car. He looked back towards the large picture window to their bedroom and noticed Kennedy watching him from the inside. It almost looked as if she was waiting for him to leave. She just stood there until Troy waved good-bye to her. She waved back and left the window.

Chapter 32

The moment Troy pulled out of the driveway Kennedy pulled out her cell phone and called the DNA testing center back to get the rest of the details she needed. She needed someplace for the testing kit to be mailed, so she called the only person she could trust with this information, conveniently leaving out details about the rape and blackmail. Mrs. Divine didn't appear to be surprised and promised Kennedy that as soon as the package came, she would let her know.

"Does Andre know that there is a chance that Zola could be his?" Mrs. Divine asked.

"Yes. He's the main reason why I need to find out. He won't leave me alone. And I don't need for Troy to find out anything just yet. Plus, I don't want to live some soap opera lie for years. I'd have to try and hide this. I need to know for sure myself. My only problem is getting Troy to take the test."

"That's going to require some creative thought," Mrs. Divine retorted.

"Who are you telling?" Kennedy paused a moment. "Ma, you are the only person I could trust with this information. That's why I called you, so please…"

"Oh, Kennedy, please. Who do you think I'm going to tell? Troy or his fat-assed mama?"

"Ma!"

"Well she is fat," Mrs. Divine burst out laughing.

"Anyway. Just let me know when the package comes.

Between now and then I'll figure out a way to get him to take the test."

"Okay. Just be careful because Troy's no dummy."

"I know, Ma. Let me go before he comes back. Talk to you later."

"Okay pumpkin. I'll see you later. And remember we need to talk about planning your anniversary gala. You know I've already completed the guest list."

"What guest list? You don't know all of my friends."

"Girl, what friends? Dina and Angel? They're on the list."

"Very funny. I have other people I intend to invite. But right now I can't think about any of that. All I'm worried about is getting the information I need and taking care of this baby."

"You're right. Let me worry about the list. That's why I started it already. This list is chock full of the old, the elite and the wealthy. People your age aren't big spenders. They don't know any better. With the folks I'm inviting, you're liable to make a few thousand off of this engagement. Even the ones who can't make it will send you a little something. You can put that into your little secret account." Mrs. Divine must have amused herself because she roared with more laughter.

197

"Bye, Ma." Kennedy hung up.

A week later, Mrs. Divine called to let Kennedy know that the package had arrived. Kennedy had to tell her mother to hold on to it until further notice because Troy had yet to return to work. Kennedy hadn't realized that Troy had arranged to take a few weeks off of work to be with her and the baby. She actually appreciated the gesture but wished he would go to work so she could handle her business. She was still trying to figure out how to get him to take the test without letting on what the test was for.

The first day Troy went back to work, Mrs. Divine left work early to bring the kit to Kennedy's house. After examining the kit and reading every word of the enclosed material, Kennedy snapped her finger. She had a light bulb moment, and figured out how she could get Troy to take the test. She immediately put her plan in action.

The next weekend Kennedy invited a few friends over to see the baby, including Dina and Carl, Angel and Patrick and Troy's favorite cousins. Since Kennedy had little energy due to nursing and the baby's erratic sleeping pattern, Mrs. Divine agreed to keep Evan and the girls came over early that evening to help Kennedy prepare for her guests. Dina and Angel ended up handling everything while Kennedy nursed and napped before the guests arrived.

When the doorbell rang, Troy traipsed downstairs to greet his guests while Kennedy stayed in the room to finish getting dressed. When all was clear, Kennedy pulled the DNA kit from under the mattress on her side of the bed. She extracted something that looked like a large cotton swab in protective wrapping, and placed it in the pocket of her jeans. Then she went to join the get-together.

The night went well. The men eventually flocked down to the playhouse to listen to music, shoot pool and drink like fish while the girls stayed up in the large family room. After a while Kennedy checked on Zola upstairs then took the girls to the basement to ensure that the boys, especially Troy, were getting good and juiced up.

"Hey Barry. Look what I've got." Kennedy had to yell

in order to be heard over the music. She pulled out a bottle of Tequila which happened to be Barry's favorite drink.

Barry, one of Troy's cousins from Virginia, was in town for the weekend. A burly fun-loving guy with a pot-belly and a pleasant demeanor, his dark, beady eyes were now glazed over from the liquor he'd consumed since his arrival.

"That's what I'm taking about." Barry grabbed the bottle from Kennedy and turned towards Troy. "Come on now, cuz. You know you have to take a shot with me to celebrate."

"Man, you know I don't mess with that stuff. Give me some scotch or something, anything but tequila. Kennedy why did you even show that dude that stuff." Troy said.

Kennedy smiled innocently and sat on Troy's lap.

"Ah, come on, man, I know you are not going to punk out on me now. How often do we get to see each other these days? You got to have at least one shot with your boy. Come on, man."

"I've had enough as it is, B."

"Troy you know you are going to have to have at least one shot with Barry," Kennedy coaxed. "Don't over do it Barry, because you aren't sleeping here tonight," Kennedy said and everyone, including Barry shared a hearty laugh.

"I know you're not going to leave me hanging. It's a celebration, man. Celebration time, come on," Barry broke out into the chorus of the old-school song by Kool & The Gang.

"Okay. Okay. I'll only take a shot if you stop singing," Troy said and laughed. "But just one. I remember the last time I let you talk me into taking shots of tequila with you. I woke up on my mother's front lawn in the middle of the night next to a pool of vomit. When I woke up again, I was in my room wondering why I was burning up until I realized that I was wrapped up in my comforter with all of my clothes on, including my boots, coat, and hat." Laughter filled the playhouse.

"That's my man. Here you go." Barry swiftly walked around to the other end of the bar to retrieve a couple of shot glasses.

"Well I'll leave you gentlemen to your bottle. Don't get too wasted," Kennedy said and gathered with the rest of the women in a separate area of the playhouse.

The men began consuming the tequila, shot by shot. This was just what Kennedy needed to get her results from Troy without him knowing. By the time the last guest left the tequila bottle was empty, and Troy was sprawled across the mocha-colored micro suede sectional. Kennedy nudged Troy a few times in an attempt to wake him. Troy was out cold, sleeping with his mouth wide open as drool hung from the corner of his lips. Kennedy pulled out her testing equipment and carefully inserted the swab into Troy's mouth. Troy shut his mouth, moaned, and turned his face towards the back of the couch, clamping the swab between his teeth. Kennedy drew her finger back quickly to avoid getting bit.

She struggled to pry the tester from his grip without waking him. To her advantage, Troy repositioned himself and was once again facing her. She sat watching him, hoping that he would fall further into his stupor so that she could get it over with. Troy let out a loud snore, which caused Kennedy to jump. Now she knew he was in his deepest sleep. His mouth fell wide open as he continued to snore. For a moment, Kennedy thought he would choke on his own breath. She grabbed the tester, quickly rubbed it against his cheek several times, and pulled it out before he could shut his mouth again. She carefully placed it in its casing, sealed it, and ran up to her room to secure it in the package provided by the testing center. She checked on the baby once more before tipping back to the basement to place a cover over Troy. Her plan worked perfectly. Tomorrow she would have her mother pick up the package and send if off. Within a week she would know for sure which man really fathered her daughter.

Chapter 33

Carl and Dina had just settled on the couch in Kennedy's den to enjoy a movie after their scrumptious meal. Dina had prepared shrimp scampi over rice with sautéed green beans. Once again, she was setting the mood for a sensual evening of romance and hopefully baby making. She'd been trying to get pregnant for months and didn't quite understand why she'd been unsuccessful. The reproductive specialist assured her that she was indeed capable of reproducing but advised her that it could still take several months to conceive. The specialist also recommended that she advise Carl to go for testing to make sure he was capable of reproducing. Dina assumed that wasn't necessary since he already had a daughter. Plus, she wanted to surprise him with the pregnancy. Dina decided to increase their sexual activity during the time of the month when she was due to ovulate. Based on the body temperature chart the doctor gave her to use in determining this, she knew she was right at her most fertile time of the month.

After a few glasses of wine with dinner, Dina began to feel a little giddy. On several occasions she thought about bringing up the idea of having a baby with Carl but didn't because she thought the surprise would be fun. As far as she was concerned, if he didn't want children, he wouldn't have started to have unprotected sex with her—even though they'd been together off and on for about two years. In the beginning they both insisted on using condoms. Living together for a few months last year had changed all of that. Now that they were officially back together, Dina was determined to keep him around. She just knew that having his baby would most likely prompt him to marry her.

The relaxing influence of the wine began to take effect, and Dina was ready to get started on yet another night of passion. Carl had just pressed the play button on the DVD remote. Dina took the remote from him, pressed pause, and looked longingly into Carl's eyes. Her lips curled into a sultry smile, giving Carl an idea of what she was thinking. Carl smiled back and gently cupped Dina's full, pert breast in his hand. The heat of passion filled the atmosphere then quickly dissipated when strong hard knocks accompanied by the constant ringing of the doorbell imposed upon their foreplay.

"Who the hell could this be?" Dina yelled. "Just wait right here while I get rid of whoever it is." Dina kissed Carl full on his lips and pried herself from him. When she stood she gave him a quick flash of her ample breast and hard nipple while she backed out of the room. A wicked smile spread across Carl's face, and he began to disrobe. Dina shrieked and ran to the door.

"Hurry up," Carl prompted.

"You got it," Dina yelled back as she raced for the door.

The anxious guest continued with the urgent ringing and knocking. Dina yanked the door open, prepared to give the person on the other side a piece of her mind if it wasn't an emergency. When she saw who it was, her throat closed, preventing anything audible from coming out. Her eyes stretched and her mouth hung wide open.

Dionne smirked, obviously amused by Dina's reaction, then sauntered toward her younger sister and pushed Dina's mouth closed.

"Nice to see you too, sis. How long has it been—a year, two, maybe more," Dionne asked and laughed.

Dina didn't respond. In fact she wasn't sure what to say. It had been years since she had laid eyes on her sister.

Dionne released that chuckle Dina hated so much. The one that she held in her throat. Dina sighed and still held the door open. A part of her wanted Dionne to stay, yet her loins nudged her and made her wish Dionne would leave and drop in another time. She had business to take care of in the other room with Carl.

"Some greeting! I'm fine, baby sis, and how are *you?*" Dionne mocked as she slowly eyed the townhouse. "Nice place. I hear it's Kennedy's. Still living in her shadow huh?"

Dina took a deep breath as if to draw strength from the air. "Why are you here, and what do you want, *big sis,*" Dina returned the mocking gesture, accentuating the words big and sis.

Secretly Dina was happy to see Dionne but wondered what actually made her, of all people, stop by unannounced at this particular time.

"I think I'm going to take a look around," Dionne said placing her mink jacket and matching mink purse on the chaise lounge in the living room.

Dina cut her eyes and shook her head.

"This place is really nice. Almost looks better than mine. That bitch Kennedy always did have good taste. Honestly she could rival mine any day. Had we ever liked one another, we probably would have been a hell of a team as friends." Dionne walked off in the direction of the den.

Dina sighed, slammed the door to shut out the frigid air, and hastened her steps in Dionne's direction. Dionne and Kennedy never got along, probably because they were alike in a lot of ways.

Dionne waltzed into the den following the voices from the TV to find Carl laying across the comfortable looking couch completely naked, stroking his family jewels while anticipating Dina's return. Dionne entered the room and smiled. Dina was right on her heels. When Dina saw Carl's naked body she screamed.

"Carl! Oh my goodness!"

Dina's cry captured Carl's attention and he noticed they were not alone. He tried to cover his manhood with both his hands, but it was too late. Dionne had already begun walking toward him.

"You must be Carl. Nice to meet you. I'm Dionne, Dina's older sister." Dionne stood above Carl eyeing his nakedness with her hand stretched out to greet him.

Carl looked slightly embarrassed yet removed one hand to return Dionne's greeting, giving her a firm handshake. As if he was fully clothed, Dionne took a seat right next to Carl and patted the space beside her on the couch.

"Come sit, little sis. We need to talk." Then she turned toward Carl. "By the way, nice package! I can see why my sister likes you."

"Thanks," Carl said before getting up to gather his clothes. He dressed right in front of the sisters, picked up the TV remote, and settled across the nearby chaise.

No longer phased by Dionne's presence, Dina finally

found her voice. "So what brings you by, Didi?" She used her nickname from their childhood.

"I just wanted to see my baby sister, that's all. Will you believe that?"

"No!"

Dionne laughed loud. Dina stared at her, waiting for her to finish enjoying her own joke. Even though she longed for a relationship with her sister at times, she knew better than to think that Dionne simply missed her.

"Well," Dina said.

"Okay, here goes. For one, I'm moving back."

Dina reared her head back. "You're moving in with Ma?"

"Oh, hell no! I'm moving back to Queens. I couldn't wait to get out of that house. Why would I ever move back?" Dionne shook her head at Dina.

"To be honest, I didn't know you weren't in Queens."

Dionne chuckled again. "Has it been that long? Anyway, I've been in Brooklyn for the past few years. But now that I'm pregnant, I want my child to grow up with a backyard. So I found a house out in Laurelton for my baby's daddy to buy for me. We should close by the end of next month."

Dina's eyes bulged as she eyed Dionne's svelte frame, tight jeans, and fitted shirt. Then she looked down at her stiletto boots and back at Dionne's face.

Dionne appeared to have read her mind. "I just found out recently. I'm only three months. So you're going to be an auntie."

"I can deal with that," Dina said and sat back.

She was genuinely happy for her sister. Maybe this would

bring Dionne and her closer than they had been in years. As children they were allies. As teenagers their relationship became strained until Dionne finally decided she'd had enough of her family and went out on her own at the early age of seventeen. Since then they had only seen each other passing through their mother's house on occasion. Dionne didn't come around much. Dina kept up with Dionne's life through the bits and pieces of information their mother fed her occasionally. Since she and her mother didn't engage in productive conversations often, information about Dionne came sparingly.

"So listen, Dionne, does that mean you are going to be around more?" Dina sounded hopeful.

"Possibly. But I also came to tell you that mom is pregnant too."

Dina almost fell off the couch when she heard the news. She couldn't believe it. Their mother was a mere nineteen years older than her and only eighteen years older than her sister and was due to turn fifty this year. This was devastating to Dina on many levels. For one, she would have a sibling thirty years younger than her. Second, her new sibling would have a mother that would often be mistaken for it's grandmother. Her new niece or nephew would be the same age as their aunt or uncle. She wondered if her mother planned on keeping it but assumed she would since she'd told Dionne about it. Why hadn't she said anything to her?

Thoughts ran through Dina's mind like the horses running in the midst of a stampede. This was embarrassing. Furthermore, Dina was disturbed by the fact that once again everyone seemed to get the things they wanted, and yet again she was left out in the cold. First Kennedy, and now this. As much as she wanted a baby and as hard as she'd been trying, what was the problem? Her long-lost sister shows up at her door, looking like she'd just stepped off the pages of Black Vogue and announces that not only is she pregnant, but their old-assed mother was too. And who the hell was the father? That jerk Mrs. Jacobs brought to Thanksgiving dinner who couldn't take his eyes off Mrs. Divine the entire evening. Dina felt a headache coming on.

"Earth to Dina," she heard Dionne repeating over and over again. Each time it was said, the words rang through louder and clearer.

"I can't believe this. When did you find out?" Dina asked

She could see Carl pretending not to pay attention to their conversation.

"Well, believe it. It's true. And get over it," Dionne commanded.

Dionne still didn't answer Dina about when she found out. That question was burning Dina under the surface. Then she thought about what her sister had just said to her about getting over it.

"Get over it? What's that's supposed to mean?" Dina asked.

"I may not have been around for a while, but you're my sister, and I know you. Stop calculating everything that you think is wrong with this picture. We never had the perfect family environment before. Why should you expect anything different now? By this point in life, nothing should surprise you, especially when it comes to your mother. We are going to have a new brother or sister soon. Accept it."

"I hope she does a better job with this one than she did

with us," Dina said.

"That's not my problem. The baby will survive just like we did. She's probably having this baby for the same reason she had us. Anyway, it's time for me to get out of here. I've got things to do and people to see." Dionne rose from the couch and Dina caught her by the arm.

"What do you mean by that? What's the reason?"

"Dina, where the hell have you been? You know your mother will do anything to keep a man, including having a damn baby at the ripe old age of forty-nine."

"Are you telling me that Ma had us to hold on to Daddy?"

"Yep. I guess she figured that would be one way to keep him from his wife.

Dina's mouth hit the floor and her hands involuntarily massaged her temples. That headache was getting stronger by the minute. She wanted to cry but had to get the rest of the story while she was still coherent.

"They were never married?" the concept finally dawned on her.

"No!" Dionne stretched the word out and looked at Dina like she was crazy.

"But we all have the same last name. I remember when he lived with us before he left," Dina seemed to plead as if it could change the harsh reality of the situation. She wanted to scream.

Dionne looked at Dina and shook her head as if she felt sorry for her. Dina's expression seemed to cry out for clarity.

"I don't get it," Dina said and grabbed handfuls of hair in both hands.

"Ma gave him what his wife couldn't, so he stuck around. At least that's what Ma thought. I guess having me wasn't insurance enough that he would stick around, so she made sure that by the time she went back for her postnatal checkup she was pregnant again. It worked for a while, a few years in fact, until his once barren wife miraculously became pregnant. She made him move halfway across the country to keep him away from Ma and us, and the sorry bastard picked up and left us all behind. I guess the wife couldn't deal with the competition. As far as the last name goes, Ma didn't want to be embarrassed so she changed her last name legally to match ours. It goes to show that having a baby don't necessarily get you the man."

Dionne's last statement hit home for Dina. She glanced over at Carl to see if there was a response from him in any way. This was too much heavy information at one time. She decided to steer the conversation in another direction.

"Dionne, when did Ma tell you about her pregnancy?"

"Last week. Why?" Dionne made an expression indicating that she had now understood the question. "Oh, you're wondering why she told me and hadn't said anything to you yet. Well, believe it or not, she tells me a lot more than you would think. Somewhere along the line it's like we've switched roles. She's always calling to tell me her business or to ask advice about some new dude she's seeing. I give it to her straight. I think she likes that. Besides, you know she never had any friends anyway. She was always too trifling to keep anyone around for too long without getting into a fight." Dionne put her finger to her lip and thought for a moment before asking, "Now where did I put my coat and bag?"

"In the living room," Dina said and shook her head.

"Right." Dionne walked off in the direction of the living room. "Bye, Carl. Nice meeting you. Take good care of that package."

When the sisters reached the living room, Dionne retrieved her coat and bag and headed for the door. Just before she walked out, she turned to Dina for one last comment.

"Oh, did I tell you who the daddy is?" Dionne asked.

"No, but you told me he's buying you a house in Queens."

"Not my baby's daddy, Ma's."

"Oh. No, you didn't mention it."

"Remember Mr. and Mrs. Ellis across the street from Ma's house?"

Dina nodded and said, "Yeah, Mike and Tasha's parents."

"Yeah, well, Mr. Ellis is the daddy. So chances are Ma may need a place to stay and I'll tell you right now, it won't be with me! See you later." Dionne started out of the door then turned back once more and said, "Maybe you can throw us a baby shower at the same time," then fell into a fit of laughter.

Dina shut the door right in her face, cutting off her laugh. She needed to speak to that unbelievable woman she called a mother right away. Dina ran to the den where Carl was still watching TV.

"Carl, baby, I'm sorry, but I've really got to go!"

She spun around, grabbed her hot pink ski jacket, matching Coach boots, then snatched her keys from the small table in the entry, and headed for her mother's house.

Chapter 34

Kennedy had just finished her conversation with her former boss. Only the boss didn't know he would not see her at their place of work ever again. Although she hadn't announced it to anyone, she had no intentions of returning. As Troy's wife and mother to his two children, she looked forward to being a stay-at-home-diva forever.

The baby was asleep and Kennedy wondered what she would do until it was time to pick up Evan from the after-school program. She decided she would go browse around the stores in Americana Mall in Manhasset, which was located on the north shore of Long Island. Kennedy packed up the baby's belongings and headed out to peruse the upscale shops. She pulled into a parking spot alongside a brand new Hummer H2. Impressed with the outside, Kennedy admired the interior through the passenger-side window and decided right then and there to tell Troy that she wanted one for herself and the kids. The rugged look of the vehicle appealed to her the most. People didn't usually expect a beautiful and very feminine woman to step out of that type of vehicle and Kennedy always enjoyed being one to shatter expectations.

Just as she rounded the car to take the baby out, her cell phone rang. Mrs. Divine's home number appeared across the screen. At first Kennedy hesitated then decided to take the call. Kennedy flipped the phone open.

"What's up, Ma?" she asked quickly as she continued to

release the straps holding Zola down.

"It's here. Can I open it?" Mrs. Divine asked. Kennedy could tell by her voice exactly how anxious her mother was.

"Of course not! I'm on my way right now," Kennedy said and replaced the straps around Zola, securing her in the infant car seat once again. "I guess that new Gucci baby bag will have to wait." Kennedy flipped her phone closed.

The drive to Kennedy's mother's house seemed like a blur. The day had come for Kennedy to find out for sure who Zola's real father was. The fact that she was only minutes away from finding out kept her mind occupied for the entire ride. Kennedy pulled halfway into her mother's driveway, threw her Cadillac into park, jumped out and grabbed the entire car seat out of the back. Mrs. Divine anxiously waited with the front door open, holding the envelope in her hands. She pushed the door open wider for Kennedy to get in with the baby.

Kennedy carefully placed the sleeping baby in the center of the kitchen table and returned to the living room with her mother. For several minutes the two women watched the envelope as if it would open itself until Kennedy finally snatched it from her mother's hands and ripped it open. The top page held the information she was looking for. Both held their breath while reading the contents of the letter. Kennedy finally broke the silence when she yelled, "Yes!" she held her heart to steady her breathing.

"I am so glad that baby belongs to Troy. This just saved you a world of trouble, Ken. Don't get yourself into another situation like this again. You almost gave me a heart attack," Mrs. Divine dramatically held her heart.

"Well how do you think I felt?" Kennedy asked. Then she

had an epiphany. "Ma, I need you to watch the baby for a little while. I'll be right back."

Kennedy ran through the front door before her mother could ask where she was going. Kennedy knew that calling Andre wouldn't suffice, she needed to deliver the DNA test results to him in person to bring closure to the situation. She drove fast enough to break several traffic laws along the way.

When Kennedy arrived at Andre's office she noticed the name on the awning had been changed to Lewis & Co Brokerage. When she walked in she noticed a few more changes. The receptionist was out, but a mug half-filled with coffee and a pack of mints left in her place indicated that she would probably return soon. Boxes of letterhead, envelopes, and business cards sat on the receptionist's desk. Kennedy looked around and saw that the office was in a bit of disarray as a result of an apparent remodeling project. The office was being transformed into a sophisticated navy and gray color scheme, Andre's favorite colors. No other brokers were present. She spotted Andre talking on the phone through the glass window on the wall that separated his private office from the rest of the cubicles. Andre hadn't noticed her, so she took it upon herself to inspect the boxes on the desk. Everything had been changed to reflect the new name of the business. Andre must have bought his partner out.

Kennedy strolled towards the office with a smirk on her face and her full length mink, courtesy of Troy, sweeping the newly carpeted floor. She walked slowly to ensure that Andre noticed her before she actually reached his office. When he looked up and saw her, he quickly completed his conversation, hung up the phone, and met her at the door to his office.

Kennedy stopped and posed right in the doorway. For a moment, Andre didn't speak as he stood studying Kennedy. Subconsciously she pulled in her slightly pouted stomach and straightened her posture. Even after giving birth a few short weeks ago, she knew she looked good in her red, fitted, cashmere sweater, expensive, close-fitting jeans, and stiletto boots. Andre finally diverted his attention with a gesture towards one of the chairs in front of his desk.

"Would you like to sit?" he politely asked.

"No, thank you. I won't be long."

"What brings you by?"

"These," Kennedy said and tossed the papers on his large, mahogany desk. The baby's not yours. See for yourself. As I told you before, the baby belongs to my husband. Now you can leave me alone."

Andre crunched his brows and retrieved the papers from the desk. He reviewed them carefully while Kennedy secretly admired his handsome build. This was apparently not a typical work day for Andre since he was dressed more like a contractor than a mortgage broker. But something about his jeans, work boots, and t-shirt seemed to stir old feelings inside of Kennedy. Although she loved for her men to possess a strong sense of style, there was something undeniable about the rugged look that Andre sported. Kennedy tried to shift her focus by looking around his office. Her eyes settled on a large framed photo of a cute, little baby. It had to be his child. She noticed there were no pictures of his wife, Indira, and remembered that there had never been any in his office.

Andre finally looked up from the papers and sighed.

Kennedy walked over to the credenza and picked up the baby picture.

"Cute kid."

Andre didn't respond, so she looked his way and caught him staring at the floor. She rolled her eyes, wondering what his problem was.

"Well, that's all I came for," Kennedy said and reached for the papers.

Andre slowly put the papers back in Kennedy's outstretched hand, but before she could pull back, he grasped her forearm gently. A spark seemed to have ignited in the space between them, and a moment passed before Kennedy pulled away from him.

"I wanted the baby to be mine," Andre nearly whispered.

"You can't be serious, Andre. You raped me, remember? Must I remind you?" Kennedy couldn't believe her ears.

Andre didn't respond. Instead he moved toward her, closing her in between his body and the mahogany credenza. Kennedy backed up until she felt herself pinned against the piece of furniture.

"I'm sorry for that." Andre's apology was calm.

"Sorry!" Kennedy shouted.

Andre didn't move. In fact he came so close to her that she could feel his breath on her face. Initially Kennedy felt uncomfortable, but she shook that feeling of uncertainty. She knew Andre wouldn't hurt her again, especially since he knew what she was capable of. Still, she was surprised by his admission and desire for the baby to be his.

Andre stared into her eyes. "Tell me you feel nothing at all for me, and I'll leave you alone for good."

Kennedy sucked her teeth and tried to push passed him. Andre didn't budge.

"Please just tell me that."

Kennedy shook her head but didn't respond.

"You have the information you were looking for. Now I have to..."

Andre pressed his full lips against hers. Kennedy leaned back, but Andre moved with her, never separating his lips from hers. He pulled away and looked into Kennedy's eyes. She attempted to speak, and he pressed his lips against hers once more. This time his tongue teased her lips, coaxing her to let him in. Kennedy's lips parted slightly. Andre held her by the sides of her face and pulled her to him, then kissed her with more passion. Kennedy could feel her resolve melt away as she began to give in. She remembered how much of a sensual lover he was but considered the kiss one for the road. After all, she didn't anticipate having to be bothered with him anymore unless she wanted to.

217

Still holding Kennedy's face tenderly in his hands, Andre said, "It's still there, I can feel it."

Again Kennedy didn't respond. She wasn't quite sure what she wanted to say. What she did know was that her nipples had begun to tighten and her vagina had become moist. A longing from somewhere deep inside had found its way to the surface. Andre had always been one of her best lovers. He gave her more satisfaction in bed than her conservative husband, and he knew her body well.

Andre closed in on her once again and kissed her with more intensity than he had before. She met his intensity, and his hands moved from her face to her ample breasts. Andre's hands moved about Kennedy's body as if he was looking for something she had hidden in her clothing. He lifted Kennedy's sweater and released her engorged breasts from the bra. Andre rolled her pert nipples between his fingers, using his thumb to massage the oozing milk into her soft skin. Kennedy's eyes closed, and her head fell back. Andre gently sucked each breast, tasting the natural, subtle taste of her milk. Kennedy felt fire and moisture settle in her center. Andre's erect groin rubbed against her wetness through their clothes, igniting even more heat between them.

Kennedy would allow him to tease himself but hadn't decided if she was willing to go any further, despite her body's obvious desire. Andre sucked on her breast once again. Before Kennedy realized it, Andre's hands had moved to her center, caressing her through her jeans. Moisture evaded her protests as it began to darken her pants between her legs. Kennedy's pants had been unbuckled. Andre lifted her and sat her on top of the credenza, positioning himself between her smoldering legs, he pulled her to him so their loins could connect. Kennedy found herself grinding back against him while pulling at his t-shirt. Andre took the hint and removed the shirt, exposing his strong, hairless chest and tight abs. The feel of Andre's chest enticed Kennedy to taste him, and she took his nipples into her mouth. Her vaginal muscles tightened around Andre's fingers, causing her to nibble harder on his chest. The walls of her womanhood began to pulsate, inviting her to shed her jeans. As if on cue, Andre tugged at the band of her jeans, prompting her to lift her bottom as he peeled the pants and her sexy, thong underwear off of her. Andre then removed his own pants and teased her clit with the tip of his penis before inserting the head in her opening. Together they positioned themselves for a perfect fit. Andre rubbed her clit and vulva with his manhood once more before lowering his lips to taste her. Kennedy released a muffled groan followed by a series of petite breaths. He gently coaxed her backwards to gain access to her waiting womanhood. Andre lowered himself and took her full center into his mouth, then began a titillating, suckling motion. He pressed the flat of his tongue against her vagina and licked from top to bottom. Andre held Kennedy's legs open wide as he clenched her swollen clit between his soft, full lips. His motions created a sensual friction, bringing Kennedy to a forceful climax that sent erotic shock waves through her entire body. Without affording her a chance to recover, Andre entered her and commenced to grind deep inside her cushioned walls. Kennedy's release covered Andre, and she could feel her passion walls closing in around him. Together they created a perfect rhythm, keeping the flow steady until Kennedy felt herself reaching her sexual heights again. She tightened her muscles around Andre's penis as she met his every thrust until she could feel him pulsate inside of her. She looked into Andre's face and saw the onslaught of his release. Andre's eyes closed tightly, and his head reared back when he reached his point of pleasure.

Momentarily, Kennedy snapped out of her state of bliss to remind Andre to pull out. She returned to her place of pleasure, and they reached their peaks together, bucking wildly as their orgasms took control of their bodies. Andre's fluids exploded from his body, landing over Kennedy's lower body and staining

219

the lining of her full-length mink. Afterwards, they rested upon one another's shoulders and tried to catch their breath.

For the first time since they began their forbidden escapade, Kennedy thought to look out into the office to see if anyone had come in while they were inside. Things happened so quickly, neither had bothered to close the blinds to Andre's office. Anyone coming into the establishment would have witnessed their sexual escapade.

Kennedy went to the office bathroom to clean up, and Andre joined her there.

"Is this it?" Andre asked.

"Absolutely!" Kennedy confirmed before waltzing out of the bathroom and the office without looking back.

But once she reached her car she remembered the disturbing truth. It had been less than six weeks since she gave birth, which is the most fertile time of a woman's life, and she just had great, yet unprotected sex with Andre. Even though he pulled out, there was still chance that his pre cum could be inside of her. She hadn't even had sex with her husband since the baby was born. She only hoped that she wouldn't have to deal with anymore secrets. She'd better not be pregnant. If she was, there would be no question who the father was.

Chapter 35

Dina drove as fast as she possibly could. Her nerves were a wreck. Between the frantic telephone conversation with her mother and a few close calls with nearby vehicles, she couldn't wait to get to her mother's house and park the car. After finding out what her mother thought was so urgent, Dina would stay just long enough to get her nerves together and go back home. Her mom was difficult enough to deal with on a normal day. Pregnancy had made her unbearable and Dina was certainly in no mood for her mother's hormones. It was hard enough to accept the fact that the woman was actually pregnant and as serious as AIDS about keeping the baby despite the fact that it was fathered by her married neighbor.

221

As Judy's stomach grew, it became harder for Dina to stay in denial. Now she was just thoroughly embarrassed. She couldn't believe her mothers audacious attitude about being forty-nine with two grown daughters and a baby on the way. As she approached her mother's block, she could see a small crowd gathered near her mother's home. Dina closed her eyes briefly and said a silent prayer for her dysfunctional family. She had stopped praying for a normal family long ago.

Dina pulled up and saw that the crowd consisted of her mother's next door neighbor, who appeared to be holding Mrs. Jacobs back, a couple of nosey neighbors, Mrs. Ellis, and another neighbor from across the street. Mr. Ellis, the baby's daddy, was nowhere in sight. The women were screaming at one another at the top of their lungs. One of the neighbors tried her best to pull Mrs. Ellis away from the uncouth scene, but she refused to budge. Dina threw the car into park, jumped out, and made her way through the crowd.

"What the…" was all she could manage.

Mrs. Ellis and her mother were going at it in the center of the gathering, slinging insults at one another.

"Bitch, don't you ever bring your whoring ass to my doorstep again," Mrs. Ellis commanded with her forefinger dangerously close to Mrs. Jacob s' nose.

"Get your damn hand out of my face. Quit calling my damn house with your bullshit and I won't have reason to come to your doorstep. And as long as I am carrying your so-called husband's baby, I'll show up on your raggedy-assed doorstep whenever I damn well please. I don't know who you think you fooling, that…"

Dina had pushed through the crowd, grabbed her mother and dragged her in the house ranting and raving.

"Ma, I can't believe the two of you out there carrying on like that. Is that what you called me for?"

"Yes, if you hadn't showed up, I swear I would have knocked that woman's head off of her body."

"Ma, you can't be serious." Dina searched the kitchen for tea or something else to calm her mother's nerves. "You have no business trying to fight in your condition. I really can't believe you." Dina found what she was looking for and filled the tea kettle with water. "Ma! You are pregnant and way too old for all of this. That's reason enough not to be out here acting like some foolish teenager. I can't believe the two of you. What if something happened?" Dina stopped for a moment and thought about the entire ordeal. "Actually, I am in awe!" she said, then fell out laughing.

Mrs. Jacobs looked at her as if she was crazy. Dina caught the look on her mother's face and laughed even harder. This was pathetic. Her mom and her neighbor were out on the street ready to brawl over a man as if they were in their teens. What was the world coming to? Despite the craziness of the situation, Mrs. Jacobs appeared to glow. Pregnancy was actually agreeing with her. Too bad she was so unstable.

"I don't see what's so funny," Mrs. Jacobs' said with her hands on her wide hips as she stared Dina down. Suddenly Mrs. Jacobs sighed and shook her head. "I guess I'll be raising another child by myself. I want him to come back, but there's so much going on. I just think he's having trouble handling all of it." She stopped pacing and directed her next question directly to Dina. "You think I planned on this?" Mrs. Jacobs pointed to her stomach. "Maybe this time I can get it right. Hopefully he'll come back. If not, I'll work it out. I'll do a better job than I did with you and your sister. But I deserve a good man too, don't I?"

"Where is he anyway?" Dina asked with genuine concern. The fact that her mother's new baby's daddy was missing in action was news to her.

"Oh, he'll be back soon," Mrs. Jacobs said although she sounded unsure.

Dina felt her mother's pain. She thought of Carl and her own desire to hold on to him by any means necessary. She and her mother were a lot more alike than she ever realized. Dina still had questions for her mom. She wanted badly to ask about her father and whether or not they were ever really married. She needed to know. She had every right to know. Unfortunately, that would have to wait. This obviously wasn't a good time to try to force those skeletons out of her mother's closet. Dina hung out with Mrs. Jacobs for a little while longer, then left. She didn't want to go home and be alone but she couldn't stay at her mother's house any longer without asking about her father.

On her way home she called up Angel and Kennedy to see if they wanted to come by for cocktails and a movie. Both girls agreed. When Dina arrived at home, she searched the fridge for something tasty but light to serve her friends for the evening. Since she wasn't much of a shopper, there wasn't much to choose from. Take-out menus decorated her refrigerator door, but she was low on funds since it was not her pay week. Carl was busy and she didn't want to bother him for money, so she racked her brains trying to think of a dish she could put together. Living alone didn't call for much shopping, but Dina knew she needed to keep a better stock of food in her fridge and cabinets.

Then it hit her. Dina remembered that she had a small bag of scallops stashed in the freezer. When she opened the freezer, she spotted a package of bacon and immediately knew what she wanted to make, broiled scallops wrapped in bacon. Dina pulled out the bacon and went searching for the scallops she'd put in a clear unmarked storage bag. She also pulled out a package of frozen strawberries to mix cocktails. After emptying nearly half of the food, Dina pulled on a bag that was stuck to the ice in the back of freezer. She tugged until she felt the bag loosen. Finally the scallops, she thought. But when Dina pulled out the bag, she wasn't quite prepared for what was inside.

The package was neatly filled and labeled. Dina pulled everything out and thoroughly examined the contents. Stunned by the ripped underwear and blood-stained washcloth, she quickly put the items back in the storage bag, looked over her shoulder as if she wasn't home alone, then placed it back in the rear of the freezer. She had seen all she needed to see and added this on her list of important discussions, right next to the one she needed to have with her mother about her parents alleged marriage. She needed to ponder just how to approach Kennedy with the news about what she found. Dina could understand why she would leave the evidence at her house. She certainly couldn't bring something like that into the home she shared with Troy.

Then it hit her. Dina recalled the time that Andre stopped as she was leaving and wondered if that was the day the incident occurred. If so then Dina wondered if little Zola was Troy's baby or Andre's. One way or another, she would get to the bottom of the situation, and soon.

Chapter 36

"Troy I need to go over some paperwork with you. I want to make sure your assets are protected," Mrs. Alexander said as she prepared a tuna sandwich for Evan.

"Protect my assets from what?" Troy asked.

"That woman you call a wife," Mrs. Alexander stated sharply, then looked to see if Evan was paying attention. She quickly finished up the sandwich, gave it to Evan, and ushered the young boy out of the kitchen. "You can eat out back sweetie." She watched Evan bust through the door into the brisk air and run to the picnic table in the center of the yard.

"Ma, I really don't..."

"Listen, you never know what may happen. Since you didn't even consider a prenuptial agreement, I just think you need to be careful about what happens to your money in case things get sour."

Troy was getting frustrated. Usually his mother just made snide remarks about Kennedy, but now she was implying that Kennedy might rip him off. This was not a comfortable conversation for him. Troy knew that he and Kennedy were cut from different cloths but he had no intentions of letting her get away from him a second time. He'd do whatever was necessary to keep her and his children close.

"All I suggest is that you transfer some of your accounts into your sister's name or just add Courtney's name to some of them," Mrs. Alexander recommended.

"I think Kennedy may take that the wrong way."

Mrs. Alexander's eyes stretched. "Personally, I don't give a damn about what Kennedy may think. My husband worked hard for what he had. Now I may not have been with him in the end. But I witnessed him bust his hump to build his business. And even when things went bad between us, he always made sure that his family was taken care of. I just don't want to see his money squandered if something happens between you and Kennedy. It just wouldn't be fair."

Mrs. Alexander turned towards the window to the backyard. Troy swore he heard her sniffle. His mother had taken his father's passing a little harder than he realized.

"I can understand that, Ma, but I'm not worried. Remember that Kennedy is the mother of my two children. Let me give it some thought. Now can I have one of those sandwiches you just made for Evan?"

Mrs. Alexander began making another tuna sandwich.

"The kids will be taken care of, and you know that. Their college money has already been set aside. But I think you need to move forward sooner rather than later."

"What's the big rush, Ma?"

"Nothing in particular, Troy." Mrs. Alexander sighed. "Just handle your business."

Dylan came barreling through the kitchen to greet his grandmother.

"Hi Grandma! Hey, Uncle Troy! Where's Evan?" Dylan sang.

"My goodness, boy, slow down," Mrs. Alexander teased. "Evan's outside. Did…"

Before she could ask her question, Dylan was headed outside to catch up with his cousin.

Courtney finally arrived in the kitchen just after Dylan ran out. She greeted her mother and brother warmly, and looked around the room.

"Okay, what's up?"

"Why did you ask?" Troy questioned.

"Because the two of you are too quiet."

"I told Troy he needs to do something to protect his assets and put some things in your name or add your name to some of his accounts."

Troy looked at Courtney to see whether she was on his side or not. The look on her face told him that she might side with their mother.

"Well, Troy, she makes sense. You know I don't get into the middle of these things, but I do feel you need to protect yourself."

Troy became more agitated.

"She's the mother of my two children, remember that? God forbid, if something happens she deserves something based on that alone. Despite the fact that you don't like her, you can't deny that she is a good mother to my kids."

"Troy, it's not like we are saying she's not entitled to anything. But what if things don't work out? You've been there before with her," Courtney pointed out.

"We weren't married before."

"So what? That doesn't mean that you two can't break up," Mrs. Alexander said.

"That's true, Troy," Courtney added.

"Kennedy's not going anywhere."

"I wouldn't be so sure of that," Courtney almost whispered.

"What the hell is that supposed to mean?" Troy was on his feet, and his patience was really wearing thin.

"Troy, think about it. The first time around you didn't have much to lose. Now you are considerably well off. This time around, you have a lot to lose. Namely, a lot of money. I just think Ma wants you to take precautions. Don't think of it as taking away from your kids. You can provide for them regardless," Courtney said.

"If I lost Kennedy today, do you think I would care about how much money I could lose? What's important to me are Kennedy and my kids, not money. If she didn't want to be with me, she would have never agreed to marry me," Troy huffed.

"Do you think that wench didn't realize you had money coming to you? You took her to see your father, and less than a month later the two of you were married. You don't think she saw your father's death as a payday?"

Troy was disgusted. How could they make such outrageous assumptions about Kennedy's intentions. What mattered was that he loved her, and he was sure that she loved him too. Look at all he had done for her. He knew how to keep her happy. Didn't he?

"I've had enough for one day. I need to get out of here," Troy said and turned to head for Evan outside.

As he passed by Courtney she grabbed him by his arm. "Troy, let me ask you a question."

Troy stopped and sighed. "What, Courtney?"

"Did it ever occur to you that Kennedy may have known Andre before daddy's funeral?"

"Why, Courtney?" Troy and his mother asked at the same time.

"For one, she looked awfully shocked to see him there. You may not have noticed, but as a woman, I did. I had no reason to question it at the time, so I just kept it to myself, but I saw her leaving Andre's office the other day when I went to drop off some paperwork of my own."

Troy's eyebrows tightened. Why would Kennedy be at Andre's office? he wondered. An obvious response to Courtney's point evaded him, so he simply walked out, got Evan and left.

Chapter 37

Troy arrived at home with Evan as Kennedy was preparing for her visit to Dina's house for an evening of hanging with the girls. From the master bath where Kennedy was putting the finishing touches on her exotic eyes, she could hear Troy scolding Evan about taking better care of his portable video game system. By the tone Troy used, Kennedy knew something was bothering him. She decided to work on her face a little faster so she could hurry up and get out of the house.

Kennedy quickly painted a sheer shimmery gloss across her full lips and snapped her designer makeup case closed. Just as she entered their bedroom, Troy walked in from the hallway, stopped and stared at her. The look on his face confirmed Kennedy's assumption that something was on his mind. She wanted to make her exit quickly.

"Hey, baby. Zola's asleep in the bassinet. I'm going to run over to Dina's for some cocktails, conversation, and a movie with the ladies." When Troy didn't respond she continued. "I won't be long. Zola just went to sleep, so she'll be out for a while. Her bottles are in the fridge."

Troy remained in the same spot. Kennedy wondered what was wrong with him and wished that he'd either come out with what was on his mind or move out of the doorway so she could leave.

Finally Troy spoke up in a low voice.

"Ken, I need to run a few things by you."

"Well, hurry up because I'm supposed to be on my way to Dina's by now. You know how she is. She'll keep calling until I get there. What's up?" Kennedy asked, hoping this wouldn't take long.

Troy came further into the room. First he went over to the baby's bassinet to peek in on her, then he sat on the edge of the bed.

"Hello! What do you want to talk about? I've got to go." Kennedy couldn't help herself. Everyone knew she didn't have much patience.

"Um, I need to move some money around and make some changes to our accounts," Troy said.

"So what's the problem? Do what you have to do," Kennedy said and went into their large walk-in closet to figure out what sunglasses she wanted to wear for the day. She settled on a pair of rose-tinted Chanel shades that matched the color of the short, rose-colored blazer she wore with her bootcut jeans. "Fine with me," she continued. "Let me know so I can update the accounts on the computer." She searched through her shoes for just the right pair to finish off her outfit.

"Well, I'll need to transfer some over to Courtney's account."

That got Kennedy's attention. Courtney had just as much money as Troy, she assumed. Why would he need to give her anything? The soft pink pumps got her attention because they matched the tank she wore under her blazer. Kennedy calculated her thoughts as she processed what Troy had just said. No anxious responses, she said to herself quietly before coming out of the huge walk in closet. She walked over to Troy who was now seated on the bed, and stood over him.

"Is everything okay with Courtney?" Kennedy studied Troy's face to gauge his thoughts and figure out where this was going.

"Um. She's fine. She just needs a little money."

"Really?" Kennedy asked, sounding unconvinced.

"Yeah!" Troy seemed really uncomfortable. "That's it," he said getting up from the bed. He walked to the master bath and turned on the shower water.

Something went down at Troy's mother's house, and Kennedy knew it. Those bitches probably convinced him to shuffle his assets to keep her hand away from them.. Little did they know, she had already set aside a nice little stash in the account that she had with her mother. But she wasn't finished yet.

Kennedy stood deep in thought. She didn't realize Evan had come into the room until she felt his little hands around her legs.

"Hi, mommy. Is daddy still upset?"

"Hey, pumpkin." Kennedy stooped down, kissed Evan, and began tickling him.

Evan giggled and begged his mother to stop.

"Okay," Kennedy said and stopped tickling Evan. She helped him gain his footing before continuing. "Actually, I think Daddy is still a little upset. Tell Mommy what happened."

"I lost one of my games at Grandma's house."

"What did Daddy tell you about..."

Evan interjected, "I know, I know. I have to keep up with my stuff. But it wasn't my fault. Dylan was playing it and then..."

Kennedy gently placed her index finger on Evan's little

lips, and Evan immediately stopped talking.

"No excuses. You know what you have to do. Make sure you find it or Daddy won't buy you anymore games. Okay?"

"Yes, Mommy. Are you going out? You look pretty."

"Thank you, sweetie. I'm going over to Auntie Dina's for a while, but I won't be gone long, okay?"

"Okay, Mommy."

Kennedy stood up and prepared to leave.

"Oh, and Evan, make up with your daddy," Kennedy teased.

Troy was unable to stay mad at his family for long and they both knew that it wouldn't take much for Evan to get back into his father's good graces.

Kennedy grabbed her natural-colored signature Gucci purse and called out to Troy in the bathroom.

"Troy, I'll see you later. I'm heading out now."

Troy emerged easily from the bathroom and stood in the entrance to the bedroom. Kennedy noticed he was still in a bad mood and made her way over to him to say good-bye. After a quick kiss on his cheek, she sauntered across the room, checked on Zola one last time, and turned to leave.

"How well do you know Andre Lewis?" Troy asked.

Kennedy was totally shocked, and she certainly wasn't prepared with an answer.

Chapter 38

It took forever for Angela and Kennedy to get to Dina's place. By the time they arrived Dina had already dipped into the dessert. The scallops wrapped in bacon were a hit and the strawberry inspired cocktails weren't bad either. The movie and girl talk served as a great pastime. After a fun night, Dina was ready to get down to business. Her heart was about to jump out of her chest because of the secret she was harboring. She had used every ounce of strength she could muster to keep from blurting out the details of what she had found in the freezer. Now she needed a tactful way to send Angel on her way, but keep Kennedy around to privately discuss her findings. Dina had a few questions of her own.

Much to Dina's benefit, Angel either had a case of the 'itis'" or had indulged in more cocktails than she could handle because she had begun to doze off. When Angel went into a chorus of light snores, Dina woke her and suggested she head home before she got too tired.

"You are right, girl. I am beat. My belly is full, and I'm feeling pretty good. If I don't leave now, I may have to spend the night," Angel said and laughed.

Not tonight, Dina thought.

"Are you okay or do you need a ride home," Kennedy asked.

Dina hoped that Angel would say she was all right.

"I'm good to go. The food soaked up most of the liquor.

I'm too full to be drunk," Angel said. Then they all laughed.

"That's the truth. I think we ate too much to stay tipsy," Dina added.

Angel got up and gathered her things while Dina watched. In minutes she would be alone with Kennedy to discuss the package.

"Dina, are there anymore of those scallops? I want Patrick to taste them," Angel inquired..

"Not a single one, but I'll make them again soon."

"Okay. Well, ladies, it's been fun. I'll catch up with you all during the week. Love you," Angel said and kissed each girl as her good-bye.

Kennedy stood, stretched, and looked around the room. Dina could tell that she was preparing to leave also. To keep her there, Dina ran over to Kennedy and pushed her back onto the couch.

"Wait, you can't leave yet," Dina said and ran to catch up to Angel, who was heading for the door.

Dina opened the door for Angel and said her final good-byes.

"Call me when you get home," Dina told Angel.

When she returned to the den, Kennedy looked at her questionably.

"What was that for?" Kennedy asked.

"I just didn't want you to leave yet. I have something to ask you."

Kennedy's eyes rolled up into her head.

"About what?" Kennedy asked, looking annoyed.

"Andre," Dina said quietly.

"Actually, I have bigger fish to fry than to talk about Andre. You need to sit down for this one."

Dina immediately shifted gears. She wasn't sure if Kennedy's news was bigger than her knowing what went on between Kennedy and Andre, but she certainly wanted to hear what Kennedy had to say. Maybe it would be a close second. Dina decided to contain her own suspicions and hear Kennedy out.

"Well, what's up?" Dina asked.

Kennedy got up and started pacing the room and rubbing her hands together. Dina watched her move about, wondering what Kennedy was about to lay on her. She could tell by Kennedy's body language that this wouldn't be an average conversation. Not to mention, Kennedy was wearing out the carpet with her constant pacing. The hesitancy alone was alarming. Kennedy always shot straight from the hip, no filters, and no beating around the bush. What could possibly have her pacing?

"Can I trust you, Dina?" Dina was surprised. Despite the dicey, weird friendship, at the end of the day, they were always there for each other.

"Of course you can trust me, Ken. What's up?"

"Okay. Listen closely. I'm going to ask you something. But before I do, you must vow to never allow this conversation to leave this room," Kennedy said.

Dina shifted in her seat. Whatever Kennedy was about to say must have been big if she was making Dina swear to secrecy before she even said anything.

"I swear, Kennedy," Dina said, awaiting the bomb like a child anticipating Christmas.

Kennedy stopped pacing and sat down next to Dina on

the couch. She looked into her hands, took a deep breath, and sat for another moment in silence. Finally she turned to Dina.

"I need your help," Kennedy said.

"Okay!" Dina held the word like she was singing.

"Listen closely," Kennedy said.

"Kennedy, cut the bullshit and come out with it already!"

"I need you to sleep with Troy."

"WHAT! Kennedy, you can't be serious? Troy's your husband. Why on earth would you want me to sleep with your husband?"

Kennedy stood once again. Dina was on the edge of her seat. The conversation about the package in the freezer could wait. She needed to understand where Kennedy was going with this.

"Troy's mom and sister have apparently been trying to talk Troy into turning his assets over to them. They don't want me to have anything. I don't know if Troy is going to try and leave me or not. But I need to protect myself and my kids."

"Well, what does that have to do with me sleeping with your husband?"

"So that I can have some ammunition in case they win him over." Kennedy said the word 'they' as if it burned her tongue.

"Kennedy, how on earth do you expect me to accomplish that? Troy is dedicated to you. Even a blind man can see that," Dina said.

"Unfortunately not as dedicated as I'd like to believe. Something is going on and at the end of the day, I don't want to be assed-out, broke, and alone."

"Oh my goodness, Ken," Dina's hand went to her heart.

"I didn't realize you and Troy were having problems. What happened" Dina said. She was truly surprised. "Do you really think this is really necessary? Do you think it'll work?"

Dina would never have expected this type of request to come from Kennedy and wasn't totally sure she could actually go through with something like this? It was shocking to hear that there was trouble in their perfect little paradise.

"Dee, if you don't want to do it. I'll understand. I just wanted someone I could trust and not some stranger. I wouldn't want to have to worry about some chick pursuing him beyond this deed." Kennedy paused. "Maybe I could ask Angel. She's not into stuff like this but she'd do anything for her friends."

Dina snapped out of her racing thoughts. If anyone would do something this big for Kennedy it would be her, not Angel. Besides there was no way Angel could pull off something like this. Kennedy was playing her, and she knew it. But still, she couldn't imagine Angel and Kennedy sharing a secret like this if she wasn't involved. Dina sighed.

"How do you expect me to pull this off?" Dina asked.

"Don't worry, I've got it all planned out," Kennedy said, smiling for the first time since Angel left.

"Damn, girl," Dina said and paused. "All right, I'll do it!"

239

Chapter 39

Troy pulled up to Andre's brokerage firm and quickly made his way inside. The office was bustling with potential home-owners seeking to get the best mortgage deal through their trusty brokers. Troy knew the receptionist since he had been to this office many times before. Only today, he was here for different business. Every since Courtney mentioned that she had seen Kennedy leaving Andre's office, Troy hadn't been able to shake his suspicious thoughts.

The petite receptionist cut into Troy's thoughts.

"Hi, Mr. Alexander! Mr. Lewis isn't in right now, but he should be back any moment now."

"Um...tell him...how long will he be?"

"Any minute now. He just went out to drop off some paperwork to a client."

Troy was losing his nerve and his cool. He came prepared to ask Andre a few important questions, but hadn't planned on having time to wait and think things over. Maybe he shouldn't approach Andre at all about knowing Kennedy. The idea of them possibly having a history haunted him and he needed answers. He took a seat in one of the empty chairs in the front of the office. Shortly after sitting, he stood again and told the receptionist that he would stop by later in the week.

"No problem, Mr. Alexander. I'll let him know you stopped by."

"Thanks." Troy spun around and practically ran out the

door. The moment he stepped foot outside he ran right into Andre.

"Hey, Troy! What's up? What brings you by?"

Troy hesitated. "Uh, yeah...What's up, man?" Troy returned Andre's greeting, and the two exchanged a brotherly handshake. "Can we go into your office and talk for a minute?"

Andre raised a brow. "Sure, man. Come on."

The gentlemen walked passed the receptionist, other brokers, and customers along the way to Andre's newly renovated office space. Andre placed the files in his hand on the large desk and rounded back to close his office door behind Troy.

"So, what's on your mind?" Andre asked.

Troy didn't respond right away. The words wouldn't come together, and he couldn't risk sounding or appearing desperate. Moisture pooled in the center of his hands, and he wiped them against his pants. Troy fought to bring a solitary statement to the forefront to break the ice. He looked around the office to find something to speak about other than the thoughts clouding his mind.

"I just noticed all the changes you made around here. The place looks good."

Andre looked puzzled. "Thanks, man. It was in need of some change." He paused then moved around to the back of his desk. "So is there something you wanted to talk to me about, man?"

Troy snapped out of it. "Oh...Yeah. Could I work out an agreement to combine the mortgages for a few of the properties my father left me?"

Troy decided that it wasn't Andre that he needed to get

his answers from but he didn't want to look stupid in front of the man. He could tell that Andre wasn't exactly buying the act. Kennedy would have to answer his questions, and he'd deal with her when he got home. It was time to turn the tables. Kennedy was spoiled because he allowed her to be that way. He just needed to put his foot down and demand to know what he wanted. If Kennedy became upset, she would get over it

Troy focused on Andre's moving lips until the words that were coming out of his mouth began to make sense. He hadn't realized that Andre had been going on and on about the question he'd just asked. What question had he asked anyway? Troy listened intently for a moment just to catch on to what Andre was saying. Troy caught up with the conversation and feigned interest.

"I see. Okay, let me give it some more thought, and I'll get back to you. Thanks!"

Troy stood to leave then hesitated. "Just go," said the little voice inside of him. Troy made another step to the door, paused another moment then proceeded to walk out. Andre followed him still talking.

"Just call me if you have more questions about it. I could get that going for you," Andre said.

"Sure, no problem. And thanks," Troy replied politely but had no clue what the hell Andre was talking about.

Andre walked Troy to the front door and held his hand out. At first, Troy just looked at him, finally realizing what he was doing. "Oh, sorry," he apologized. Troy took Andre's hand and shook it, "Like I said. I'll get back to you on that one." *Whatever it was.*

Troy took a step onto the sidewalk he then turned back one last time. Andre was in the door watching him.

"How well do you know my wife?" he finally asked.

"For a ..."

Before Andre could finish his statement, Troy had walked off as if he never asked.

Chapter 40

If there was such a thing as love at first sight, then Dina had finally experienced it. Upon first setting foot in the ornate but beautifully designed Italian restaurant, Dina was immediately smitten. A fireplace sparkled in the center of a rustic stone wall in the private dining room where Kennedy's reception was taking place. The rich terracotta tones and stunning Tuscan décor seemed to wrap her in its inviting warmth. Luxurious dark silk drapes framed the large floor-to-ceiling windows. The design-inspired romance that hung in the air made Dina think of the man she loved, Carl. Once again she painted the perfect family scene in her head. A family with Carl was what she wanted more than anything. No matter how long it took, she would continue to try to have his baby.

Dina felt better today than she had in a long time. She attributed her good feelings to the aura of the restaurant. The place put her at peace. Peace that lasted as long as she didn't think about what she had to do later on that evening. An entire year had passed since Kennedy and Troy had been married. Months had passed since Kennedy first asked her to do the unthinkable, but it wasn't until one day a few weeks before when Kennedy finally revealed to her just how she wanted Dina to carry out her request. Once again Dina was shocked. They were all gathered on this evening for an intimate celebration for two reasons. One, to celebrate the couple's first anniversary. Secondly, this party would also be considered their official reception since they didn't have a traditional wedding.

Kennedy was a master at her game. A game that now involved Dina. No matter what, she would be there for her friend.

Carl's svelte body looked scrumptious in his rented tux. Everyone looked gorgeous that evening. Kennedy, of course, was the belle of the ball. Her champagne colored gown was fit for the red carpet at the Oscars. When she became pregnant with Zola, she had stopped cutting her hair. Her shoulder-length tresses were pinned up in an elegant bun with delicate tendrils cascading randomly around her head. In the nine months that had passed since giving birth, Kennedy had managed to regain her figure. Needless to say, Kennedy looked incredible and Troy was the perfect handsome complement to Kennedy's unbridled beauty.

Dina was a sight herself. Carl drowned her with his attention and flooded her ego with compliments on how beautiful she looked in her cranberry, form-fitting silk dress. If she was going to be able to complete her tasks this evening, she would have to leave the reception early so that she could take care of Carl before taking care of Troy. About an hour before the party was due to end, Dina led Carl to the valet, picked up his car, and headed back to his place.

They toyed with each other's private parts during the entire half-hour ride home. By the time they made it through Carl's front door, Dina's hands were in his pants, coaxing his manhood to attention. It didn't take much encouragement before Carl became hard enough to cut diamonds. Their lips connected at the door and remained in tact as they shuffled toward the couch. Their seal wasn't broken even as they undressed one another. Shoes, jackets, dress, and underwear spotted the carpet leading to the couch.

Dina was breathless as she straddled Carl and inserted his manhood in her warm, moist canal. Carl sighed and moaned. When Dina felt Carl nearing his breaking point she shifted gears and pulled him on top of her. She gently constricted her vaginal muscles until she was snugly wrapped around Carl's shaft, then rode him to a forceful climax. Carl practically howled as he came, and his body jerked uncontrollably. Dina continued to squeeze him until she was sure that she had received every last drop of his semen. Finally he collapsed on top of Dina and the sweat of their lovemaking mingled.

Carl began a light snore. That was Dina's cue to get up and get out. After cleaning up and getting her clothes together, Dina called a cab and went home. Once at home, Dina went straight to the stash of liquor under the kitchen sink and pulled out a bottle of Grey Goose vodka. She gulped down three quick shots and headed for the shower. Sweet scents filled the bathroom as she massaged mango body wash into her skin. A soft pink kimono that left little to the imagination is what she chose to slightly cover her naked body. Then she discreetly placed condoms under the end of the couch in the den.

The Grey Goose called for her again and Dina went into the kitchen and downed two more shots before settling in the living room to await Kennedy's call.

Chapter 41

To say that Troy enjoyed himself was an understatement. The event went without a hitch and his wife looked more stunning than he could ever remember. Kennedy even seemed to truly enjoy herself. It was a good thing that his beautiful wife suggested that they get a limo to pick them up and take them home because Troy was in no condition to drive. Between his cousin and their personal waiter, Troy's glass stayed full. By the end of the party, he had no idea how much he'd drank. He just knew that he needed to get home, get some of his wife, and get to bed. A hangover was sure to force him to stay in bed a little longer the next morning.

After Troy's visit to Andre's office a few weeks back, he decided to put the issue of Kennedy and Andre's acquaintance to bed. Things were going well in their marriage, and he didn't want to be the one to rock the boat. His mother and sister were still nagging him about his assets, but during the planning of their reception, he had managed to put them off also.

Kennedy's voice caressed his ears as she called his name. At first he didn't answer so that she would continue to call him. When she seemed to be getting frustrated, he responded..

"What's up, baby?" he asked.

"My goodness, Troy. You're slurring," Kennedy acknowledged.

Troy straightened his back and asked, "Who me?"

"Yes, you. Let's go," Kennedy said and grabbed him by the arm.

Troy couldn't wait to get home and lay it on his wife. He laughed as Kennedy guided him to the awaiting car. When the fresh air hit him, he opened his eyes wider to focus on what was in front of him. For a man with 20/20 vision, everything appeared to be awfully blurry. Troy wondered if it was fog or his drunken eyesight. The thought of having to figure out which one it was made him laugh hard.

"What in the world are you laughing at, Troy?" she asked.

"Is it foggy, or have I had too much to drink?" he asked and laughed again.

"Come on, silly. Let's go," Kennedy said and pushed him into the back of the limo.

All the way home Troy roamed Kennedy's body with his hand. Kennedy pushed him away after he'd slapped a few wet and sloppy kisses on her face. He chuckled. The limo pulled up to the front of their handsome home and the driver leaped to help Troy and Kennedy out of the car.

"Drink this water," Kennedy commanded once they were inside.

Troy did but he didn't feel any different just yet. Suddenly Troy felt Kennedy shaking him and he woke with a start. Drool had made its way down the side of his mouth with some settling in the crevice of his lips.

"Troy, I need you to go over to the townhouse. Dina called. Something's wrong with the downstairs bathroom. She can't stop the water from flowing. You're going to have to go over there before the whole place gets flooded."

"Can't it wait until the morning? I'm in no condition to

drive over there tonight," Troy said with his head down.

He was tired, but he still wanted to make love to Kennedy before he lost all of his fizz, especially since Kennedy's mother took the kids home with her so that he and Kennedy could spend the night alone. The last thing he wanted to do was go out in the cool, fall air while his loins were on fire. That would surely destroy the mood and zap him of any energy he had left.

"Tell her to call Carl over there," he suggested.

He waited a few moments for her response. Just as he felt a twinge of relief, he could hear Kennedy's footsteps approaching the family room from the kitchen.

"Carl can't do anything. He doesn't know where the shut-off valve is. If you don't go now, my entire townhouse is going to be flooded. You have to go now, Troy! Dina has no idea what to do and I don't want Carl over there experimenting and screwing things up. He's no handy-man."

Troy could not believe his fate but knew there was no other choice.

"Ah, damn! Call her and tell her I'll be there shortly."

Troy managed to drag himself off of the family room couch and splash his face with cold water. It didn't help much, but he assumed the cold air would help once he got outside.

"You just be ready for me when I get back," Troy demanded. He then picked up his keys and headed for the two-car garage.

Troy could hear his speech slur a little. He resolved himself to get there and back as quickly as possible. Something metal crashed to the floor when he entered the garage. The loud clanging rang in his ears. Troy flinched and felt his way to his truck.

The garage wasn't completely dark, but Troy's vision was impaired for other obvious reasons.

"I know I have no business behind this wheel," he said as he climbed into the truck. Rugged sounds of his enhanced exhaust system roared though the two-car garage. In swift motions, Troy started the car, threw it in reverse and stepped on the gas. He crashed on the breaks, stopping just in time to narrowly miss blowing through the closed garage doors. "Oh shit," he said to no one. Troy tapped the automatic door opener clipped to his visor. As the door rose, he said a quick prayer for the safety of himself and the other people on the road. He lowered all of the windows and started out on his journey.

Chapter 42

When Kennedy called to say that Troy was on his way over, Dina ran to the kitchen for another hit of vodka. The short silky garment that she wore fell open, revealing her naked shapely body. She decided to leave it hanging. The tingling in her lips was a sign that the vodka was in full effect. Hopefully this would make the deed easier to complete. The thought made her reach for the liquor once more.

With her robe still hanging ajar, Dina filled a bucket with water, carried it to the first floor bathroom, and poured it over the commode and floor. By the time she was done, everything was soaked, the toilet tissue roll mounted on the wall, the expensive rugs that adorned the floor, and the decorative towels that usually hung from the stainless steel towel bar. Her bare feet made smacking sounds in the water as she traipsed around the bathroom. Then the doorbell rang.

251

Dina took a deep breath, closed her robe slightly, and headed for the door, stumbling once or twice along the way. Now she had *too* much to drink. After all, she had been drinking at the reception and it was never a good idea to mix alcohol. Without checking the peephole, Dina swung the door open with a little more force than she intended.

"Hey, Dina, what's up? Show me where the trouble is," Troy said but didn't move.

Dina was also stuck in her spot wondering how this would all play out. She noticed Troy glance down a few times at her thick and shapely thighs as they peeked out from under her kimono. Dina moved her leg so that the split in her robe would showcase a little more of her leg. She sized up Troy, who was still wearing his dress shirt and tuxedo pants from the party. His top three buttons were undone, giving sight to his hairless chest. Troy wasn't cut, but he was fit. There was something sexy about him looking unkempt in his crushed attire as he braved the breezy night air without a jacket. Dina finally moved aside enough to let him in.

"Come on in, Troy. It's the first floor bathroom. I don't know what happened. I went upstairs to take my shower and then came down for a glass of water. When I walked passed here, I noticed that there was water everywhere." Troy followed Dina through the house as she continued. "I have no idea where it came from. I tried to call Carl but he didn't answer his phone. Besides, I don't know if you would want him trying to repair anything around here anyway. He's nobody's handyman. In fact..." Dina realized she was rambling and decided to get to the point. "Well anyway. I called Ken and she said for me not to touch anything, and that you would be coming over to take care of it right away. I guess she didn't trust me or Carl to mess with this. I am so sorry to make you come out so late. I know you probably just wanted to get in the bed and call it a night." Dina made the last two statement sound rather sweet.

"No problem. Let me take a look at this."

Troy got down on the bathroom floor to examine the situation. When he stood, his clothing was soaked from fiddling around with the back of the commode and sink. He flushed the toilet and ran the water from the faucet, then he stepped back to check for more leaks. Dina looked everywhere he looked. Finally he washed his hands and wiped them across his trousers. Dina noticed how off balance he was and decided to use that as her lead.

"Well, whatever the problem is, it seems to have fixed itself. There's no more water coming from the sink or toilet. I need to check the basement to make sure the water didn't damage anything down there. After that I'll just have to clean up the water from the floor, and everything should be fine. I need to get back home. I am in no condition to be out here driving," Troy said.

"I can see that," Dina said.

"Man! Is it that obvious?" Troy asked.

"Kind of. I'll make you a cup of coffee before you get back on that road. That Southern State Parkway can be a beast on a good day," Dina spun around quickly and felt the air brush the base of her behind.

She knew that her robe had lifted slightly and looked back to see if Troy noticed. He did. Troy turned around immediately and darted for the basement stairs.

By the time Troy returned to the first floor, Dina was on her knees in the bathroom, attempting to get up some of the water from the alleged flood. As she moved about, her robe shifted dangerously close to showing her bare goods.

She could hear Troy walk up behind her, and she leaned forward to give him a slight view of the crack of her assets.

"Dina, I'll take care of that," Troy offered.

"Are you sure?" Dina asked sweetly.

"I've got it," Troy stated with finality in his voice.

"Okay," Dina sang and tried to get up. Troy had to help her up.

She made it to a full stand and wiped her hands on her robe, which caused it to open slightly once again. Troy turned his head then dropped to the ground to get up the water.

"I'll get that cup of coffee for you by the time you're done," Dina said and sauntered out of the bathroom.

Dina realized that her task might be easier than she thought. All of her seductive tactics had succeeded in getting Troy's attention, and his attempts to resist being affected made her feel sexy. The five shots of vodka helped a little too. This was becoming a game to her, one that she had begun to enjoy playing. After all, she was only honoring her friend's request.

"Dina," Troy called out to her when he finished in the bathroom.

"I'm in here," She called back from the den. Dina had turned the TV to a digital music Chanel that played classic R&B tunes. The soulful melodies wafted through the air. The only light in the room were flickers from the TV screen. "Come on in. I have your coffee. I assumed you wanted it straight and black."

"Thanks!" Troy said and joined Dina on the couch.

"I hope it's not cold. I didn't realize how long it would take for you to finish. Taste it and let me know."

Troy took a sip and said, "It's a little cool, but that's okay."

Dina jumped up and grabbed the cup spilling some of the contents on his white shirt and already wet pants. Troy was slow to respond, and Dina realized that he too was still quite tipsy.

"Oh, Troy, I'm so sorry. I'll be right back with something to clean that up and a fresh, hot cup of coffee."

"Dina wait…"

Dina ran off before Troy could finish.

"No. I insist," Dina yelled back. "It will only take a

moment." This time, when she reached the kitchen, instead of getting a glass, she gulped more of the bitter vodka straight from the bottle.

Dina returned after a few short minutes with a steaming cup of coffee and a wet cloth. "Here," she said as she handed the unsteady cup to Troy, who almost spilled the now blistering contents himself. Dina took the cup from him, placed it on the side table and began to gently wipe at the stains on his shirt. Then she moved to his pants. At first Troy grabbed her arm. She stopped and looked directly into his eyes. Dina seductively lowered her eyes and continued to rub the cloth across his lap, getting severely close to his groin.

"You're all wet," Dina said and tossed the cloth. "Here, want to watch something while you finish up your coffee?"

Troy just shrugged his shoulders. Instead of picking up the remote, Dina sauntered across the room, bent over slowly, and began manually sifting through channels on the TV, giving Troy full view of her rear. When she turned around, Troy's head was down, but she was sure he liked what he saw because he began to shift uncomfortably.

"Are you okay, Troy?"

"Uh…yeah, I'm fine," he stammered. "I need to finish up this coffee and get home."

Troy tried to gulp down the coffee, but it was much too hot. Drops of coffee spilled along his chin and onto his shirt once again. Dina laughed to herself as she slowly returned to the couch with her supple skin peeking through the opening of her robe. It was time. She reached over and gently wiped the dripping substance from the side of his chin. Then she moved in closer, her breast brushing Troy's slightly exposed chest, and wiped the other side of his mouth.

Troy kept his head down but didn't stop Dina from touching him. She then slid her finger across the base of his chin to capture any leftover moisture. Dina took her index finger and traced a line down Troy's neck and chest all the way to his navel. That's when Troy jumped up. But Dina didn't move, so when he stood he was standing directly in front of her. They were so close that her breast teased him through his shirt. Dina leaned in and kissed his chest. Troy's head fell back, and he exhaled loudly. He attempted to step away again, but Dina followed him. She wrapped her arms around him and nuzzled her forehead across his chest.

"Wait," she whispered, letting her loosely tied robe fall open.

Dina sensed that he wanted to get the hell out of there, but she had already aroused his libido, which made her advances hard to resist. Surely the liquor was no help. She slowly slid down until she was on level with his protruding penis. She released his manhood from the confines of his pants and licked the length of his shaft on the top, bottom, and both sides. Troy moaned. Dina knew she had him, and she worked quickly to avoid him bailing out before the deed was complete.

Dina took him into her mouth fully, and after a few, long oral strokes, Troy caught her rhythm and helped her along by pushing his pelvis back and forth. It didn't take long for him to reach his pinnacle. But before Dina would allow him to get there, she pushed him down on the couch and straddled him. Troy's sex filled her up and she rode him until her body clenched from pleasure. Troy guided her stride with his hands planted on her behind and pushed himself further inside of her cushioned walls. Dina's back arched and she screamed, "Oh...My... Damn...Please don't stop."

Troy pressed deeper and raised the intensity with long, hard, aggressive strokes. Dina wailed like a mother giving birth as she came hard. She shuddered and every muscle in her body tightened over and over again. Troy's head reared back, and he exploded. Dina collapsed onto Troy's chest and together they tried to steady their breathing and contracting body spasms. Several minutes passed before they came down off their euphoric high, and both began to snore.

Chapter 43

Kennedy woke with a start at five in the morning and realized that Troy had not made it home. She hoped he hadn't gotten into an accident since she knew he'd had too much to drink. She felt a twinge of guilt about sending him out like that, but she knew that was the only way to make him vulnerable enough for Dina to take advantage of him. Kennedy wondered what happened and decided to call Dina to make sure things went as planned.

Dina's sleepy voice picked up after eight long rings. "Hello?"

"Dina. Wake up! It's me, Ken. Is it done?"

"Oh. Um. Yeah," Dina said.

"What time did he leave?"

"Not yet."

Kennedy was angry. She sat up fully in their king-sized bed. She could tell by the way Dina answered her questions that he was right next to Dina. Kennedy pictured them in her old bedroom together and became livid.

"What do you mean, not yet?" Kennedy spat her words, not hiding how she felt.

"Let me call you right back," Dina said and hung up before Kennedy could respond.

Kennedy tossed the cordless phone across the room. Although this was her plan, Kennedy didn't like the way it was going already. Despite being intoxicated, she knew Troy fell into deep sated slumber after having good sex. She never considered that their experience might have been an enjoyable one. She picked Dina because she knew she would do it, especially after the nonsense she told her about Troy possibly leaving her. The fact was that Kennedy was ready to move on but knew that in order for her to maintain her lavish life style she couldn't just walk away. With Troy's indiscretion, he would feel guilty and would set her up for life. That's beside what she had already set aside for herself over the past year and a half.

Kennedy's imagination ran wild as she thought about how things may have gone down between Troy and Dina. She didn't like the idea, but it was too late. She would have to move on with her plan. When the time was right, she would reveal to Troy, that she had 'found out' about his infidelity and make him leave their beautiful home. Maybe she would even entertain a few more romps with Andre after all was said and done. As for now, she needed to shake the foolish feelings of jealously that were coming over her and stay focused on her plan.

A few minutes later. Kennedy's phone rang again. She raced across the floor, and answered. It was Dina.

"Ken, he's on his way." Dina said.

"Well, why the hell did you let him stay all night? What went on over there?"

"Ken, what's the matter? I just did what you asked and we fell asleep," Dina tried to assure her.

"How many times?" Kennedy asked. She'd begun to grind her teeth. That only happened when it was hard for her to control her temper.

"How many times? Ken..." Dina sighed. "Just one."

Kennedy pressed the end button, threw the phone again,

and sat in the center of the bed with her arms folded across her chest. The back of the phone flew in one direction, the battery fell out and the rest of the phone flew in another direction. Eventually, the noise of Troy's roaring exhaust let Kennedy know he was on the block. Seconds later, he pulled into the driveway. The creak of the garage door opening grated Kennedy's nerves. She tried to put her feelings in check.

By the time Troy made it through the entrance leading from the garage, Kennedy was there to receive him.

"What the hell did you have to do, build a whole new toilet?" Kennedy was fuming.

Troy looked like a deer caught in the headlights. He lowered his head and spoke near a whisper.

"Um...I fell asleep. Baby, I'm sorry. I was real messed up and shouldn't have been behind the wheel in the first place. After I fixed the bathroom and cleaned up the water, I was exhausted. Dina offered to fix me a cup of black coffee. Babe, I couldn't even drink the coffee. I just fell out. The next thing I knew, Dina was shaking me awake saying that I had to go home. I'm sorry, baby. Really I am."

Kennedy glared at Troy for a moment before stomping off to their room. She took a sheet and two pillows, threw them into the hall, and locked the bedroom door.

Troy knocked softly while calling her name, "Ken, baby."

"Sleep in the guest room!" she yelled back, rolled over, and went to sleep.

Chapter 44

Dina ran to the local pharmacy during her lunch because her period hadn't showed up this month. Hoping it wasn't another false alarm and being overly anxious, she took the test in the bathroom at the office. She stayed in the stall until the testing strip revealed her fate. When she read 'pregnant' across the little strip, she jumped for joy, banging her elbow on the hook where women hang their bags. She was in pain but didn't care. She called Carl to let him know she had great news. He practically begged her to tell him what it was but she refused. She wanted it to be special and planned the evening precisely. Dina had waited so long for this moment.

Immediately after work, Dina shot straight to Carl's house. She didn't even carry out her original plans because she was too excited to be bothered. Carl's car wasn't in the driveway when she got there, and Dina felt like she could explode. Dina let herself in, freshened up, and got ready for Carl to get home. As soon as he walked in, Dina met him at the door and jumped on him like a child would greet her father, smothering his face with big, sloppy, wet kisses.

"Hi, baby," Dina gaily addressed Carl.

Carl kissed her, looked at her and laughed, then wrapped his arms around her and walked over to the couch.

"What's up? Now tell me the good news."

Dina finally let go of him, faced him, and held both his hands.

"Baby, we are finally going to be complete. We are going to have a baby!"

Carl's mouth dropped open and his eyebrows crumpled. She jumped up and went on, pacing as she continued.

"Isn't it exciting? I can't wait. Carl, I love you so much, and I've dreamed of the day that we would get married and have children. If it's a boy, I pray that he looks just like you. We have to think of names and everything. I have a few that I like already."

Dina had been ranting so much that she never noticed the steam rising out of Carl's ears.

"So who's is it, Dina?" Carl asked through clenched teeth.

Dina stopped in her tracks and scrunched her face up at Carl.

"What?"

"Who have you been messing around with?"

"Carl, why would you say something like that? I haven't been with anybody but you."

As soon as the words came out of her mouth, she immediately thought about the encounter with Troy a few weeks back. Dina had condoms but couldn't recall using one. Those shots of Grey Goose clouded her memory.

Carl stood to his feet and hovered over her. Dina flinched, thinking he was about to hit her. She wondered if he knew about Troy.

"You're such a liar. I can't believe I got caught up with you again."

"Carl, why are you saying this? I thought you'd be happy." Dina started crying.

"Happy? Happy to find out that my girl has been screwing another man?" Carl yelled. He closed the space between him and Dina, and she took a few steps back.

Dina cried uncontrollably. "Carl, I don't understand. Why would you think that? Why would you say it isn't yours?"

"Because I had a vasectomy years ago after my ex took my daughter away." Carl started to pace the floor. "I vowed then, that nothing like that would ever happen again. So I can't make babies. Therefore that baby obviously belongs to someone else."

Through streaming tears, Dina pleaded with Carl.

"Please don't say that. It's still possible." She broke down then gathered herself together. "Why didn't you tell me? Isn't that something that I should have known?"

"Why? You never mentioned anything about having a baby. But right now it doesn't make a difference. Get all of your shit, and get the hell out of my house."

263

Carl picked up Dina's bag and keys and pushed her through the front door.

"I don't ever want to see your trifling ass again."

Dina fell down the front steps and crashed to the ground. Carl slammed the door shut while she laid on the ground whimpering, watching her tears make small, dark circles on the walkway. When she felt like she could cry no more, Dina brushed herself off, got into her car, and set out to find Troy.

She passed by Kennedy and Troy's house but couldn't tell if they were home because their cars were always parked in the garage. Dina banged on the steering wheel because she didn't know what to do next. She pulled over and cried some more. Finally, she spotted Troy's truck coming down the street in her side-view mirror. Dina quickly backed up to get Troy's attention. She threw the car in park, jumped out, and ran to his driver side window.

"I need to talk to you. It's important," Dina blurted.

"What's the matter, Dina. Is everything all right? Do you want to come inside?" Troy looked genuinely concerned.

"NO!" she shouted. "We can't talk in there."

"Um, Dina, if it's about the..."

"Troy, please. We need to talk now. Follow me to my house. It's not what you think." Tears were streaming down Dina's face now.

She ran back around the SUV, jumped back in her car, and peeled off, giving Troy no choice but to follow her. When they reached the townhouse, Dina ran inside with Troy on her heels.

"What's wrong, Dina?" Troy asked as he followed her in the front entrance. He looked around outside before securely closing the door.

Dina was stomping a hole in the carpet, marching back and forth. She stopped for a quick moment and put her palm on her head.

"Troy, I'm pregnant. And it's yours."

Troy's mouth hit the floor. "Mine? Are you sure?"

"Yes. I just told Carl and he kicked me out, asking me who was I screwing," Dina cried. "He told me he had a vasectomy a few years ago and there was no way I could be pregnant by him. That leaves you. Troy what am I going to do...I wanted this so bad. Why did it have to happen like this?"

Troy walked over to Dina and embraced her, offering her

a shoulder to cry on. Dina took advantage and her entire body shook as the tears flowed. Troy didn't speak. He let her release. Then Dina stopped abruptly as if she had a revelation. She looked at Troy with wide, hopeful eyes.

"Troy, you are a good father to Evan and Zola, I know you can be a good father to our baby."

Troy pulled back from Dina and looked at her incredulously.

"Do you hear what you are saying? Kennedy is your best friend and my wife."

"Troy, I could love you the way you deserved to be loved."

"What? Dina, I have to go."

"No, wait!" She grabbed his arm. "You can't tell me you didn't feel anything that night we were together."

"Dina, that night was a big mistake."

"Troy, your marriage to Kennedy is a mistake."

Troy snapped his neck in Dina's direction. "Watch what you say, Dina," he said, pointing a finger at her.

"No really, Troy. That's the only reason I seduced you that night. Kennedy asked me to. She said she needed ammunition in case you tried to leave her. We could work this out. Kennedy doesn't really care about you. She would never have asked me to do what she did if she loved you. You know as well as I do that Kennedy is all about what she can gain. Think about it. We are the victims here. We can be together."

Troy's face wrinkled with confusion, so Dina gave him the clarification he was looking for. She hoped he would understand why it made sense to her that they could be together. They both wanted to be loved and had plenty of love to give.

Troy's face twisted with anger. He pushed Dina out of his way and left. Dina fell to her knees and broke down once again. She'd lost two men in one day.

Chapter 45

Troy drove recklessly, cutting the twenty-minute trip in half. As much as he tried to control his emotions, tears stung his eyes all the way home. He couldn't believe what Dina had exposed to him. Kennedy had been using him all along. His mother and sister were right. Could he even remember her saying the words 'I love you?' He was usually the one who expressed any feelings. Troy thought his heart would pound through his chest. The pain had become physical. His breath shortened, and he wondered if he would make it home in one piece.

Troy carelessly whipped the SUV into the driveway so hard the front end bounded. He threw the gear into park, cut the engine off, but left the keys in the car. He didn't realize he had no keys with him until he tried to get in the house. When he ran back to retrieve the keys he noticed that he never closed the driver-side door.

Troy almost ripped the doorknob off trying to get in the house.

"Kennedy! Kennedy! Where are you?" He yelled as he stormed through the house.

Kennedy appeared at the top of the steps leading to the bedroom area. Troy took the stairs three at a time. At the top, his children came to mind. He allowed himself to wonder if Zola was actually his. An unbearable pain hit his stomach, forcing him to bend forward, clenching his gut.

"Evan!" Troy wailed.

267

Evan came running out of his room. "Yes Daddy?"

Troy stooped to his level. "Hey, partner. Go downstairs and play your games in the family room. Mommy and I have to talk."

"Okay, Daddy. I'll get out of your way so you guys can do your private talk."

Kennedy stayed put while Evan ran to his room to pick up a few games before dashing to the family room. When Evan hit the stairs, Kennedy turned to go into their bedroom. Troy was right on her heels.

"So you set me up?" Troy said with his chest heaving.

Kennedy was calm. "What are you talking about?"

"I just came from speaking with Dina. Don't lie to me, Ken. You told Dina to sleep with me so you could use that as ammunition." Troy wanted to cry but held his ground. "What kind of shit is that, Kennedy? Why did you do it?"

Kennedy went about straightening up the room as if nothing special was going on.

"So did you sleep with her?" she asked calmly.

"Kennedy, don't fucking play with me." Troy yelled and veins bulged in his neck.

Right then Troy lost it. He knew she was simply trying to manipulate him as always. This time he wasn't going for it. Dina's story made a lot of sense, and she had revealed things that she could only have known if Kennedy told her about them. Troy began ranting like a madman. Kennedy stood frozen as he paraded around her yelling.

"You've played me for far too long, Kennedy, and I am not going for this shit anymore. No other man would put up with your bullshit and still try and give you the world on a platter. And this is the thanks I get?" Troy walked up on Kennedy with swiftness and pointed his finger in her face. For the first time ever, he saw fear in her eyes.

"I'm going to take the kids to my mother's house and while I'm gone I want you to get your shit and get the hell out of my house."

Kennedy was in shock. Troy could no longer fight back the tears. To release the remainder of his pent up energy, he started trashing the room, throwing everything that belonged to Kennedy to the floor. Troy marched into Zola's room, picked up the sleeping baby, and kissed her forehead. He grabbed her baby bag, which was always packed and ready to go and flew down the steps in search of Evan.

"Hey, little man. Get your shoes. We're going to take a ride over to grandma's house," Troy said to Evan as he added empty bottles and formula to Zola's bag.

Chapter 46

Kennedy was shocked and fuming. What the hell would make Dina tell Troy everything? She had to get to the bottom of this fast. Kennedy would deal with Troy's anger later. She knew she could work on him and get him to come around. She wasn't leaving her house for anyone. Everything in and around that house was a reflection of her.

Kennedy changed into a sweat suit because she was ready to kick Dina's unstable ass. She snatched her keys off the hook, jumped into her Caddy, and hit the highway with speed. When she arrived at her townhouse, she found the door unlocked. Kennedy ran through the first floor searching for Dina and calling her name. The more she called, her the madder she got. Everything was messed up because of Dina's big mouth. Kennedy had worked too hard to gain all that she had, and, she wasn't about to lose it all because big-mouth Dina grew some kind of conscience.

Kennedy raced up the stairs and could hear stirring from her old master bedroom, which was now Dina's room. She walked into the room and heard Dina in the master bath. Kennedy burst through the door and pounced right on top of Dina as she sat on the toilet with her head in her hands.

"You bitch! How could you do this to me?"

Kennedy pounded away on Dina. The poor woman barely had a chance to defend herself, let alone clean herself up. All Dina could manage to do was scream.

"Kennedy, please stop."

She held her arms up to shield her body from Kennedy's barrage of punches. Kennedy struck Dina in the face and started to kick her. By then Dina had just balled up into a fetal position and took the strikes. Kennedy wore herself out and charged into the bedroom huffing and puffing.

"I can't believe you! How could you do this to me? Troy wants me out. You ruined everything."

Dina was still balled up on the bathroom floor weeping.

"Shit!" Kennedy yelled and grabbed handfuls of hair in her hands. Then she broke down and began to cry.

"Kennedy," Dina called through her tears.

"What?" Kennedy snapped.

"I didn't tell him everything." Dina whimpered. She hadn't moved from her spot on the bathroom floor.

"Oh yeah. Well, what could you have possibly left out?" Kennedy's statement dripped with sarcasm.

"I didn't tell him about the evidence in the freezer."

Once again Kennedy was quiet.

"Kennedy?" Dina called again.

"What do you want?" Kennedy screamed.

"I'm pregnant, and the baby is Troy's."

"Bitch!" Kennedy ran into the bathroom and gave Dina one last, swift kick in her back before turning to leave.

Kennedy jumped back in her SUV and wondered where she could go. She pulled from her house only to pull over a few blocks later. The only person that came to mind was her mother. But Kennedy couldn't drive. Tears flooded her eyes and her body rocked as she cried hard for the loss of love she didn't realize she had.

Chapter 47

With nowhere else to turn, Dina crawled to the phone and called Angel.

"Help me, please," Dina pleaded between sniffles and tried to tell Angel as much as she could about the events of the day. It seemed as though it only took Angel minutes to come to her rescue. But in fact it took much longer than that. Dina was mentally, physically, and emotionally drained.

Dina could hear Angel when she entered the house, her sweet voice calling her name. But Dina couldn't respond. She was in a daze.

"Sweetie, where are you? Dina? Talk to me, honey."

All Dina could manage was a moan. Fortunately it was loud enough for Angel to realize that she was in the bedroom. The thumping from Angel's firm steps against the carpet echoed in Dina's ears.

"Oh my God! Dina, honey what happened?"

Angel found her laying in her own vomit. She ran to Dina and lifted her head.

"Come on Dee. We've got to get you cleaned up. What happened to you?"

The red brightness caused Dina to squint before she fully opened her eyes. The bright lights shining down on her let her know that she was no longer home. She felt extremely groggy and struggled to open her eyes fully. When she did, Angel, Kennedy, Dionne, and her very pregnant mother were by her hospital bedside.

Once Dina got her head together Kennedy's presence put everything else in perspective for her. She remembered the physical and emotional pain that served as the catalyst for her hospital stay. Tears stung her eyes. A part of her wished she had succeeded in killing herself, but truthfully she was glad that she hadn't. She felt like she had a second chance, and wanted to make the best of it.

Angel spoke up first as she rubbed Dina's messy hair. "Did you rest well? The doctor said you are going to be just fine. You threw up all the pills and they just wanted to hold you for a while to monitor you. You will be able to go home in a few days."

Home, Dina thought, where was that? Kennedy's house was probably off limits. Dionne would never let her stay with her and her mother was the last person on earth she'd ever want to stay with, especially since Mr. and Mrs. Ellis decided to get back together and move out of the house on her mother's block. Mrs. Jacobs was bitter about that, and between her resentment and moodiness, Dina wouldn't get a day of peace. Dina closed her eyes squeezing out more tears. Shook her head.

273

"Kennedy!" Dina sniffled, "I am so sorry... How did you know I was here?" Dina whispered.

"Angel called me," Kennedy replied but hadn't acknowledged Dina's apology. However, she did take Dina's outstretched hand in hers.

"What the hell went down?" Dionne asked loudly.

Everyone looked at one another, but no one answered.

"Okay, now that I know you are going to be okay, I'm going to go on home. My back is killing me. Come by if you need to. I'll see you all later," Mrs. Jacobs said before waddling out of the room.

"You two really need to talk," Angel said. "But I guess that can wait until you are home. Dina, sweetie, you can stay with me if you need to." Angel spoke to Dina but looked at Kennedy.

Kennedy didn't respond.

"I'm here. She can stay with me. I mean, I am her sister," Dionne stated.

The doctor snagged all of their attention when he entered the room to examine Dina.

"How are we feeling Ms. Jacobs?" Dr. Carter asked.

"Okay, I guess," Dina whispered.

"Well, you look great," Dr. Carter said. Dina was suddenly conscious of her appearance and pressed her hair down as the doctor continued. "We just need for you to hang with us a little longer to complete a few more evaluations. "We'll have you out of here in just a few days and then we'll get you started with your sessions at the center."

"Okay, thank you, Dr. Carter."

He gave her a warm smile and patted the back of her hand before exiting the room.

Angel asked Dionne if she could excuse them for a moment. Dionne sucked her teeth and left the room.

"Dina, I can't believe what you just went through. I'm hoping the two of you will agree to join me for church next Sunday," Angel said.

Kennedy scrunched up her face and looked at Angel. Dina just sighed.

"I'm serious. Kennedy, you are here, so despite the fact that you are upset with Dina, you still care about her. Not to mention, it's partly your fault that she's in here, between this thing with Troy and the fight. Dina, you have serious issues that you need to work out, and whether you realize it or not going to church a time or two can help."

"Whatever," Kennedy said.

"I'll just keep bugging you until you both agree," Angel said.

"I'll think about it, Kennedy said."

Dina took a deep breath and exhaled loudly. "I have something to say," she said, and the room fell silent. She took a deep breath and cleared her throat before continuing. "I'm not going to have this baby." Her voice was still low and groggy.

Angel gasped, and Kennedy turned away and began her pacing ritual.

"Are you sure you want to do this? Have you considered giving the baby up for adoption?" Angel asked Dina, taking her by the hand.

"No. I can't handle going through nine months of pregnancy and giving my baby away. It's hard because I'm not crazy about the idea of abortion, but this is all wrong. I need time to work on me before I screw up someone else's life."

Dina swiped at a lone tear sailing down her cheek. Angel squeezed Dina's hand, and Kennedy continued pacing.

"But Dina..." Angel began pleading.

Dina held up her free hand. "That's it. My decision is final," she answered Angel but looked at Kennedy. "Besides, if I'm going to get my life and friends back on track, then I need to do this. I'm sorry." Dina lowered her head.

Moments went by without a single sound from anyone.

Angel and Dina were both crying, and Kennedy had yet to stop pacing.

"And, Angel, about church next Sunday, count me in."

True to her word, the following week Dina called Angel early Sunday morning and asked her to pick her up from Dionne's house on her way to church. Dina was actually enjoying the service. She even felt somewhat rejuvenated with a renewed sense of hope. The church was jumping as the choir sang an upbeat gospel song. People were swaying and lifting their hands. Some were clapping, others crying. The pastor approached the pulpit and asked everyone to stand and bow their heads for the sermonic prayer.

After prayer, the congregation was seated. Angel pulled out her Bible and flipped to the section noted by the pastor. The title of the sermon for the day was "Be Guided by Love." The preacher spoke about loving yourself, knowing that you are worthy of love, and being guided by love in all that you do. Dina felt as if the pastor was speaking directly to her until he got to the part where he mentioned that allowing oneself to be misguided will always lead to self-destruction. Dina wished Kennedy was there to hear that part. She shed a few more tears for Kennedy's sake.

Feeling hopeful, Dina looked back towards the door, wishing to see Kennedy walk in. Instead she was surprised to actually see Kennedy seated right behind her. Tears then flooded her eyes and blurred her vision. When she looked at Angel, she noticed tears in her eyes as well. For once in her life, Dina felt a sense of inner peace. She wished that feeling would last forever.

Chapter 48

After service, Kennedy ran out of the church before anyone could notice that she was gone. The powerful sermon had reached her core and sparked something deep inside. She decided to head home for the first time since the events of the past week and a half. Although she was nervous, she knew what she had to do. The very first thing she did was destroy the rape evidence in the freezer at the townhouse. In order to move forward, she had to let go of the past. She vowed to leave Andre to his wife forever.

Kennedy resolved to work things out with Dina and rebuild their friendship. Dina's attempt at suicide and the preacher's sermon helped her put many things into perspective. Her revelation shocked her because she never thought she would see life the way she did now. Despite Dina's issues, Kennedy couldn't help but acknowledge the fact that Dina was not the only one at fault in the situation. She also realized it took a lot for Dina to arrive at the tough decision to get rid of her baby. With her mother and sister about to give birth, Dina's coming nephew and little sister would surely serve as permanent reminders of the child that she never had. Dina had more serious issues to deal with as she traveled the road to emotional recovery. Eventually she'd also have to confront her mother about the lies she grew up believing. She started by forgiving her mother for lying to them about their father all these years.

Kennedy also admitted that after all was said and done

she truly did love Troy. He was everything a woman could ever wish for in a man. She was lucky to have had him, even if she never got him back. Troy didn't deserve to be mistreated and if Kennedy got the chance, she'd spend her days treating him like she should have been treating him all along. Unfortunately, her mind was so wrapped around what she could gain from him financially that she never stopped to realize that she already had all she ever needed with him. She missed her kids and wanted so badly to hold them in her arms. When she pulled up to the house, she noticed the front door was open. Kennedy hoped Troy hadn't changed the locks. She slowly walked up to the door and peered inside. At first she didn't see anyone until Evan noticed her standing outside the door. Evan was dressed in a wife beater and sweats with no socks. Kennedy imagined Troy trying to 'keep house' and laughed. Then she fought a threat of tears.

Evan came barreling through the living room to the front door chanting, "Mommy's here!" all the way. Kennedy opened the door and let Evan fall into her arms. She thought she'd never let go. When she opened her eyes, the tears fell and Troy stood behind Evan.

Kennedy closed her eyes again and spoke through the tears and the pain. Her first words were ones she couldn't recall saying in years.

"I'm sorry."

Troy stepped back and let her in.

END

Reading Group Guide

1. Who were your most favorite and least favorite characters and why?

2. What was the most memorable scene in the book for you?

3. Kennedy's love of money and tendency to be very superficial became her downfall. Why do you think she turned out that way?

4. When Kennedy went to Andre's office to deliver the paternity test results, she ended up having sex with him. Why do you think she allowed that to happen?

5. Troy went to Andre's place of business to find out how well Andre and Kennedy knew one another. When he got there, he changed his mind. Why do you think Troy abandoned his plan?

6. Dina had some very deep-rooted issues. What were some of her issues, and from where do you think they come?

7. If you were Kennedy would you remain friends with Dina through all they endured, especially at the end?

8. If you were Dina, would you have remained friends with Kennedy?

9. When Dina found the bag of evidence in the freezer she didn't mention it to Kennedy right away. Should she have said something about it to Kennedy sooner, or should she have kept it to herself?

10. What do you think about Troy accepting Kennedy back at the end, and why do you think he allowed her back?

11. Now that Dina's mother, Judy Jacobs, is pregnant again, do you think she will make a better mother this time around?

12. What do you think about Dina's decision to abort Troy's baby?

13. What was your impression of each character's parents?

Miss-Guided

A Novel by

Renee Daniel Flagler

Renee Daniel Flagler is a native New Yorker and marketing professional, currently residing in Long Island, NY. Professionally, she has written several articles and ads which have appeared in a number of B2B publications and consumer magazines. Renee also authored the novel *Mountain High, Valley Low* and she's currently hard at work on her third novel.